THE PULL OF THE STARS

THE
PULL
OF THE
STARS

EMMA DONOGHUE

PICADOR

First published 2020 by Little, Brown and Company,
a division of Hachette Book Group, New York

First published in the UK 2020 by Picador
an imprint of Pan Macmillan
The Smithson, 6 Briset Street, London EC1M 5NR
Associated companies throughout the world
www.panmacmillan.com

ISBN 978-1-5290-4615-1

1 3 5 7 9 8 6 4 2

A CIP catalogue record for this book is available from the British Library.

Printed and bound by CPI Group (UK) Ltd, Croydon, CR0 4YY

Visit www.picador.com to read more about all our books
and to buy them. You will also find features, author interviews and
news of any author events, and you can sign up for e-newsletters
so that you're always first to hear about our new releases.

CONTENTS

I. Red   1

II. Brown   93

III. Blue   163

IV. Black   233

Author's Note   293

I

RED

STILL HOURS OF DARK to go when I left the house that morning. I cycled through reeking Dublin streets that were slick with rain. My short green cape kept off the worst, but my coat sleeves were soon wet through. A waft of dung and blood as I passed a lane where livestock were waiting. A boy in a man's coat shouted something rude at me. I pedalled faster, past a motor car creeping along to eke out its petrol.

I left my cycle in the usual alley and clipped the combination lock onto the back wheel. (German manufacture, of course. How would I replace it when its mechanism rusted up?) I let down the side tapes of my skirt and took my rain-soaked bag out of the basket. I'd have preferred to cycle all the way to the hospital, and it would have brought me there in half the time the tram took, but Matron wouldn't hear of her nurses turning up in a sweat.

Emerging onto the street, I nearly walked into a disinfection cart. Its sweet, tarry tang marked the air. I ducked away from the masked men who were spraying the gutters and feeding their hose through the grating of gully after gully.

I passed an improvised war shrine—a wooden triptych draped with the Union Jack. There was a chipped azure Virgin Mary for good measure and a shelf below overflowing with decaying flowers. The names painted on were just a few dozen Irishmen out of the tens of thousands lost so far, out of hundreds of thousands who'd enlisted. I thought of my brother, whom I'd left at home finishing a piece of toast.

At the tram stop, the pool of electric light was becoming watery as dawn approached. The lamppost was pasted with advertisements: DEPLETED AND DEBILITATED FROM LIVING TOO QUICKLY? FEELING OLD BEFORE ONE'S TIME?

Tomorrow I'd be thirty.

But I refused to flinch at the number. Thirty meant maturity, a certain stature and force, no? And the suffrage, even, now they were extending it to women over thirty who met the property qualifications. Though the prospect of voting felt unreal to me, since the United Kingdom hadn't had a general election in eight years and wouldn't till the war was over, and God alone knew what state the world would be in by then.

The first two trams whizzed by, crammed to bursting; more routes must have been cut this week. When the third came, I made myself push onto it. The steps were slippery with carbolic, and my rubber soles could get no purchase. I clung to the stair rail as the tram swayed through the fading darkness and hauled myself upwards. The riders on the balcony section looked soaked through, so I ducked in under the roof, where a long sticker said COVER UP EACH COUGH OR SNEEZE... FOOLS AND TRAITORS SPREAD DISEASE.

I was cooling fast after my bike ride, starting to shiver. Two men on the knifeboard bench moved a little apart so I could wedge myself between them, bag on my lap. Drizzle slanted in on us all.

The tram accelerated with a rising whine, passing a line of waiting cabs, but their blinkered horses took no notice. I saw a couple arm in arm below us hurry through a puddle of lamplight, their bluntly pointed masks like the beaks of unfamiliar birds.

The conductor inched along the crowded top deck now. His torch—a flat one, like a whiskey flask—spilled a wavering radiance over knees and shoes. I gouged the sweaty penny out of my glove and dropped it into his sloshing tin, wondering whether the inch of carbolic would really wash the germs off.

He warned me, That'll only bring you to the Pillar.

So the penny fare's gone up?

Not at all, there'd be ructions. But it doesn't take you as far now.

In the old days I would have smiled at the paradox. So to get to the hospital...

A halfpenny more on top of your penny, said the conductor.

I dug my purse out of my bag and found him the coin.

Children carrying suitcases were filing into the train station as we swung past, being sent down the country in hopes they'd be safe. But from what I could gather, the plague was general all over Ireland. The spectre had a dozen names: the great flu, khaki flu, blue flu, black flu, the grippe, or the grip... (That word always made me think of a heavy hand landing on one's shoulder and gripping it hard.) *The malady,* some called it euphemistically. Or *the war sickness,* on the assumption that it must somehow be a side effect of four years of slaughter, a poison brewed in the trenches or spread by all this hurly-burly and milling about across the globe.

I counted myself lucky; I was one of those who'd come through practically unscathed. At the start of September I'd taken to my bed hurting all over, knowing enough about this brutal flu to be rather in a funk, but I'd found myself back on my feet in a matter of days. Colours appeared a bit silvery to me for a few weeks, as if I were looking through smoked glass.

Apart from that, I was only a little lowered in spirits, nothing worth making a fuss about.

A delivery boy—matchstick legs in shorts—whizzed past us, raising a peacock's fan of oily water. How slowly this tram was trundling through the sparse traffic—to save electricity, I supposed, or in line with some new bylaw. I'd have been at the hospital already if Matron let us cycle all the way there.

Not that she'd know if I broke her rule; for the past three days she'd been propped up on pillows in a Women's Fever ward, coughing too hard to speak. But it seemed sneaky to do it behind her back.

South of Nelson's Pillar, the brakes ground and squealed, and we came to a halt. I looked back at the charred carapace of the post office, one of half a dozen spots where the rebels had holed up for their six-day Rising. A pointless and perverse exercise. Hadn't Westminster been on the brink of granting home rule for Ireland before the outbreak of world war had postponed the matter? I'd no particular objection to being governed from Dublin rather than London if it could come about by peaceful means. But gunfire in these streets in '16 hadn't brought home rule an inch closer, had it? Only given most of us reason to hate those few who'd shed blood in our names.

Farther down the road, where firms such as the bookshop where I used to buy Tim's comics had been razed by British shellfire during that brief rebellion, there was no sign of any rebuilding yet. Some side streets remained barricaded with felled trees and barbed wire. I supposed concrete, tar, asphalt, and wood were all unaffordable as long as the war lasted.

Delia Garrett, I thought. *Ita Noonan.*
Don't.

Eileen Devine, the barrow woman. Her flu had turned to pneumonia—all yesterday she'd coughed up greenish-red, and her temperature was a kite jerking up and down.

Stop it, Julia.

I tried not to dwell on my patients between shifts since it wasn't as if I could do a thing for them until I was back on the ward.

On a fence, specifics of a variety concert with CANCELLED stamped diagonally across them; an advertisement for the All-Ireland Hurling Finals, POSTPONED FOR THE DURATION pasted on it. So many shops shuttered now due to staff being laid low by the grippe, and offices with blinds drawn down or regretful notices nailed up. Many of the firms that were still open looked deserted to me, on the verge of failing for lack of custom. Dublin was a great mouth holed with missing teeth.

A waft of eucalyptus. The man to my left on the tram bench was pressing a soaked handkerchief over his nose and mouth. Some wore it on their scarves or coats these days. I used to like the woody fragrance before it came to mean fear. Not that I had any reason to shrink from a stranger's sneeze, being immune now to this season's awful strain of flu; there was a certain relief to having had my dose already.

A man's explosive cough on the bench behind me. Then another. Hack, hack, a tree being axed with too small a blade. The mass of bodies leaned away. That ambiguous sound could be the start of the flu or a convalescent's lingering symptom; it could signify the harmless common cold or be a nervous tic, caught like a yawn just by thinking about it. But at the moment this whole city was inclined to assume the worst, and no wonder.

Three hearses in a row outside an undertaker's, the horses already in harness for the morning's first burials. Two aproned men shouldered a load of pale planks down the lane to the back—for building more coffins, I realised.

The streetlamps were dimming now as day came. The tram rattled past an overloaded motor launch that looked tilted, askew; I saw two men kick at the rear axle. A dozen passengers in mourning wear still sat pressed together on its benches, as if stubbornness might get them to the funeral mass on time. But the driver, despairing, let her forehead rest on the steering wheel.

The man sitting jammed against my right elbow trained a little torch on his newspaper. I never had a paper in the house anymore for fear of upsetting Tim. Some mornings I brought a book to read, but last week the library had recalled them all for quarantine.

The date at the top reminded me that it was Halloween. The front page was offering hot lemonade, I noticed, and life insurance, and *Cinna-Mint, the Germicidal Throat Tablet.* So many ex-votos sprinkled among the small ads: *Sincere thanks to the Sacred Heart and the Holy Souls for our family's recovery.* The man turned the page, but his newspaper was blank inside, a great rectangle of dirty white. He let out a grunt of irritation.

A man's voice from the other side of him: Power shortages— they must have had to leave off printing halfway.

A woman behind us said, Sure aren't the gasmen doing their best to keep the works up and running, half staffed?

My neighbour flipped to the back page instead. I tried not to register the headlines in the veer of his shaky beam: *Naval Mutiny Against the Kaiser. Diplomatic Negotiations at the Highest Level.* People thought the Central Powers couldn't possibly hold out much longer against the Allies. But then, they'd been saying as much for years.

Half this news was made up, I reminded myself. Or slanted to boost morale, or at least censored to keep it from falling any further. For instance, our papers had stopped including the Roll of Honor—soldiers lost in the various theatres of war. Irishmen who'd signed up for the sake of king and empire, or the just cause of defending small nations, or for want of a job, or for a taste of adventure, or—like my brother—because a mate was going. I'd studied the roll daily for any mention of Tim during the almost three years he'd been posted abroad. (Gallipoli, Salonika, Palestine—the place-names still made me shudder.) Every week the columns had crawled another inch across the newspaper under headings with the ring of categories in a macabre parlor game: *Missing; Prisoner in Enemy Hands; Wounded; Wounded—Shell Shock; Died of Wounds;* and *Killed in Action*. Photographs, sometimes. Identifying details; appeals for information. But last year, casualties had grown too many and paper too scarce, so it had been decided that the list should from that point on be made public only for those who could pay for it as a threepenny weekly.

I noticed just one headline about the flu today, low down on the right: *Increase in Reports of Influenza*. A masterpiece of understatement, as if it were only the *reporting* that had increased, or perhaps the pandemic was a figment of the collective imagination. I wondered whether it was the newspaper publisher's decision to play down the danger or if he'd received orders from above.

The grand, old-fashioned silhouette of the hospital reared up ahead against the pallid sky. My stomach coiled. Excitement or nerves; hard to tell them apart these days. I struggled to the stairs and let gravity help me down.

On the lower deck, a man hawked and spat on the floor. People twitched and drew back shoes and hems.

A female voice wailed, Sure you might as well spray us with bullets!

Stepping off the tram, I saw the latest official notice in huge letters, pasted up every few feet.

A NEW FOE IS IN OUR MIDST: PANIC.
THE GENERAL WEAKENING OF NERVE POWER
KNOWN AS WAR-WEARINESS
HAS OPENED A DOOR TO CONTAGION.
DEFEATISTS ARE THE ALLIES OF DISEASE.

I supposed the authorities were trying to buck us up in their shrill way, but it seemed unfair to blame the sick for *defeatism*.

Written across the top of the hospital gates, in gilded wrought iron that caught the last of the streetlight: *Vita gloriosa vita.* Life, glorious life.

On my first day, when I'd been just twenty-one, the motto had made me tingle from scalp to toe. My father had stumped up the fees for the full three-year course at the Technical School for Nurses, and I'd been sent here for ward work three afternoons a week; it was in this hulking, four-storey building—handsome in a bleak, Victorian way—that I'd learnt everything of substance.

Vita gloriosa vita. The serifs were tipped with soot, I noticed now.

I crossed the courtyard behind a pair of white-coiffed nuns and followed them in. Religious sisters were said to make the most devoted, self-abnegating nurses; I wasn't sure about that, but I'd certainly been made to feel second best by a few nuns over my years here. Like most of the hospitals, schools, and orphanages in Ireland, this place couldn't have run without the expertise and labour of the various orders of the sisters. Most of the staff were Roman Catholics, but the hospital was open to any residents of the capital who needed care (though Protestants usually went to their own hospitals or hired private nurses).

I should have been down the country. I'd been due a whole three days off, so I'd arranged to go to Dadda's farm for a little rest and fresh air but then had to send him a telegram at the last minute explaining that my leave was cancelled. I couldn't be spared, since so many nurses—including Matron herself—had come down with the grippe.

Dadda and his wife's farm, technically. Tim and I were perfectly civil to our stepmother and vice versa. Even though she'd never had children of her own, she'd always kept us at a slight remove, and I supposed we'd done the same. At least she had no reason to resent us now we were grown and supporting ourselves in Dublin. Nurses were notoriously underpaid, but my brother and I managed to rent a small house, mostly thanks to Tim's military pension.

Urgency girdled me now. Eileen Devine, Ita Noonan, Delia Garrett; how were my patients getting on without me?

It felt colder inside the hospital than out these days; lamps were kept turned down and coal fires meagrely fed. Every week, more grippe cases were carried into our wards, more cots jammed in. The hospital's atmosphere of scrupulous order—which had survived four years of wartime disruption and shortages and even the Rising's six days of gunfire and chaos—was finally crumbling under this burden. Staff who fell sick disappeared like pawns from a chessboard. The rest of us made do, worked harder, faster, pulled more than our weight—but it wasn't enough. This flu was clogging the whole works of the hospital.

Not just the hospital, I reminded myself—the whole of Dublin. The whole country. As far as I could tell, the whole world was a machine grinding to a halt. Across the globe, in hundreds of languages, signs were going up urging people to cover their coughs. We had it no worse here than anywhere else; self-pity was as useless as panic.

No sign of our porter this morning; I hoped he wasn't off sick too. Only a charwoman sluicing the marble with carbolic around the base of the blue-robed Virgin.

As I hurried past Admitting towards the stairs to Maternity/Fever, I recognised a junior nurse behind her mask; she was red-spattered from bib to hem like something out of an abattoir. Standards were really slipping.

Nurse Cavanagh, are you just out of surgery?

She shook her head and answered hoarsely: Just now, on my way here, Nurse Power—a woman insisted I come see to a man who'd fallen in the street. Quite black in the face, he was, clawing at his collar.

I put my hand on the junior's wrist to calm her.

She went on in gulps. I was trying to sit him up on the cobblestones and undo his collar studs to help him breathe—

Very good.

—but he let out one great cough and...Nurse Cavanagh gestured at the blood all over her with widespread, tacky fingers.

I could smell it, harsh and metallic. Oh, my dear. Has he been triaged yet?

But when I followed her eyes to the draped stretcher on the floor behind her, I guessed he was past that point, beyond our reach. Whoever had brought a stretcher into the road and helped Nurse Cavanagh carry him into the hospital must have abandoned the two of them here.

I crouched now to put my hand under the sheet and check the man's neck for a pulse. Nothing.

This weird malady. It took months for the flu to defeat some patients, sneaking up on them by way of pneumoniac complications, battling for every inch of territory. Others succumbed to it in a matter of hours. Had this poor fellow been a stoic who'd denied his aches, fever, and cough until he'd found all at once, out in the street, that he couldn't walk, couldn't speak, could only whoop out his lifeblood all over Nurse Cavanagh? Or had he felt all right this morning even as the storm had been gathering inside him?

The other day an ambulance driver told me an awful story: He and his team had motored off in response to a phone call from a young woman (in perfect health herself, she said, but one of her fellow lodgers seemed very ill and the other two not well), and when the ambulance arrived, they found four bodies.

I realised that Nurse Cavanagh hadn't felt able to leave this passage outside Admitting even to fetch help in case someone tripped over the corpse. I remembered being a junior, the paralysing fear that by following one rule, you'd break another.

I'll find some orderlies to carry him down to the mortuary, I promised her. Go and get yourself a cup of tea.

Nurse Cavanagh managed to nod. She asked, Shouldn't you have a mask on?

I went down with flu last month.

So did I, but...

Well, then. (I tried to sound kind rather than irritated.) One can't catch it twice.

Nurse Cavanagh only blinked uncertainly, a rabbit frozen on a railway line.

I went down the corridor and put my head into the orderlies' room.

A knot of smokers in crumpled round caps and in white to the knees, like butchers. The waft made me long for a Woodbine. (Matron broke all her nurses of the filthy habit, but once in a while I relapsed.)

Excuse me, there's a dead man at Admitting.

The one with the metal half-face snorted wetly. Come to the wrong place, then, hasn't he?

Nichols, that's who the orderly was—Noseless Nichols. (A ghastly phrase, but such tricks helped me remember names.) The copper mask that covered what had been his nose and left cheek was thin, enamelled, unnervingly lifelike, with the bluish tint of a shaved jaw and a real moustache soldered on.

The man beside him, the one with the trembling hands, was O'Shea—Shaky O'Shea.

The third man, Groyne, sighed. Another soul gone to his account!

These three had all been stretcher-bearers. They'd enlisted together, the story went, but only O'Shea and Nichols had been sent up the line. Equipment shortages at the front were so awful that when bearers ran out of stretchers, they had to drag the wounded along on coats or even webs of wire. Groyne had been lucky enough to be posted to a military hospital and was never sent within earshot of the cannon; he'd come back quite un-marked, a letter returned to sender. They were all mates still, but Groyne was the one of the threesome I couldn't help but dislike.

Anonymous at Admitting, we'll call him, Groyne intoned. Gone beyond the veil. Off to join the great majority.

The orderly had a bottomless supply of clever euphemisms for the great leveller. *Turned up her toes,* Groyne might say when a patient died, or *hopped the twig,* or *counting worms.*

Something else I held against him was that he fancied himself a singer. *Goodbye-ee,* he crooned lugubriously now, *goodbye-ee...*

Nichols's nasal, echoey voice joined in on the second line: *Wipe the tear, baby dear, from your eye-ee.*

I set my teeth. Despite the fact that we nurses had years of training—a theory diploma from the technical school as well as a practical one from the hospital and a third in an area of specialty—the orderlies liked to talk down to us, as if feminine weakness made us need their help. But it always paid to be civil, so I asked, Could two of you possibly bring Anonymous below when you have a moment?

O'Shea told me, Anything for you, Nurse Power.

Groyne reached towards the overflowing brass ashtray, stubbed out his fag, and put it in his breast pocket for later, singing on.

Don't cry-ee, don't sigh-ee,
There's a silver lining in the sky-ee.
Bonsoir, old thing, cheerio, chin chin,
Napoo, toodle-oo, goodbye-ee.

I said, Thanks ever so, gentlemen.

Heading for the stairs, I found I was a little dizzy; I hadn't eaten anything yet today.

Down into the basement, then, not right towards the mortuary but left to the temporary canteen that had been set up off the kitchen. Our ground-floor dining rooms had been commandeered as flu wards, so now staff meals were dished up in a windowless square that smelled of furniture polish, porridge, anxiety.

Even with doctors and nurses having to muddle in together in this ad hoc canteen, there were so few of us still on our feet and reporting for duty that the breakfast queue was short. People leaned against the walls, wolfing down something egg-coloured with an obscure kind of sausage. Roughly half were wearing masks, I noticed, the ones who hadn't had the grippe yet or (like Nurse Cavanagh) who were too rattled to do without the sense of protection offered by that fragile layer of gauze.

Twenty hours' work on four hours' sleep!

That from a girlish voice behind me. I recognised her as one of this year's crop of probies; being new to full-time ward work, probationers lacked our stamina.

They're bedding patients down on the floor now, a doctor grumbled. I call that unhygienic.

His friend said, Better than turning them away, I suppose.

I glanced around, and it struck me that we were a botched lot. Several of these doctors were distinctly elderly, but the hospital needed them to stay on till the end of the war, filling in for younger ones who'd enlisted. I saw doctors and nurses who'd been sent home from the front with some harm done but not enough for a full service pension, so here they were again despite their limps and scars, asthma, migraines, colitis, malarial episodes, or TB; one nurse from Children's Surgical struggled with a chronic conviction that insects were crawling all over her.

I was two from the head of the line now. My stomach rumbled.

Julia!

I smiled at Gladys Horgan, squeezing towards me through the knot of bodies at the food table. We'd been great pals during training almost a decade ago, though we'd seen less of each other once I went into midwifery and she into eye and ear. Some of our class had ended up working in private hospitals or nursing homes; between those who'd left to marry or who'd quit due to painful feet or nerve strain, there weren't many of us still around. Gladys lived in at the hospital with a gang of other nurses, and I lodged with Tim, which was another thing that had divided us, I suppose; when I went off shift, my first thought was always for my brother.

Gladys scolded: Shouldn't you be on leave?

Nixed at the eleventh hour.

Ah, of course it would be. Well, soldier on.

You too, Gladys.

Must rush, she said. Oh, there's instant coffee.

I made a face.

Have you tried it?

Once, for the novelty, but it's nasty stuff.

Whatever keeps me going . . . Gladys drained her cup, smacked her lips, and left the mug on the dirty-dishes table.

I didn't want to stay without anyone to talk to, so I collected some watery cocoa and a slice of war bread, which was always dark but varied in its adulterations—barley, oats, and rye, certainly, but one might find soya in there too, beans, sago, even the odd chip of wood.

To make up some of the time I'd lost finding orderlies to bring Anonymous down to the mortuary, I ate and drank as I climbed the stairs. Matron (currently in Women's Fever) would have been appalled by the lapse in manners. As Tim would have said—if he were able to say anything these days—everything was entirely arsewise.

Full day had broken without my noticing; the late October light stabbed in the east-facing windows.

I put the last of the bread in my mouth as I went through the door that bore a handwritten label: *Maternity/Fever*. Not a proper ward, just a supply room converted last month when it became clear to our superiors that not only were expectant women catching this grippe in alarmingly high numbers, but it was particularly hazardous to them and their babies.

The ward sister was a lay nurse like myself. Sister Finnigan had overseen my diploma in midwifery, and I'd been flattered last week when she'd chosen me to staff this tiny room with her. Patients admitted with the flu who were well on in pregnancy got sent here, and Maternity, up on the second floor, transferred down any women who had fevers, body aches, or a cough.

We'd had no actual deliveries yet, which Sister Finnigan said was a sign of divine mercy, given that our facilities were so primitive. There was a line from our training manual that always stuck in my head: *For a woman with child, the surroundings should be such as will promote serenity.* Well, this makeshift ward was more conducive to irritation; it was cramped, with battery-powered lamps on each bedside cupboard instead of electric night-lights. At least we had a sink and a window for air, but there was no fireplace, so we had to keep our patients warm by bundling them up.

We'd had only two metal cots at first, but we'd crammed in a third so we wouldn't have to turn away Eileen Devine. My eyes went straight to her bed, in the middle, between Ita Noonan, who was snoring, and Delia Garrett, who (in a dressing jacket, a wrap, and a scarf) was reading. But the middle cot was empty, with fresh bedding pulled tight.

The crust of bread turned to a pebble in my throat. The barrow woman was too ill to have been discharged, surely?

From over her magazine, Delia Garrett gave me an angry stare.

The night nurse heaved herself off the chair. Nurse Power, she said.

Sister Luke.

The Church considered it immodest for nuns to serve in lying-in wards, but given the shortage of midwives, Matron—who happened to be from the same religious order as Sister Luke—had managed to persuade their higher-ups to lend this experienced general nurse to Maternity/Fever. *For the duration,* as everyone said.

I found I couldn't control my voice enough to ask about Eileen Devine. I drained the cocoa that now tasted like bile and rinsed the cup at the sink. Is Sister Finnigan not in yet?

The nun pointed one finger at the ceiling and said, Called to Maternity.

It had the ring of one of Groyne's playful synonyms for death.

Sister Luke adjusted the elastic band of her eye patch, a puppet pulling its own strings. Like quite a few nuns, she'd volunteered at the front, and shrapnel had sent her home with one eye gone. Between her veil and her white mask, the only skin showing was the hinterland around the other eye.

She came over to me now and nodded at the stripped cot. Poor Mrs. Devine slipped into a coma around two a.m. and expired at half past five, *requiescat in pace.*

She sketched a cross on the stiff, snow-white guimpe that covered her broad chest.

My heart squeezed for Eileen Devine. The bone man was making fools of us all. That was what we kids called death in my part of the country—the bone man, that skeletal rider who kept his grinning skull tucked under one arm as he rode from one victim's house to the next.

I hung up my cape and coat without a word and swapped my rain-soaked straw hat for a white cap. I unfolded an apron from my bag and bound it on over my green uniform.

Words burst out of Delia Garrett: I woke up to see men toting her away with a sheet over her head!

I walked over to her. How upsetting, Mrs. Garrett. I promise you, we did our utmost for Mrs. Devine, but the grippe had lodged in her lungs, and in the end it stopped her heart.

Delia Garrett sniffed shakily and pushed back a smooth curl. I shouldn't be in hospital at all—my doctor said this is only a mild dose.

That had been her constant refrain since arriving yesterday from her gracious Protestant nursing home where the two midwives on staff had been knocked out by the flu. Delia Garrett had walked in here wearing a ribboned hat and gloves rather than the old shawl typical of our patients; she was twenty years old, with a genteel South Dublin accent and that sleek air of prosperity.

Sister Luke tugged off her mackintosh sleeves and took her voluminous black cape from the peg. Mrs. Garrett's passed a comfortable night, she told me.

Comfortable! The word made Delia Garrett cough into the back of her hand. In this poky cubby on a backbreaking camp bed with people *dying* left and right?

Sister only means your flu symptoms are no worse.

I tucked a thermometer as well as my silver watch, attached by its fob chain, into the bib of my apron. I checked my belt, my buttons. Everything had to fasten at the side so as not to scratch a patient.

Delia Garrett said: So send me home today, why won't you?

The nun warned me that her pulse force—an indication of blood pressure—was still bounding.

Sister Finnigan and I hadn't been able to decide if Delia Garrett's flu was to blame for this hypertension; we often found the pulse force surged after the fifth month of pregnancy.

Whatever the cause, there was no treatment but rest and calm.

I said, I do sympathise, Mrs. Garrett, but it's best if we keep an eye on you till you're quite well.

I scrubbed my hands at the sink now, almost relishing the sting of the carbolic soap; if it didn't hurt a little, I wouldn't trust it.

I looked over at the sleeper in the cot on the left. And how's Mrs. Noonan been, Sister?

Much the same.

The nun meant Ita Noonan was still away with the fairies. Since yesterday, the woman had been so dazed, she wouldn't have noticed if the pope had come from Rome to pay her a visit. The only mercy was that her delirium was of the low type, not the high kind that could make sufferers chase, whack, or spit at us.

The night nurse added, I poulticed her just before she dropped off, so that'll need changing by eleven.

I made myself nod. The messy rigmarole of preparing hot, moist linseed and plastering it on the chests of congested patients was the bane of my life. The older nurses swore by poulticing, but I couldn't see that it achieved any more than a hot-water bottle.

I asked, When will Sister Finnigan be in?

Oh, I'm afraid you're on your own, Nurse Power. She pointed at the ceiling. Sister Finnigan's in charge of Maternity today—four deliveries on the go at once up there, and only Dr. Prendergast left.

Physicians were as rare as four-leaf clovers. Five of ours had enlisted and were serving in Belgium or France; one (caught up in the rebel cause) was in a Belfast prison; six were off sick.

Dry-mouthed, I asked: So I'm acting ward sister?

A shrug from Sister Luke. At a moment like this, *ours not to reason why.*

Our superiors might be making unwise decisions, did the nun mean? Or was she just saying that I shouldn't baulk at any new burden laid on my shoulders?

She added, Nurse Geoghan's missing in action too.

I sighed. Marie-Louise Geoghan would have been a great help. She was skilled at patient care, even if she still knew little of midwifery; in the current crisis, she'd been allowed to get her nursing certificate early. I said, I presume I'll be sent a junior, or a probie as a runner?

I'd presume nothing, Nurse Power.

The nun straightened her wimple and hooked her black cape at the throat, ready to depart.

A volunteer, at the very least? Another pair of hands?

I'll have a word with Staff on my way out, see what I can do for you.

I forced myself to thank Sister Luke.

As the door closed behind her, I was already rolling my sleeves up past my elbows despite the chill in the room. I buttoned on a pair of long starched cuffs. *In sole charge,* I told myself. *Needs must. No time for whining.*

More light, first. I went over to the small, high window and tilted the green slats towards me. I spotted a blimp hovering high over Dublin Port, watching for German submarines.

I'd been taught that each patient should have one thousand cubic feet, which meant a ten-by-ten-foot space per bed. In this improvised ward, it was more like ten by three. I wound the handle and angled the window half open at the top to let more air in.

Delia Garrett complained: As if there weren't already a draught.

Ventilation's crucial to recovery, Mrs. Garrett. Shall I get you another blanket?

Oh, don't fuss.

She went back to her magazine.

The tight-sheeted cot between her and Ita Noonan was a reproach, a tomb blocking my path. I called up Eileen Devine's drooping face; she'd kept her dentures in a glass by her bed. (Every baby seemed to cost these inner-city women a handful of teeth.) How she'd loved the hot bath I'd drawn her two days ago—the first she'd ever had, she'd told me in a whisper. *Luxury!*

I wished I could wheel Eileen Devine's empty cot out onto the landing to make a bit of room, but people would only bump into it. Also, I had no doubt we'd be getting another pregnant grippe case to fill it soon.

Eileen Devine's chart from the wall behind the bed was gone already, presumably tucked into the corner cabinet under *October 31.* (We filed by date of discharge, which sometimes meant death.) If I'd been the one to write the concluding line in the regulation tiny lettering that filled both sides of her sheet, I'd have been tempted to put *Worn down to the bone.* Mother of five by the age of twenty-four, an underfed daughter of underfed generations, white as paper, red-rimmed eyes, flat bosom, fallen arches, twig limbs with veins that were tangles of blue twine. Eileen Devine had walked along a cliff edge all her adult life, and this flu had only tipped her over.

Always on their feet, these Dublin mothers, scrimping and dishing up for their *misters* and *chisellers,* living off the scraps left on plates and gallons of weak black tea. The slums in which they somehow managed to stay alive were as pertinent as pulse or respiratory rate, it seemed to me, but only medical observations were permitted on a chart. So instead of *poverty,* I'd write *malnourishment* or *debility.* As code for *too many pregnancies,* I might put *anaemia, heart strain, bad back, brittle bones, varicose veins, low spirits, incontinence, fistula, torn cervix,* or *uterine prolapse.* There was a saying I'd heard from several patients that struck a chill into my bones: *She doesn't love him unless she gives him twelve.* In other countries, women might take discreet measures to avoid this, but in Ireland, such things were not only illegal but unmentionable.

Concentrate, Julia. I said the phrase in my head to scare myself: *Acting ward sister.*

Let Eileen Devine go; I had to bend all my efforts to the living now.

One always checked the sickest patient first, so I went around the skeletal frame of Eileen Devine's empty cot and took down the chart on the left. Good morning, Mrs. Noonan.

The mother of seven didn't stir. Ita Noonan had been wheeled in six days ago without the grippe's characteristic cough, but feverish; head, back, and joints as sore as if she'd been knocked down by a bus, she'd said. That was when she could still speak coherently.

She'd told us all about her job at the shell-filling factory, where her fingers had been yellowed by handling the TNT. She'd return to it as soon as she was over this flu, despite what she referred to lightly as her gammy leg. (The right was swollen to twice the width of the left since her last birth; it was hard and chill, the skin chalky and nonpitting. Ita Noonan was supposed to stay off it—keep it elevated, in fact—but sure how could she do that during the working day?) Once she was delivered in January, she'd return to the shell factory again for the grand wages and the cheap meals too; she'd have her eldest girl bring the baby in for feeds, she assured us. Mr. Noonan had been jobless ever since the lockout, when the bosses had broken the workers' union; he'd tried to join the British army but was turned away for having a hernia (even though his pal with a withered arm had kept his jacket on and been accepted), so he went around with a barrel organ now. Ita Noonan chafed to know how her kids were getting on; visitors weren't allowed in because of the influenza, and her husband wasn't one for writing. Oh, she was full of chat and jokes and strong views too; she went off on a rant about the Rising in '16, how her Canary Girl crew—all loyal to His Majesty—hadn't missed a day and had filled eight hundred shells that week.

But yesterday her breathing had turned noisier and her temperature had swooped up, jumbling her mind. Despite Sister Luke giving her high doses of aspirin, she'd spiked a fever twice last night, I read, hitting 103.7 and then 104.9.

I tried to slip the thermometer under Ita Noonan's tongue without waking her, but she roused, so I yanked it out before her remaining teeth could clamp together. Every nurse made that mistake once, had a patient spitting glass and mercury.

The woman blinked her pale blue eyes as if she'd never seen this room before, and writhed against the tapes binding the hot poultice to her chest. The shawl slid off her head; her thin hair cropped inches from the scalp stood up, the prickles of a hedgehog.

It's Nurse Power, Mrs. Noonan. I see you've had a haircut.

Delia Garrett muttered, Sister Luke put it in a paper bag.

Some of the older nurses maintained that cutting a fever patient's hair had a cooling effect and that if you cut it, it would grow back after, whereas if it fell out on its own, as often happened with this flu, it'd never return. Superstition, but I didn't think it worth a quarrel with the night nurse.

Delia Garrett touched her fingertips to her own elegant head and said, If it never comes back and the poor creature's left as bald as an egg, I suppose she can have a hairpiece made of it.

Let me just take your temperature, Mrs. Noonan.

I loosened the collar of the woman's nightdress. A thermometer under the arm needed two minutes rather than one and gave a reading one degree lower, but at least there was no risk of the patient biting the glass. On a chain Ita Noonan wore a tin crucifix, I noticed, no bigger than the top joint of my finger. People were all for holy things these days—talismans against terror. I tucked the thermometer into her humid armpit. There we go.

A little breathless, Ita Noonan answered randomly: Rashers! That's right.

I knew never to dispute a point with a delirious patient.

Could she be hungry for her breakfast? Unlikely, in her state; patients with serious flu cases had no appetite. Haggard at thirty-three years old, pale but for those flame-red cheeks, her belly a hard hill. *Eleven previous deliveries,* it said on Ita Noonan's chart, *seven children still living,* and this twelfth birth not expected for another two and a half months. (Since Mrs. Noonan had been able to tell us nothing about when she might have conceived or when she'd felt the quickening, Sister Finnigan had had to make a stab at the due date based on the height of the uterus.)

My job wasn't to cure all Ita Noonan's ills but to bring her safe through this particular calamity, I reminded myself, to push her little boat back into the current of what I imagined to be her barely bearable life.

I placed my first two fingers on the skin between tendon and bone on the thumb side of her wrist. With my left hand, I pulled out the heavy disk of my watch. I counted twenty-three beats in fifteen seconds and multiplied by four. *Pulse rate 95,* at the upper end of normal; I jotted it down in minute letters. (Wartime policy, to save paper.) The rhythm was *Regularly irregular,* I noted, which was typical during a fever. *Pulse force normal,* a small mercy.

I drew out the thermometer from under Ita Noonan's arm; its glass dragged at her tired skin. The mercury stood at 101, the equivalent of 102 taken orally, which was not too alarming, but temperatures were generally at their lowest in the early morning, and hers would climb again. I penciled the point on the graph. Many an illness had a characteristic line of exposure, incubation, invasion, defervescence, convalescence—the silhouette of a familiar mountain range.

Ita Noonan turned confiding now. She wheezed, said in her thick inner-city accent: In the wardrobe, with the cardinal!

Mm. Just lie quiet, we'll take care of everything.

We? I remembered I was on my own today.

Ita Noonan's chest strained to rise and fall, her breasts two windfalls rotting on dropped branches. Six breaths in fifteen seconds. I multiplied and wrote down *Respirations 24.* That was still rather high. *Mild nasal flaring.*

She beckoned me closer with her gaudy stained fingers. I leaned in and got a whiff of linseed from her poultice and something else...a bad tooth?

Ita Noonan whispered: There's a baby.

I wasn't sure how old her youngest was; some of these women were unlucky enough to produce two in a year. You've a little one at home?

But she was pointing down, secretive, not quite touching the drum under her sweat-dampened nightdress or even looking at it.

Oh yes, another one on the way, I agreed, but not for a good long while yet.

Her eyes were sunken; was she dehydrated? I lifted down the kettle to make her some beef tea. In this cramped space, we had only a pair of spirit lamps for cooking, so on one of them we kept a kettle always simmering, and on the other a wide pan for sterilising, in the absence of an autoclave to steam things clean. I picked up the jug of cold boiled water and poured some into the beef tea so it wouldn't scald Ita Noonan. I put the lidded cup into her hands and waited to make sure that in her confusion, she remembered how to suck from the hole.

A hard shake to the thermometer drove the mercury down into its glass bulb. I dipped it in the basin of carbolic, then rinsed it and put it back in my bib.

Delia Garrett slapped down her magazine and let out an angry cough behind her polished fingernails. I want to get home to my little girls.

I took one of her plump wrists and counted the beats, my eyes on the silver-framed family portrait on the miniature bedside table. (Patients' effects were meant to be kept in the drawer, for hygiene, but we knew when to turn a blind eye.) Who's looking after them while your husband's at the office?

She swallowed a sob. An older lady up the avenue, but they don't like her and I hardly blame them.

Pulse rate nothing out of the ordinary, the rhythm just a little syncopated. No need for the thermometer because her skin was the same temperature as mine. What concerned me was the pressure of her blood against my fingers. *Pulse force bounding,* I wrote down. Hard to tell how much was due to her agitation.

I observed her respiratory rate now.

Isn't it a mercy you've only a light dose, Mrs. Garrett? I was the same myself back in September.

I was trying to distract her because one never let a patient know one was counting her breaths or self-consciousness would alter the rhythm. *Respirations 20,* I wrote.

Delia Garrett narrowed her pretty eyes. What's your name—
your Christian name?

It was against protocol to share any personal information;
Sister Finnigan taught us to maintain gravitas by staying aloof.
If you let patients become familiar, they'll respect you less.

But these were strange times and this was my ward, and if
I had to run it today, I'd do it my way. Not that it felt as if I
were running anything, exactly; just coping, hour by hour.

So I found myself saying, It's Julia, as it happens.

A rare smile from Delia Garrett. I like that. So did they jam
you in a storeroom, Julia Power, between a dying woman and
one who's off her head?

I found myself warming to the wealthy Protestant for all her
obstreperousness. I shook my head. I was nursed at home, by
my brother, actually. But when you're expecting, this flu can
lead to...complications.

(I didn't want to spook her by listing them: miscarriage,
premature labour, stillbirth, even maternal death.)

Any headache this morning?

A bit of pounding, Delia Garrett admitted with a surly look.
Where?

She swept her hands from her bosom up to her ears as if
brushing away flies.

Problems with your vision at all?

Delia Garrett blew out air. What's there to look at in here?

I nodded at her magazine.

I can't settle to reading; I just like the photographs.

She sounded so young then.

Is the baby giving you a lot of bother—kicking and such?

She shook her head and covered a splutter. It's just the cough
and the aching all over.

Perhaps you'll get another note from Mr. Garrett today.

Her lovely features darkened. Where's the sense in forbidding our families to visit when the whole city's riddled with this grippe anyway?

I shrugged. Hospital rules.

(Though I suspected it wasn't so much about quarantining our patients as sparing our skeleton crew the extra trouble.)

But if you're the acting sister today, you must have authority to give me a cough mixture and let me out of here, especially since the baby's not coming till Christmas!

Unlike our poorer patients, Delia Garrett knew exactly when she was due; her family physician had confirmed the pregnancy back in April.

I'm sorry, Mrs. Garrett, but only a doctor can discharge you.

Her mouth twisted into a knot.

Should I spell out the risks? Which would be worse for her thumping blood, the frustration of feeling confined for no good reason or the anxiety of knowing that there were grave reasons?

Listen, you're doing yourself harm by getting worked up. It's bad for you *and* the baby. Your pulse force—

How to explain hypertension to a woman with no more than a ladylike education?

—the force with which the blood rushes through the vessels, it's considerably higher than we like it to be.

Her lower lip stuck out. Isn't force a good thing?

Well. Think of turning a tap up too high.

(The Garretts would probably have hot water laid on day and night, whereas most of my patients had to lug babies down three or four flights to the cold trickle of the courtyard tap.)

She sobered. Oh.

So the best thing you can do to get home as soon as possible is keep as quiet and cheerful as you can.

Delia Garrett flopped back on the pillows.

All right?

When will I get some breakfast? I've been awake for hours and I'm *weak*.

Appetite is a splendid sign. They're understaffed in the kitchens, but I'm sure the trolley will be up before long. For now, do you need the lavatory?

She shook her head. Sister Luke brought me already.

I scanned the chart for bowel movements. None yet; the flu often caused the pipes to seize up. I fetched the castor oil from the cupboard and poured a spoonful. To keep you regular, I told her.

Delia Garrett screwed up her face at the taste but swallowed it.

I turned to the other cot. Mrs. Noonan?

The befogged woman didn't look up, even.

Would you care for the lavatory now?

Ita Noonan didn't resist as I lifted the humid blanket and got her out of bed. Clutching my arm, she staggered to the door into the passage. Dizzy? I wondered. Along with the red face, that could mean dehydration. I reminded myself to check how much of her beef tea she'd managed to drink.

I felt a twinge in my side as Ita Noonan leaned harder. Any nurse who denied having a bit of a bad back after a few years on the job was a liar, though any nurse who griped about it had a poor chance of staying the course.

Once I had her sitting down on the lavatory, I left the stall and waited for the tinkle. Surely even when her mind was wandering, her body would remember what to do?

What a peculiar job nursing was. Strangers to our patients but—by necessity—on the most intimate terms for a while. Then unlikely ever to see them again.

I heard a rip of newsprint and the soft friction as Ita Noonan wiped herself.

I went back in. There now.

I pulled down her rucked nightdress to cover the winding rivers of veins on her one bloated leg in its elastic stocking and her skinny one in ordinary black.

Ita Noonan's eyes in the mirror were vague as I washed her hands. Come here till I tell you, she murmured hoarsely.

Mm?

Acting the maggot something fierce.

I wondered who she could be thinking of.

Back in the ward, I got Ita Noonan into bed with the blankets pulled up to her chest. I wrapped a shawl around her shoulders, but she scraped it off. The lidded cup still felt half full as I set it to her lips. Drink up, Mrs. Noonan, it'll do you good.

She slurped it.

Two breakfast trays sat side by side on the ward sister's tiny desk, protruding over its edges. (*My* desk today.) I checked the kitchen's paper slips and gave Delia Garrett her plate.

A wail went up when she lifted the tin lid. Not rice pudding and stewed apple again!

No caviar today, then?

That won half a smile.

And here's yours, Mrs. Noonan...

If I could persuade her to take something, it might bolster her strength a little. I straightened her legs, the huge, swollen one (very carefully) and the ordinary one. I set the tray down in her lap. And some lovely hot tea, if you prefer that to the beef?

Though I could tell the tea was lukewarm already, and far from lovely; given the price of tea leaves these days, the cooks had to brew it as transparent as dishwater.

Ita Noonan leaned towards me and confided in a ragged whisper, The boss man's out with the rossies.

Really?

She might be thinking of Mr. Noonan, I supposed. Though *boss man* seemed an odd epithet for a fellow pushing a barrel organ around town to support a sick wife and seven children. Was there almost a relish in delirium, I wondered, at getting to say exactly what floated through one's head?

Delia Garrett leaned out of bed to ogle Ita Noonan's tilted plate. Why can't *I* have a fry-up?

Nothing fatty or salty, remember, because of your blood pressure.

She snorted at that.

I perched on Ita Noonan's cot—there was no room to fit a chair between this one and the next—and cut one of the sausages into small bites. What would Sister Finnigan say if she could see me break her rule about sitting on a bed? She was gliding about upstairs, too busy catching babies to tell me the thousand things I needed to know and had never thought to ask.

Look, lovely scrambled eggs.

I put a forkful of the nasty yellow stuff—obviously powdered—to Ita Noonan's lips.

She let it in. Once she realised this was a fork I was setting in her hand, she gripped it and went to work. Wheezing a little, pausing to strain for breath between bites.

I found my eyes brooding over the empty cot in the middle. The nail on which Eileen Devine's chart had hung was loose, I remembered. I stood up now to ease it out of the wall. I pulled on the chain of my watch and weighed the warm metal disk in my palm. Turning away so neither woman would notice what I was doing, I set the point of the nail to my watch's shiny back and scratched an only slightly misshapen full moon among the other marks, this one for the late Eileen Devine.

I'd formed this habit the first time a patient died on me. Swollen-eyed, at twenty-one, I'd needed to record what had happened in some private way. A newborn's prospects were always uncertain, but in this hospital we prided ourselves on losing as few mothers as possible, so there really weren't that many circles marked on my watch. Most of them were from this autumn.

I replaced the nail in the wall. Back to work. Every ward had intervals of peace between rushes; the key was to snatch these opportunities to catch up. I boiled rubber gloves and nailbrushes in a bag in a saucepan. I crossed to the opposite wall and studied the contents of the shallow ward cupboard, acting competent, if not feeling it. All these years, I'd been expected to set my judgement aside and obey my ward sister; such an odd sensation, today, to have no one telling me what to do. A measure of excitement to it, but a choking feeling too. I went to fill in requisitions at the desk. Since the war, one never knew what would be in short supply, so all one could do was ask politely. I didn't bother requesting cotton pads and swabs, as they'd disappeared *for the duration*. Some supplies had been back-ordered for weeks already, I found from Sister Finnigan's list.

When I finished my slips I remembered I had no runner to deliver them, and I couldn't leave this room. I swallowed down my anxiety and tucked them in my bib pocket for now.

Ita Noonan was staring off into the corner of the room, egg on her chin. Most of the cut-up sausage was still on her plate, but the whole one was gone. Could Delia Garrett have knelt on the vacant cot and stolen food off her neighbour's plate?

Avoiding my eyes, the younger woman wore a faint smirk.

Well, one sausage—whatever it was made of these days—wouldn't kill her, and Ita Noonan didn't seem to want it.

The delirious woman skewed sideways all of a sudden, and her tray clattered down between her cot and the medicine cabinet. Tea spilled across the floor.

Mrs. Noonan! I stepped over the mess and studied the sheen across her scarlet cheeks; I could sense the sizzle of her skin. My thermometer was already in my hand. Pop this under your arm for me?

She didn't respond, so I hoisted her wrist myself and tucked the thermometer into her armpit.

As I waited, I took out my watch and counted Ita Noonan's noisy breaths and her pulse—no change. But the mercury had bumped up to 104.2. Fever did have power to burn off infection, though I hated to see Ita Noonan like this, sweat standing out along her intermittent hairline.

I stepped around her upturned breakfast to get ice from the counter, but the basin held only a puddle around a solitary half cube. So instead I filled a bowl with cold water and brought it over with a stack of clean cloths. I dipped them into the bowl one by one, squeezed them out, laid them over the back of her neck and on her forehead.

Ita Noonan twitched at the chill but smiled too, in instinctive politeness, more past me than at me. How I wished the woman still had wits enough to tell me what she needed. More aspirin might lower her temperature, but only a physician could order medicine for a patient; Dr. Prendergast was the one obstetrician on duty, and when was I likely to lay eyes on him this morning?

Now that I'd done all I could think of for Ita Noonan, I bent to pick up the tray and the plate. The handle was off the cup, in two pieces. I mopped up the puddle before someone could slip in it.

Shouldn't you call someone to do that for you? Delia Garrett asked.

Oh, everyone's swamped at the moment.

Technically, a spill came within the orderlies' remit if one had no ward maid, probie, or junior nurse, but I knew better than to ask them. If one called those fellows in over a splash of tea, they might take offence and turn a deaf ear next time, when it was wall-to-wall gore.

Ita Noonan's fiery face on the pillow seemed preoccupied. Lovely day for a dip in the canal!

Did she believe she was bathing? Something made me check under her blanket, and—

She'd flooded the sheets. I withheld a sigh. She mustn't have passed water at all when I'd taken her to the lavatory. Her bed needed making now, and a pair of nurses could do it if the patient was co-operative, but there was just one of me, and Ita Noonan so unpredictable.

I had the machine on hire purchase, she complained, only they dropped it off the balcony...

The delirious woman was caught up in some old or imagined disaster.

Come on, now, Mrs. Noonan, just hop out of bed for a minute so I can strip these wet things off you.

Smashed my holies, so they did!

Delia Garrett announced, I need the lavatory.

If you could wait just a minute—

I really can't.

I was tugging a top corner of Ita Noonan's sheet off the mattress. I'll give you a bedpan, then.

She poked one pale foot out and said, No, I'll go on my own.

I'm afraid that's not allowed.

Delia Garrett let out a harsh cough. I'm perfectly able to find my way, and I need to stretch my legs anyway, I'm stiff from lying here like a sow.

I'll bring you, Mrs. Garrett. Give me two ticks.

I'm simply bursting!

I couldn't block the door or chase her into the passage. I said sternly, Please stay where you are!

I abandoned Ita Noonan and her sodden bed and nipped into the passage. The nameplate on the first door said WOMEN'S FEVER.

All seemed calm inside. Excuse me, Sister...Benedict?

Unless it was Sister Benjamin? The tiny nun looked up from her desk.

I'm in charge of Maternity/Fever today, I told her. My voice came out too high, more cocky than careworn. I jerked my thumb over my shoulder as if to suggest that she mightn't have heard of our little temporary ward. I should have introduced myself first, but I'd missed the moment. Sister, I wonder if you could ever spare me a junior or probie?

She was well-spoken, her voice soft. How many patients have you in Maternity/Fever, Nurse?

I felt myself flush. Just two at the moment, but—

The ward sister cut me off. We have forty here.

I glanced around, counting; she also had five nurses under her. Then could you at least get a message to—

Not Matron, I reminded myself. On this topsy-turvy day, Matron might be in one of these cots; I scanned the rows. Mind you, I wasn't sure I'd recognise her out of uniform.

Could you ask whoever's standing in for Matron? I really need assistance rather urgently.

I'm sure our superiors are well aware, said Sister Benedict. One does one's bit. Everyone must pull together.

I said nothing.

Like a curious bird, the nun put her head to one side as if making a note of exactly how I was failing so she could report to Sister Finnigan later. You know, I always say a nurse is like a spoonful of tea leaves.

I couldn't answer in case my words came out in a roar.

A hint of a smile for the punch line: Her strength only shows when she's in hot water.

I made myself nod at this wise saw so Sister Benedict wouldn't write me up for insubordination. I shut the door soundlessly behind me, then remembered the papers in my bib and had to double back and open it again. If I could leave you my supply requisitions, Sister, to pass on to the office?

Certainly.

I pulled out the fistful of curling slips and dropped them on the counter.

I half ran back to my ward.

Ita Noonan hadn't stirred from her urinous bed. The younger woman's need was more urgent, I decided. Let's get you to the lavatory then, Mrs. Garrett.

She sniffed.

I steered her by the elbow. As soon as we were in the passage she began to scuttle, a hand clamped to her mouth. Oh, hurry, Nurse!

Halfway along the passage, she bent in two and threw up.

I couldn't help noticing telltale pieces of sausage.

I fished a clean cloth out of my apron to wipe Delia Garrett's mouth and the top of her nightdress. You're all right, dear. This nasty illness can disrupt digestion.

Now I really needed to find an orderly to mop this vomit up, but Delia Garret gripped her belly and cantered away towards the lavatory. I followed, my rubber soles slapping the marble behind her slippers.

The sounds from behind the stall door told me she had diarrhea now too.

As I waited for Delia Garrett, arms crossed, my gaze was caught by a word on a poster still damp from the printer's: *bowels.*

PURGE THE BOWELS REGULARLY.
CONSERVE MANPOWER
TO KEEP IN FIGHTING TRIM.
INFECTION CULLS
ONLY THE WEAKEST OF THE HERD.
EAT AN ONION A DAY TO KEEP ILLNESS AT BAY.

So we'd come to this—Anonymous had spewed his lifeblood all over Nurse Cavanagh in the street, and the government in its wisdom was prescribing onions? And as for the *culling of the weakest,* what cruel absurdity. This flu was nothing like the familiar winter bane that snuffed out only the very oldest and frailest. (If that one turned to pneumonia, it generally took them off so gently that we'd nicknamed it Friend to the Aged.) This new flu was an uncanny plague, scything down swaths of men and women in the full bloom of their youth.

Silence, now, behind the stall door. Mrs. Garrett, if I might just check the pan before you flush...

(Dark matter would reveal internal bleeding.)

Don't be disgusting!

Water roared from the overhead tank when she yanked the chain.

Delia Garrett seemed shaky as I led her back to the ward. I

hoped an orderly might have happened by and mopped up the sick-spattered marble, but no. I steered her around it, reminding myself that a mess was less important than a patient. A sponge bath in your bed and a new nightie, I murmured, and you'll feel more like yourself. I just need to see to Mrs. Noonan first.

The delirious woman was blank, unresisting; she let me move her off her wet bed to the chair at its foot and wipe her clean. I got a fresh nightdress over her head and used the cloth tapes to draw it closed all down her side.

Delia Garrett complained that she was freezing.

I pulled a folded blanket from the cupboard and handed it to her. I swathed Ita Noonan in a second one to keep her warm until I had a dry bed for her.

This reeks!

That means it's safe, Mrs. Garrett. They hang them over racks in an empty room, and they burn sulphur in a bucket to make a gas strong enough to kill every last germ.

She murmured, Like the poor Tommies in the mud.

Every now and then this spoiled young woman surprised me.

At least my brother had never been gassed. Tim had twice collapsed from heatstroke in Turkey, and he'd caught trench fever, but he'd managed to get over it, whereas many soldiers carried it in them, a cup of embers that could flare up at any time. That was the joke of it—physically, my brother was still the man he'd been before the war, when he'd worked in a haberdashery firm (gone out of business now) and went to the roller rinks with his pal Liam Caffrey every chance he got.

The door swung open, and I jumped.

Dr. Prendergast, in his three-piece suit, on his rounds at last. I was glad to see him but mortified by the timing. *Please let him not ask why both my patients are huddled on chairs. And could that be a spatter of Delia Garrett's vomit on his polished shoe?* If Sister Finnigan heard how things were falling apart on my first morning of holding the fort, she'd never entrust me with the responsibility again.

Prendergast was preoccupied with tying the strings of a mask at the back of his head. Oddly plentiful hair for a man of his age, a bog-cotton shock of white.

You heard we lost Mrs. Devine in the night, Doctor?

His voice was flat with fatigue. I certified the death, Nurse.

The man had been up since yesterday morning, then. He held on to the stethoscope around his neck with two hands as a swaying passenger on a tram might grip an overhead strap.

The cunning of this malady, he murmured. When a patient shows every sign of being on the mend, I've told the family not to worry, and then...

I nodded. But these days nurses had strict instructions not to waste a second of a physician's time, and here we were fretting over a dead woman. So I grabbed Ita Noonan's chart off the wall and handed it to him. Mrs. Noonan's twenty-nine weeks on, Doctor.

Dr. Prendergast caught his yawn in his hand. Mildly cyanotic, I see. How's her breathing?

Rather effortful. Delirious for two days now, temperature ranging up to a hundred and five.

Her blanket was trailing, I saw; I snatched it up and wound it around her. *Let him not notice that she wet herself.* I asked, Should she have more aspirin?

(Nurses weren't supposed to have any views on medicine, but this man was so tired, I thought I'd nudge him along.)

Prendergast sighed. No, the high doses seem to be poisoning some patients, and quinine and calomel are just as bad. Try whiskey instead, as much as she can take.

Whiskey? I asked, confused. To reduce fever?

He shook his head. For soothing discomfort and anxiety and promoting sleep.

I wrote down the instruction in case another doctor were to query me about it later.

Now, how's Mrs. . . .

His gaze was foggy.

Garrett, I reminded him as I handed over Delia Garrett's chart. Recent emesis and diarrhea, and her pulse force, ah, still seems high.

I had to phrase that tactfully so he wouldn't bristle at the implication that a midwife could tell with her fingers what a physician relied on fancy equipment to determine.

Prendergast hesitated, and I feared he was going to say he hadn't time to take a reading. But he got the sphygmomanometer out of his bag.

I slid Delia Garrett's pink hand through the cuff and tightened it around her upper arm, then he inflated the cuff with the hand pump. The process was little more complicated than tightening a rope; it occurred to me that any of us could be taught to use this thing.

Ow!

Just a minute more, Mrs. Garrett, I said.

She coughed discontentedly.

He fitted the yellowed tips of the stethoscope into his ears, pressed the flat disk against the soft crook of her elbow, let the cuff deflate, and listened.

After a minute, Prendergast dictated: Systolic blood pressure is one hundred and forty-two. A few moments later, he said: Diastolic is ninety-one, Nurse.

Diastolic BP 91, I added to the chart.

Prendergast didn't seem that impressed by the figures. A bounding pulse is common in the last months of pregnancy, he murmured as I packed up the device for him. If she gets very agitated you could give her bromide.

Hadn't the man heard me say Delia Garrett had just thrown up? A sedative was so hard on the stomach, I'd prefer not to inflict that on her...

But I'd been taught never to contradict a doctor; it was held that if the chain of command was broken, chaos would be unleashed.

Prendergast rubbed his eyes. I'm off home now.

While you're gone, I asked, which obstetrician—

They're bringing in a general practitioner to help out in the women's wards.

A GP in private practice—so, not the specialist we needed. I asked uneasily: Is he at the hospital yet?

Prendergast shook his head. At the door he said, Dr. Lynn's a lady, by the way.

I thought I heard a touch of disdain. There were a few female physicians these days, though I hadn't yet served under one. What I needed to know was, till this substitute presented herself, who could I call on for my patients?

Delia Garrett jumped up. Nurse Julia, can you get me out of this filthy thing now?

Yes, the minute I've dosed Mrs. Noonan, but do stay off your feet, won't you?

She subsided in the chair.

I made up a lidded cup of hot whiskey and water for Ita Noonan, sugared to be more palatable. After the first sip she sucked it down like mother's milk. Then I went to fetch a clean nightdress from the press for Delia Garrett.

Uncovered, her belly was silvered with the snail trails of her previous two pregnancies as well as this one.

I hadn't yet felt that broodiness older women had warned

me I would. I'd specialised in midwifery because the drama of it drew me in, but I'd never imagined myself as the woman at the centre of the mystery, the full moon rounding, only as the watchful attendant.

Thirty tomorrow. That ring of being past one's best.

But thirty wasn't so very old, I told myself. By no means too late to marry and have children; only, on the balance of probabilities, unlikely. And even less likely, I supposed, now so many men had been lost in the war, either facedown in some foreign field or just not interested in finding their way back to this small island.

I got Delia Garrett's nightdress on and tied the side tapes, then tucked her back into bed and wrapped her up well against the autumn air whistling in the high window.

I finished stripping Ita Noonan's mattress. I was relieved that the mackintosh drawsheet had caught all the urine; the cotton sheet and underblanket beneath it were still dry.

What I couldn't quite put my finger on was whether I wanted a husband. There'd been possibilities along the way, pleasant young men. I couldn't reproach myself with having thrust opportunities away, but I certainly hadn't seized them.

Would you be Nurse Power?

I whipped around to see a youngster in civvies in the doorway, brassy hair scraped back and oiled down but a frenzy of curls at the back. Who are you?

Bridie Sweeney.

No title, which told me she wasn't even a probie. So many young women were being rushed through basic first-aid training these days.

Delia Garrett asked, And what might you be, Miss Sweeney, a volunteer nurse?

44

The stranger grinned. I'm not any kind of nurse.

Delia Garrett threw up her eyes and went back to her magazine.

Bridie Sweeney turned to me. Sister Luke's after sending me to lend a hand.

So this was all the night nurse had managed to dig up for me—unqualified; uneducated, by the sounds of her accent; and with a clean, new-hatched look like nothing had ever happened to her. I could have slapped this Bridie Sweeney from sheer disappointment.

I said, The hospital has no funds left for casual staff. I hope Sister Luke told you there's no pay?

I wasn't expecting any.

She was the pale, freckle-dusted type of redhead, light blue eyes, brows almost invisible. Something childlike about her translucent ears; the one on the left angled a little forward, as if eager to catch every word. Thin coat, broken-down shoes; on an ordinary day, Matron would never have let her in the door.

Well, I said, I could do with a runner to fetch and carry, so I'm glad you're here. This is Mrs. Garrett. Mrs. Noonan.

Good day, ladies, Bridie Sweeney said with a bob.

I took a folded apron down from the press.

The volunteer was a scrap and looked even thinner once she'd taken her coat off; she had to wrap the apron's ties around her waist twice. With frank curiosity, she watched Ita Noonan rocking on the little chair by her cot, wheezing a song. She remarked, I've never been in a hospital.

By the way, Miss Sweeney, I assume you're immune?

The young woman didn't seem to know the word.

To the flu, the grippe. Since you've walked into a fever ward without a mask—

Oh, I've had the grippe.

But this year's one, the bad one, I specified.

Got over it ages ago. Now, what do you want doing, Nurse Power?

It was a relief to be asked that. Let's start by making up Mrs. Noonan's bed.

I checked the base layers were all smooth, the wire-spring mattress in its canvas cover sitting just so on the boards, the hair mattress in its cotton one on top. A ruddy tan waterproof mackintosh base fitted tight, then an underblanket, then a sheet.

Aromatic with whiskey fumes, Ita Noonan tried to climb on.

Just another minute, I said as I blocked her gently with my arm.

I got a fresh drawsheet, under and upper sheets, and blankets from the bedding cupboard. I said, We pull every layer smooth and crisp, see, so there'll be no wrinkles to hurt Mrs. Noonan's skin.

Bridie Sweeney nodded.

As I helped Ita Noonan in, she heaved a breath and cried, Such malarkey!

The newcomer asked, What is?

I shook my head.

Her face froze. Sorry—am I not allowed to talk to them?

I smiled. I only meant, don't worry if Mrs. Noonan makes odd remarks. I tapped my scalp and said, A high temperature can rattle the pot.

I wound one shawl around the sick woman's shoulders and draped another over the back of her head to keep draughts off.

Ita Noonan swatted at the air with her sipping cup. Awful yahoos, left my delph in smithereens!

Did they now? Bridie Sweeney fixed the pillows.

The young woman had a nice bedside manner, I decided; that couldn't be taught.

I pushed the ball of soiled bedding down into the laundry bucket and jerked my thumb towards the passage. This goes down the chute—the one marked *Laundry*, not *Incinerator*.

Bridie Sweeney hurried out with the bucket.

Delia Garrett asked, Did that girl just walk in here off the street?

Well, if Sister Luke recommended her...

A snort.

We're so short-staffed that I'll gladly accept any help, Mrs. Garrett.

She muttered into her magazine, I never said you shouldn't.

When Bridie Sweeney came back in, I took her through the distinctions between various gauze dressings (squares, balls, six-foot strips in tins), flax-tow swabs, single-use cloths, ligatures, and catgut.

The actual guts of cats?

Sheep, actually. I don't know why it's called that, I admitted.

She beamed around her. So these ladies are here for you to cure their grippe?

I let out a breath. I only wish I knew how to do that, but there's no cure as such. The thing has to run its course.

For how long?

Days or weeks. (I was trying not to think of those it killed with little warning, in the street or on their own floorboards.) Or it can linger for months, I admitted. To be perfectly frank, it's a toss-up. All we can do is keep them warm and rested, fed and watered, so they can put what force they have into beating this flu.

My young helper seemed fascinated. She said under her breath, Why's Mrs. Noonan that colour?

47

Ah, here was something simple I could teach. I told her, They go dark in the face if they're not getting quite enough oxygen into their blood. It's called cyanosis, after *cyan*—the shade of blue.

She's not blue, though, said Bridie Sweeney. More like scarlet.

Well, I said, it starts with a light red you might mistake for a healthy flush. If the patient gets worse, her cheeks go rather mahogany. (I thought of the turning of the leaves in autumn.) In a more severe case, the brown might be followed by lavender in the lips. Cheeks and ears and even fingertips can become quite blue as the patient's starved of air.

Horrible!

I remembered to turn to the other patient and say, Don't worry, Mrs. Garrett, you're not in the least cyanotic.

She gave a little shudder at the idea.

Bridie Sweeney asked, Is blue as far as it goes?

I shook my head. I've seen it darken to violet, purple, until they're quite black in the face.

(Nurse Cavanagh's fallen Anonymous this morning, as dark as cinders by the time she ran up to him in the street.)

It's like a secret code, Bridie Sweeney said with pleasure. Red to brown to blue to black.

Actually, in our training, we made...

I wondered if she'd know the word *mnemonic*. Or *alliterative*.

...little reminders to commit medical facts to memory, I told her.

Like what?

Well... the four Ts that can cause postpartum haemorrhage— bleeding after birth—are *tissue, tone, trauma, thrombocytopenia*.

You know an awful lot, Nurse Power.

I gave the young woman a tour of the other shelves and cupboards. If I hand you a metal instrument that's been used, you can take for granted that I want it sterilised, Miss Sweeney. Lower it into this pot of boiling water with these tongs here and leave it for ten minutes by your watch.

Sorry, I haven't—

There's a clock on the wall over there. Then lay out a fresh cloth from this brown-paper packet and use the tongs to set the instrument on the cloth. Anything you haven't time to boil can be disinfected in this basin of strong carbolic solution instead.

Right.

But was she grasping the importance of what I was saying?

When each item has air-dried, I went on, you move it with the tongs to a sterile tray up on this shelf, where everything's sterile—thoroughly clean, ready for a doctor. Never touch any of them unless I tell you to, understood?

Bridie Sweeney nodded.

Delia Garrett let out a series of coughs that turned into whoops.

I went over to check her pulse. How's your stomach now, Mrs. Garrett?

A little steadier, I suppose, she conceded. I blame what happened on that nasty castor oil.

I very much doubted the dose I'd given her could have liquefied her at both ends.

It's ludicrous keeping me shut up here for a touch of flu! My babies pop out the week they're due and not before, and I spend no more than half a day in bed, no fuss. Why's this chit gawping at me?

Bridie Sweeney's hand shot up to cover her grin. Sorry, I didn't know you were...

Delia Garrett glared, hands on her belly. You thought this was pure fat?

I pointed out, It says *Maternity/Fever* on the door, Miss Sweeney.

She muttered, I didn't know what that meant.

I was taken aback by her ignorance.

Well, I said. Now I'll show you how to wash your hands.

Amusedly: I think I know that much.

I asked a little sharply, You've heard of childbed fever?

Of course.

It can come on a woman anytime from the third day after birth, and it used to kill them at a terrible rate. Our only modern defence is asepsis—that means keeping germs from getting into patients. So now do you see how cleaning one's hands thoroughly could save a life?

Bridie Sweeney nodded, abashed.

I told her, Roll your sleeves all the way up so you don't wet them.

She seemed hesitant. When she bared her right forearm, it had a melted look. She saw me notice and she muttered, A pot of soup.

That must have hurt.

Bridie Sweeney shrugged, a monkeyish little movement.

I hoped she wasn't the clumsy sort. She didn't seem so. Her hands were reddish, which told me she was used to hard work.

First we pour out boiling water from this kettle, Miss Sweeney, and add cold from the jug.

She immersed her hands in the basin. Lovely and warm!

Take this boiled nailbrush and scrub your hands well, especially the nails and the skin around them.

I waited for her to do that.

Then rinse them in fresh water to get all the soap off. Finally, soak them in a third basin of water...with a full capful of this carbolic here.

I poured it out for her and added, Antiseptics such as carbolic can actually be dangerous—

—if you swallow them or splash them in your eyes, I know, she said eagerly.

I corrected her: If one relies on them lazily instead of taking care to scrub really well.

Bridie Sweeney nodded, hands dripping.

I gestured to a stack of clean cloths so she wouldn't try to dry them on her apron.

No one had been back to collect the breakfast trays yet. I said, I wonder could you take these to the kitchen?

She asked, Where's the—

In the basement, two floors down.

When she was gone I checked temperatures, pulses, respirations. No change. That was reassuring in Delia Garrett's case, worrying in Ita Noonan's. The whiskey might be providing some comfort, but that was all.

Thanks, I said when Bridie Sweeney came back in. It's a real help, having another pair of hands.

She looked down at her knuckles and scratched their reddened, swollen backs.

Chilblains?

She nodded, sheepish. Driving me wild.

Thin girls were susceptible, for some reason. I said, Here, this should soothe the itching.

I got the medicated balm down off the shelf but she made no move to take it, so I scooped a fingerful from the jar, reached for her hands, and rubbed it well into the scarlet patches. On the back of the left one, there was a raised, red circle—ringworm, the brand of poverty I saw on so many patients. But it was fading, so no longer contagious.

Bridie Sweeney breathed in a giggling way, as if what I was

doing tickled. The scent of eucalyptus filled the room. Apart from her fingers, the rest of her was so white, almost blue.

I told her, Don't let your hands get cold or wet in the winter. Always wear warm gloves when you're out.

I'm not often out.

Delia Garrett coughed pointedly. Whenever you two are finished titivating, I'm gasping for a cup of tea.

I directed Bridie Sweeney to the kettle and took down the caddy and pot from the shelf. Patients can have as much tea as they like.

She said, Very good. With sugar, Mrs. Garrett?

Two spoons. And milk. Or, no, actually—that condensed stuff is so horrid, black will do.

I told Bridie Sweeney, Offer arrowroot biscuits with tea if the patient has any appetite.

Unlike plump-armed Delia Garrett, our poorer mothers came in here with too little flesh on their bones, and in Maternity our policy was to feed them up as much as possible before their time of trial.

Bridie Sweeney was a skinnymalinks herself, but the tough, wiry kind that food went through like water, I supposed. And you can make us each a cup while you're at it, Miss Sweeney.

I seized my chance to nip out. But at the door, I turned and said, I hope you know enough to know that you know nothing?

Bridie Sweeney stared—then nodded, head bobbing, a flower on its stem.

I told her, I was taught that being a good nurse means knowing when to call a doctor. So being a good runner means knowing when to call a nurse. If these ladies need a cup of water or another blanket or a clean handkerchief, give it to them, but if they're in any distress at all, run out to the lavatory and fetch me.

She made a small, comical salute.

I won't be two ticks, I said and dashed off.

What would Sister Finnigan say about my leaving the ward in the hands of this greenhorn? Well, I was doing my best. So were we all.

After the lavatory, I found myself thirsty for a glimpse of the outside world, so I went to the window and stared down at the sparse passers-by. The rain had cleared up but the day had a damp cling to it. A lady in full-length furs—an odd getup when it wasn't even November yet—stepped down from a cab and glided in the gates with a large leather bag in one hand and a cumbersome wooden case in the other. She shook back her lavish hood, baring two old-fashioned coils of hair. Well, I supposed the porter would explain the visitor ban to her.

Back in the ward, Bridie Sweeney was draining her tea, crumbs in the corner of her mouth. Delicious!

I didn't think she was being sarcastic. I raised my own cup to my lips and tasted ashy sweepings off some faraway floor.

Ita Noonan was muttering, It's all bockedy, banjaxed.

Bridie Sweeney came over to murmur in my ear, Is she by any chance an alco?

No, no, Dr. Prendergast ordered that whiskey for her flu.

She nodded and tapped her temple. Will her pot stay rattled permanently now?

I assured her that delirium was only temporary.

So...she'll get better?

I found myself crossing my fingers so tightly it hurt. A silly habit, I knew. I told Bridie Sweeney in a low voice: These mothers are often stronger than they look. Once her fever breaks...I'd lay money she'll get through this and have her twelfth in January.

Her twelfth?

The young woman's tone was so appalled, I didn't mention that only seven of the Noonan children were alive. I said instead, Do you know that saying, *She doesn't love him unless she gives him twelve*?

She grimaced. I couldn't stand that.

With a small shiver, I admitted, Me neither. Well, they'll put up no statues to the pair of us.

That made Bridie Sweeney snort with laughter.

The day had darkened again, and rain was fretfully spattering against the slanted glass. Trickles ran down from the partly open window.

Delia Garrett asked, Can we have that shut so we don't get drenched?

Sorry, I said, but air is vital, especially for respiratory complaints.

She buried her head under the pillow.

I set Bridie Sweeney to catching the drips with a cloth before they got near the beds. Then I sent her off to the supply room for ice from the electric refrigerator. It's a big box of a machine, I explained, and the cubes should be behind a little door at the top. If there's none left, go up one floor and ask.

I checked temperatures, pulses, respirations. I changed my patients' handkerchiefs and adjusted their pillows; I propped up Ita Noonan so she was in the semi-upright position that seemed to ease her breathing a little.

By that time Bridie Sweeney was back with a basinful of ice, so I left her in charge while I brought each woman in turn to the lavatory.

She seemed gentle and trustworthy enough for a little patient care, so I got her to show me she remembered how to wash her hands—she didn't forget a single step—and then I set her to sponging Ita Noonan's face and neck with ice water. Let me know once she's finished her whiskey, won't you?

Delia Garrett coughed in a bored way. Can I have some of that instead of this awful tea?

Alcohol was a helpful relaxant in pregnancy, but...Sorry, I told her, only if the doctor says so.

(Not that my patients had a doctor supervising their treatment at the moment. When did this Lynn person mean to show her face?)

Would you like a hot lemonade instead, Mrs. Garrett, or some barley water?

Ugh!

On the other side of the room, Ita Noonan yanked Bridie Sweeney's hands down onto her own belly.

Dread seized me. What is it, Mrs. Noonan?

My young helper was having to kneel on the cot so she wouldn't fall. She stared down at the mound under her palms. Ita Noonan was clutching her wrists and humming, but as if she were excited rather than in pain.

Astonishment filled the redhead's face. It's *moving*. Banging away in her insides!

Delia Garrett said with mild scorn, What did you expect?

I told Bridie Sweeney, Every unborn baby swims and somersaults.

Get away! As if it's alive?

I frowned. Could she be pulling my leg? Well, of course it's alive, Miss Sweeney. I corrected myself: Alive inside its mother, part of her.

I thought it only came to life once it was out.

I stared, thinking what a conjuring trick that would be—God

making Adam of mud and blowing his spirit into him all in a moment. But I knew I shouldn't be surprised; some patients came in here ready to give birth with almost as little grasp of the state of things.

I took *Jellett's Midwifery* down from the shelf and lifted the delicate onionskin to show Bridie Sweeney the frontispiece captioned *The full-term uterus*.

Her eyes widened. Janey mac!

It took me a second or two to deduce that she thought this was a drawing of a woman who'd been sliced in half. No, no, it's a cutaway—sketched as if we can see right through her. You notice how the baby's all curled up?

And upside down!

I smiled. Much happier that way too, I imagine. You're learning a lot for one day, aren't you, Miss Sweeney.

She murmured, It's a little acrobat.

But fast asleep most of the time.

Delia Garrett broke in to say, My second one wasn't. Clarissa kicked like a mule night, noon, and morning. But this one's a good girl, aren't you?

She rubbed her bump with a rueful fondness.

Bridie Sweeney suggested, Or a good boy, maybe?

Delia Garrett shook her head. I don't care for boys, and besides, my mother-in-law can always tell by how I'm carrying. Show me that picture?

When I passed her *Jellett's Midwifery,* Delia Garrett grimaced at the frontispiece but with a certain pride. Look how her innards are squeezed aside! No wonder my stomach's been dicky.

I put the book back on the shelf. Almost eleven already; time to change the poultice Sister Luke had put on Ita Noonan. I heated the linseed over a spirit lamp. It had to be thick enough that a spoon would stand up in the mixture. I opened the tapes of her nightdress, unwound the bandage around her chest, and peeled back the old caked crust. Her face was looking drawn and yellowish. I wiped her reddened collarbones clean with flax-tow swabs and soapy water while Bridie Sweeney stood close, handing over supplies as I asked for them.

Ita Noonan wheezed, Come here till I tell you.

I leaned in towards the dark odour of her breath while I took her pulse. But the woman said nothing more. Her heart rate was rather faster than it was earlier, but the pulse force felt a little weaker.

I spread the cooked linseed onto lint, laid a gauze dressing over that, and placed a layer of sterilised linen over the gauze. I flipped the whole thing between her limp breasts and covered it with a flannelette bandage. The tails needed tying behind her back and around her slumped shoulders, but between us, Bridie Sweeney and I made short work of it. I wouldn't have begrudged the time spent on all this fiddly faff if I'd believed that poulticing was any real use.

Ita Noonan's breath heaved and creaked. I gave her a spoon of ipecac syrup as an expectorant to loosen her congestion, hoping it wouldn't make her throw up. She screwed up her face at the taste but didn't fight me.

A minute later she coughed up some seaweed-coloured sputum. I caught it in her handkerchief, which I gave to Bridie to throw down the incinerator.

Bridie took a while to come back, so when she did, I asked, Got lost? Fell down a chute?

Bridie Sweeney admitted, Sorry, I lingered in the water closet. The little bolt on the door so you can be private, and lashings of gorgeous hot water, and such nice squares of paper. I'm liking hospital.

That made me laugh.

Especially the smells.

I thought, *Eucalyptus, linseed, carbolic? Whiskey, at the moment?* For me they couldn't cover up the faecal, bloody tang of birth and death.

I told her, It's usually much more orderly here. You've caught us on the hop, rather. More than twice as many patients as usual and a quarter of the staff.

Her face lit up, I supposed because I was including her in the word *staff*, as a helper.

It struck me that she was a beauty in a white-faced, bony way; a precious bead winking in a dustbin. I wondered where Sister Luke had found her. Do you live near by, Miss Sweeney?

Only around the corner.

Tone a little evasive. Still with her parents, I assumed from how young she seemed. How old are you, do you mind my asking?

She shrugged. About twenty-two.

A coy way of putting it, *about* twenty-two. Well, I didn't want to poke my nose in.

She surprised me by asking, Would you call me Bridie, maybe?

Certainly, if you prefer.

I didn't quite know what to say after that, so I checked my watch. It's getting on towards noon, so you should have your lunch now.

I didn't bring one, but I'm all right.

No, no, meals are laid on for us in a canteen beside the kitchen.

She still hesitated. What about you?

Oh, I'm not hungry yet.

There was nothing to be done about her frock or shoes,

but... You might just roll down your sleeves and tidy your hair before you go down.

Flushing, Bridie felt for the fuzz of bright curls that had escaped and pulled them back out of her face.

I regretted mentioning it; she was here only for the day, after all, so how much could her grooming matter?

She wrestled with the rubber band.

I asked, Don't you have a comb with you?

She shook her head.

I went to my bag and found her a hard rubber one.

Bridie made her head smooth, then held out the comb. Thanks for the lend.

Keep it, I said.

No!

Really, I much prefer my other one. It looks like tortoiseshell but it's made of celluloid.

Stop wittering, Julia, I told myself.

A baritone crooned in the passage—Groyne.

Are ye right there, Michael, are ye right?
Do you think that we'll be there before the night?

Delia Garrett complained: That awful man who brought me in yesterday.

The orderly pushed through the door backwards. He reminded me of that macabre servant out of *Frankenstein*.

In lieu of a greeting, I commented, Always a song on your lips, Groyne.

He sketched a music-hall bow in my direction, then spun the wheelchair around to present the new patient. A young woman—a girl, I'd have said, except for her bump—with coal-black hair and a face full of fear.

Another lovely for your select sisterhood. Baby coming soon, but Maternity wouldn't have her on account of her cough.

I glanced at the chart Groyne handed me. Just one line scribbled at the top: *Mary O'Rahilly, age seventeen, primigravida.*

Women who'd given birth before were known quantities even if one could never be quite certain what would happen on the day. A first-timer such as Mary O'Rahilly was a different story. The admitting physician hadn't even estimated a due date; he must be hard-pressed today.

Mrs. O'Rahilly, let's get you out of that wheelchair.

She stood for me with no apparent difficulty but trembled. Chills, I wondered, or nerves, or both? Short and slim, dwarfed by her great bulge. I patted the chair at the end of the middle cot and said, Sit here till we get you changed.

The orderly pushed the empty wheelchair towards the door.

Groyne, any word of when we can expect to see this new doctor?

Ah, the lady rebel!

Gossip was meat and drink to the man. I wasn't in the habit of encouraging tittle-tattle, but this time I couldn't stop my eyebrows from arching.

He asked, Haven't you heard of her?

You're implying she's one of the Sinn Féiners?

(The Gaelic phrase meant *us-aloners.* They went around ranting that home rule wouldn't be enough now; nothing would content them but a breakaway republic.)

Implying nothing, Groyne told me. Miss Lynn's a vicar's daughter from Mayo gone astray—a socialist, suffragette, anarchist firebrand!

This sounded improbably lurid, and the orderly did tend to bad-mouth any woman set over him. But the details were so specific.

A vicar's daughter, I asked, really?

Most of those green-wearing Erin-lovers may be Catholics like ourselves, but there's the odd Proddy eccentric in their ranks, he said disgustedly. (He didn't notice the cold look Delia Garrett gave him.) This one was a she-captain, no less, back in the Rising. It was her stitched up the bullet wounds of those terrorist pups on the roof of City Hall.

He pointed up towards the office on the third floor and added, Top brass must be really scraping the barrel, all right.

Well, I said uncomfortably, I suppose it's hardly a time to be picky.

The new patient's eyes were bulging as she said, The hospital's hired a criminal?

The orderly nodded. Miss Lynn was deported with the rest of the pack, locked up in Britain—but then weren't they let out last year, for all the blood on their hands, and came slinking back?

I had to rein in this conversation before panic spread.

Politics aside, I said, I'm sure *Dr.* Lynn wouldn't have been called in today if she were not a capable physician.

My emphasis on her title made Groyne smirk. Ah, I'll say no more.

That was the orderly's inevitable phrase when he had a great deal more to say. He was settling in now, leaning on the handles of the wheelchair as if on a bar. These days, a fellow can't let slip a word against the gentler sex—so called! A female delivering my post, munitionettes, girls putting out fires, even. Where will it all end?

We mustn't keep you, Groyne.

He took my hint. Best of luck, Mrs. O'Rahilly.

He waltzed off, warbling to the wheelchair: *Are ye right there, Michael, are ye right?*

Bridie remarked, He's a gas, that fellow.

My lips twisted.

Don't you care for him, Nurse Power?

Groyne's humour is a little dark for my taste.

She said, Well, you have to laugh.

The two of us got Mary O'Rahilly's shawl, dress, and drawers off, though we left her stockings on for warmth. She shivered and shuddered. We drew a nightdress over her smooth black hair. *So you'll be more comfortable*, I always said, but changing their clothes was really a matter of hygiene; some patients came in crawling with lice. In a properly equipped ward, I'd have steamed Mary O'Rahilly's own clothes, just in case, but as it was, all I could do was tell Bridie to wrap them up in paper and put them on the top shelf. I showed her how to draw the tapes of the nightdress closed at the patient's sides. I got a bed jacket on the girl and a hospital shawl wrapped around her neck.

Mary O'Rahilly's face creased up and she stiffened.

I waited till it was over. How strong was that pang, dear?

(We were trained not to call them *bad*.)

Not too strong, I suppose.

Then again, I thought, a first-timer had no basis for comparison. I asked, Do you know when your baby's due?

Faintly: My neighbour says November, maybe.

Your last menses?

Her face flickered with confusion.

Your monthly?

She went pink. I couldn't tell you, sorry. Last winter sometime?

I wouldn't bother trying to reckon from when she'd felt the first foetal movements, because a primigravida rarely registered the quickening till it was too late to be a useful marker.

And these pangs—whereabouts have you been feeling them mostly?

Mary O'Rahilly gestured vaguely to her belly.

I knew that was more typical of false labour; warning shots, rather than the full onslaught, which tended to hit in the back. This girl might be weeks from delivery still.

I pressed her: How much of a break do you get between them?

An unhappy shrug.

Does it vary?

I can't remember.

Irregularity, stopping and starting—that all sounded like false labour. And tell me, Mrs. O'Rahilly, how long have you been having these pangs?

I don't know.

Hours?

Days.

One day and night for the dilating of the cervix was common enough. But surely, if this was the real thing, Mary O'Rahilly would be farther along after *days* of it?

A catch in her voice: Does that mean it's coming?

Ah, we'll see soon enough.

But that man said—

I couldn't restrain a small snort. Groyne was a military stretcher-bearer, I told her. He picked up a lot about wounds and fevers, no doubt, but not much about childbearing.

I thought that might make Mary O'Rahilly smile, but she was too rigid with worry. Like most of my patients—even the multigravidas—she'd probably never been admitted to hospital before.

As I carried on taking her history, I was looking out for hints of problems ahead. Rickets, above all, such a curse in the inner city—children's teeth came in late, they didn't walk until two, they had curvature of the ribs or legs or spine. But no, Mary O'Rahilly was only small, with a pelvis in proportion to the rest of her. No puffiness to suggest her kidneys were acting up. She'd had a perfectly healthy pregnancy until she'd caught this grippe.

She shivered, coughed into the back of her little hand. I've been so careful, Nurse. Gargling with cider vinegar and drinking it too.

I nodded neutrally. Some placed their trust in treacle to ward off this flu, others in rhubarb, as if there had to be one household substance that could save us all. I'd even met fools who credited their safety to the wearing of red.

I rested my hand with the watch in it on Mary O'Rahilly's chest so I could count her breaths without her noticing. The rate of respiration was up somewhat, between her spluttering coughs. I tucked a thermometer under her tongue. *Pulse regular but slightly weak*, I added to her chart. By the way, these blue marks on your wrist, did you have a fall? Were you dizzy, was that it?

She shook her head. I just bruise easy, she mumbled.

When I checked the mercury after a minute, her temperature was only a little above normal. I told her, Yours isn't a bad case at all.

Bridie and I helped her into the middle cot. (Eileen Devine's deathbed.)

Stop, don't think that way, would you jinx this poor girl?

Mary O'Rahilly said, in her breathy murmur, People are afraid to go near each other, it can pounce so fast! The other day, the peelers smashed down a door in the tenement behind ours and found a whole family expired on the one mattress.

I nodded, thinking it rather awful that the neighbours hadn't gone near them before that point…but how could one judge in times of such general dread?

I needed her on her back so I could feel her abdomen. It might hurt if the bladder was full, so I asked if she wanted the lavatory first.

She shook her head.

Delia Garrett snappishly: *I* need to go, as it happens.

Bridie offered to bring her.

I dithered. All right, I suppose, if you keep a firm hold of Mrs. Garrett so she won't fall.

Why on earth would I fall?

When they were gone, I checked on Ita Noonan, who was still in her vaporous daze.

Back to Mary O'Rahilly. I lifted up her nightdress but covered her privates and thighs with a sheet. Like many an adolescent mother, she had dramatic purple claw marks on the underside of her bump; tight young skin wasn't used to being stretched so. However, the good thing about her age was that her body should bounce back afterwards.

I sat on the edge of the bed, facing her head. I rubbed my palms hard to take the chill off them, but she jumped when I put them on her.

Sorry, they'll warm up. Try to relax your belly for me.

I slid my hands from one spot to the next without lifting them; crucial not to tap as if playing piano because that made the muscles contract. I shut my eyes and tried to picture Mary O'Rahilly's inner landscape based on what my hands told me. There it was, the firm top of the uterus, six finger-widths above her navel; she was full term or close to it. So the flu hadn't managed to shake this particular nut out of its shell early, thank God.

One foetus only. (We dreaded twins.) Normal presentation,

THE PULL OF THE STARS

head down and facing the spine. I found the small bottom and traced the arc of the back downward. Your baby's in just the right position.

It is?

The head seemed nicely lodged in the pelvis. Not that this told me whether she was in true labour or not, because in first-timers, the skull could lock into place a full month before birth.

Bridie came back in with Delia Garrett, perched on the bed on the other side of Mary O'Rahilly, and took her hand without asking. What are you doing now, Nurse Power?

If you'll get me that thing on the top shelf that looks like an ear trumpet, I'm going to listen to the baby's heartbeat. Nice deep breaths for me, Mrs. O'Rahilly.

I placed the wide end of the wooden horn against her belly on the side where I'd felt the back but below the midpoint, and I put the narrow end to my ear.

What—

That was Bridie; I shushed her with a finger to my lips. I counted, staring at the second hand on my watch.

Foetal heart rate 138 beats per minute, I recorded, quite normal.

A cough spasmed through Mary O'Rahilly, so I got her sitting up and sent Bridie over to the kettle to make her a hot lemonade. In the meantime, I had the young mother drink a tall glass of water. When her next pang started, I checked my watch—twenty minutes since the last. I settled her on her left side and told her to breathe in for a count of three, out for three, and repeat. If these were only warning shots, the combination of water, position, and breathing should ease them.

I checked on Ita Noonan—still asleep.

All right, Mrs. Garrett? Any more looseness?

She clucked her tongue. Quite the other way around, I'm all bunged up now.

It puzzled me how she could be feeling constipated so soon after diarrhea.

Mary O'Rahilly's small, uneasy humming stopped.

I asked, Would you say that that one was about the same or milder?

She answered confusedly: About the same?

Probably true labour, I decided. But if her pangs were still coming at only twenty-minute intervals after more than a day...oh, dear, the girl could have a long way to go still.

Though of course, the last thing I wanted was for one of my patients to start delivering in this cramped little room when there wasn't a single obstetrician in the hospital.

An internal examination to find out how far the cervix was dilated would tell me more, but I was holding off because it had been drilled into me that every time one's hand went inside a woman, one ran some risk of infecting her.

When in doubt, I'd been taught, watch and wait.

You know what might help is if you felt able to walk around, Mrs. O'Rahilly.

(That could help the cervix dilate, and it distracted the woman and gave her something to do.)

Startled, she asked: Walk where?

I wracked my brain. I couldn't send infectious patients to roam the corridors, but there wasn't room to swing a cat in here...Just up and down, around your bed. Here, we'll get these chairs out of the way. Sip your lemonade as you go.

Bridie had the chairs stacked and tucked in under the desk before I could ask.

Mary O'Rahilly stepped cautiously around the bed and back again in a U.

All right? Are you warm enough?

Yes, thank you, miss.

Nurse Power, I corrected her gently.

Sorry.

No bother.

Mary O'Rahilly was clutching her bump through the night-dress, poking one finger into her navel.

I asked, Is that where it hurts?

She shook her head and caught a cough with the back of her hand. Just wondering how I'll know when it's about to open.

I stared. Your belly button?

Her voice trembled as she paced. Does it do it on its own or will the doctor have to . . . force it?

I was embarrassed for her. Mrs. O'Rahilly, you know that's not where the baby comes out?

The girl blinked at me.

Think of where it got started. I waited, then whispered: Below.

The information shook her; she opened her mouth wide, then clamped it shut and coughed again, eyes shiny.

Bridie was standing on Mary O'Rahilly's other side holding *Jellett's Midwifery*, which she hadn't asked if she could take down. Here, look, you can see the top of the baby's head, and in the next . . .

She flipped the page.

. . . it's sticking right out of her!

Mary O'Rahilly flinched at the graphic images but nodded, absorbing the lesson. Then walked away as if she couldn't bear to see any more.

Thanks, Bridie.

I made a little gesture for her to put the book back before she noticed the more disturbing sections: malpresentations, anomalies, obstetrical surgeries.

Mary O'Rahilly was stumbling back and forth around the bed, blinded by fright.

Puritans who thought ignorance was the shield of purity—they made me angry. I said to her, Your mother should really have explained. Didn't she bring you into the world this way? I've seen it happen dozens—no, hundreds of times—and it's a beautiful sight.

(Trying not to think of all the ways it could go wrong. Of the young blonde I'd encountered in my first month here who'd laboured for three days before the doctor had pried out her eleven-pounder by caesarean section; she'd died of the infected wound.)

Mary O'Rahilly's voice was barely there: Mammy passed when I was eleven.

I regretted what I'd said about her mother. I'm so sorry. Was it…

Having my last brother, or trying to.

Her voice was very low, as if it were a secret, and a shameful one, rather than the most ordinary tragedy ever told. Even if this girl was ignorant of the mechanics of birth, she knew the fundamental fact about it: the risk.

I supposed that was why I found myself telling her, My mother went the same way.

They were all looking at me now, these three women.

Mary O'Rahilly seemed almost comforted. Did she?

I said, In our case, I was four, and the baby did live.

Bridie was watching me, her eyes crinkling in sympathy.

Mary O'Rahilly sketched a cross, touching her forehead, shoulders, and breastbone, before resuming her walk.

I felt as if I were adrift in a leaking boat with these strangers, waiting out a storm.

A grunt burst out of Delia Garrett. My bowels—I need to move them, Nurse, but I know it won't come!

I looked at her hard. I'd been so focused on the newcomer, it had completely slipped my mind that constipation could be an early hint of labour. But Delia Garrett wasn't due for almost eight weeks, I argued with myself. This being her third go, surely she'd recognise those pangs?

Except that she was so reluctant to stay in hospital, she'd be likely to deny any hint that she might be slipping into that state. And wasn't this flu becoming infamous for expelling babies before their time?

She let out a volley of coughs.

Tell me, Mrs. Garrett, when you get the urge, does your whole middle tighten up?

Like a drum!

That was another sign.

I laid her down on her back with her knees drawn up a little and began palpating. The baby's bum was up, head down; that was good. Bridie, the horn?

Delia Garrett tried to sit up, eyes wild. You're not prodding me with that thing.

It won't hurt.

I can't bear anything pressing on me right now.

Very well, I can use my ear.

So I set my cheek against her bump and asked her to take a deep breath.

I tell you I'm desperate for the lavatory!

I really don't think it's that, Mrs. Garrett, but you can try a bedpan.

Bridie rushed to fetch one.

I put my ear back to the hot, stretched skin. I found a pulse...but I could tell without counting that it was too slow to be anything but Delia Garrett's.

Her cough resounded in my head.

Let me try a different spot...

But the young woman kept thrashing about and protesting that I was pressing too hard, and I couldn't make out the pattering beat I was seeking, the foetal rhythm that should be almost twice as a fast as its mother's.

Please, Mrs. Garrett, don't move for a minute.

It hurts to stay flat on my back!

I spoke lullingly, as if to a spooked horse: I understand.

Delia Garrett's voice went shrill: How could you, a spinster?

Bridie's eyes widened and met mine.

I smiled and shook my head to show I hadn't taken it personally. Labouring women often turned cranky as things came to the crunch; in fact, it was a useful sign.

Delia Garrett's face screwed up again and she began to moan.

I noted the time.

Waiting for her pang to finish, I checked on Ita Noonan, who was still scarlet-faced and dozing.

Between their two cots, Mary O'Rahilly paced like a ghost, three steps towards the window, three steps back, trying to keep out of the way.

Mrs. O'Rahilly, how are you doing?

All right. Could I sit a bit, maybe?

Certainly, whatever you like.

I went around her to Ita Noonan and gently pulled up the woman's lip to insert a thermometer under her tongue; she didn't stir.

Back to kneel on Delia Garrett's bed, because I knew there was one more bit of proof I needed: Was the head fixed in the pelvis yet or still floating?

Hold steady on your back for just a minute more, please, Mrs. Garrett.

Facing her glossy bump, I moved my right hand into Pawlic's grip, taking hold just above the pubic bone, sinking my fingers in as if around a huge apple, and gently trying to shift the small skull from side to—

Argh!

Delia Garrett kneed me away violently.

I rubbed my bruised rib, calculating. The head hadn't budged at all under my fingers, so, yes, this woman was in labour, two months early.

Bridie pointed.

Mrs. Noonan had let the thermometer drop out of her mouth, and it had fallen onto her blanket.

Pick it up for me, would you, Bridie? Quick, before it cools.

She scuttled between the two cots.

Show me?

Bridie put the thermometer up to my face, vertically.

Flat! So I can read the figures.

She turned it.

I read the number: 105.8. Climbing again.

Check she still has some whiskey in her cup, would you?

Bridie reported: Plenty.

You could try ice-cold cloths on the back of her neck, then.

She hurried to do that.

I tugged lightly on Delia Garrett's drawers and said, These have to come off.

She huffed but lifted her hips so I could slide them down.

Let your knees fall apart, would you, just for a minute?

I didn't even need to touch her. The pubic curls were crusted with red, what we called bloody show, the surest sign.

Behind me, Bridie let out a gasp of shock, but it was covered up by Delia Garrett's groan.

I closed her legs and pulled out my watch; barely five minutes since the last pang. This was all going much too fast. Born at thirty-two weeks would mean severely premature. All we could do with those babies was keep them in the warm box upstairs for the week, send them home wrapped in cotton wool with an eyedropper for feeding, and cross our fingers—especially if they were boys, notoriously weaker—that they'd somehow live through the first year.

My most urgent task was to look after the mother, I reminded myself. To keep Delia Garrett's blood pressure from going through the roof.

I took her wrist now. Under the pads of my fingertips, her pulse leapt, a river in spate. I plumped her pillows. Sit up and lie back on these, dear.

Blinking, she did.

Bridie was still standing there with the thermometer, open-mouthed.

I asked her to disinfect it just to get her over to the sink. I followed her and murmured in her ear, You know what part of a nurse is the most important?

Bridie looked blank. Her hands? Her feet?

I pointed to my face and made it serene. If a nurse looks worried, patients will worry. So guard your face.

She nodded, absorbing that.

I went back to Delia Garrett. I believe you're on your way, dear.

Fear in her voice, for the first time. I can't be! She's supposed to be a Christmas baby.

As lightly as I could, I said, Well, she seems to believe she's a Halloween one.

Ah, no!

I turned to see Bridie with an appalled face, one hand trickling scarlet. I demanded, What have you done?

73

She cringed. Sorry, I set the thing, I put it down in the hot pot, but it must have hit something—so I took it out again—

I'd meant her to dip the thermometer in the basin of carbolic. What kind of eejit didn't know that boiling water would crack a delicate glass bulb?

But I bit my tongue. I could hardly expect this young woman to pick up the basics of nursing in a couple of hours.

Excuse me a minute, Mrs. Garrett.

She buried her face in the pillow and moaned.

I crossed the room, took Bridie's hand, and shook it a little over the bubbling water till she released the shards. I dried the bleeding finger on a sterile cloth and gave the cut a dab with a styptic pencil from my apron to seal it up so she wouldn't go off dripping scarlet like a murderess in a play.

There you go. Now, could you run upstairs to the maternity ward and find Sister Finnigan? Tell her I have a precipitate premature labour—

Damn it, Bridie would never hold on to those unfamiliar words.

A *rapid* premature labour, I said instead.

(Would I be better off taking the time to write a note?)

Tell Sister Finnigan that Mrs. Garrett's pangs are less than five minutes apart and we need a doctor. If the lady one isn't in yet, then anyone else at all. Will you remember?

Bridie echoed in a thrilled voice: Rapid, five minutes, any doctor.

She scurried off.

I called after her, Don't actually run.

Delia Garrett grunted crossly. I keep telling you, I need to go.

I reached for the bedpan Bridie had brought over.

Not that!

You have to rest and conserve your strength, Mrs. Garrett.

(What I was thinking was, what if her baby dropped out in the passage or in the toilet?)

Mutinous, she allowed me to pull her nightdress up and get the bedpan under her, but as I'd expected, nothing came out. I said, While I have you here, let me clean you.

She didn't object, just shut her eyes as she crouched miserably on the pan. I gave her soft parts a thorough going-over first with soap and water, then with warm, dilute disinfectant, to get rid of the germs that could infiltrate her or contaminate the baby as it came out.

As the next pang took Delia Garrett, she hung her head and let out a guttural sound that turned into a racking cough. Something for the pain, Nurse Julia?

I'm sure when the doctor comes—

Now!

I'm afraid nurses don't have authority to order medicine.

Then what bloody use are you?

I had no answer for that.

Let's get you lying down now, Mrs. Garrett. On your left, that helps.

(If the labouring woman turned on her right, the uterus might compress the vena cava and reduce blood flow to her heart.)

I urged, Take long breaths.

I took a clean cloth from the packet and dipped it in boiling water. When it had cooled enough, I wrung it out, folded it smaller, and went over to where Delia Garrett lay on her side. Slide your knees up towards your chest for me, so your rear's sticking out?

She grumbled but did it.

Here's a hot compress, I said, then pressed the cloth to her perineum.

A sob.

That pressure behind, that'll be the baby's head you're feeling.

Make it stop!

I wondered, *For how many millennia have women been vainly asking that?*

No, no, I assured her, it means you don't have long to go.

(And where, oh, where was the blasted lady doctor?)

In the middle bed, young Mary O'Rahilly was coiled around her own slow, unceasing pains. A little damp across the forehead, her hair a black oil slick; dark underneath the eyes. Birth was such a roll of the dice, I thought; labour could keep a woman in painful limbo for days on end or strike her as hard and fast as lightning.

I simply couldn't give hands-on care to two women at once, and Delia Garrett's need was more urgent. But when Mary O'Rahilly straightened again, I asked softly, Was that a bad one, Mrs. O'Rahilly?

A hapless shrug, as if the seventeen-year-old were unqualified to measure what was being done to her. She let out a series of small coughs.

When Bridie Sweeney gets back, I'll have her make you more hot lemonade.

Delia Garrett cried out.

I kept pressing on the hot compress with one hand, and I checked my watch with the other. Her pains were close to three minutes apart now. I fingered the silver disk as if I could smooth away the terrible scratches. I pushed it back into my bib pocket.

Delia Garrett wailed, It wasn't like this the other times, Nurse Julia. Can't you give me something?

And why was I not allowed to do that in a pinch when half the protocols had been thrown out the window?

Instead, I threw the compress into the waste bucket and got

behind her. Let's see if this helps, Mrs. Garrett. Up on your hands and knees?

She grunted angrily but heaved herself into a cow-like position. With the heels of my hands, I pressed hard on her two sitz bones, pushing the very base of her pelvis forward.

Oh, oh!

I hoped that meant I was taking the edge off the pain.

For the next contraction, three minutes later, I tried thumbing the last few vertebrae on both sides of her spine, but that did nothing for her. I switched to the dimples of Venus at the base of her back; I set my knuckles into them and leaned hard.

Any better?

Delia Garrett sounded preoccupied: A bit.

These tricks of counterpressure weren't in any manual, just passed down, midwife to midwife, though the more stern of our profession didn't approve of anything done to relieve pains they considered natural and productive. But I was firmly in favour of whatever helped a woman keep up her strength and get through.

In the silence, Delia Garrett sank back against the pillows and pulled her nightgown down. Her eyes were shut as she muttered, I didn't want this baby.

A sound of footsteps behind me. I could see by Bridie's face that she'd caught that.

I took Delia Garrett's hot hand with its manicured nails. It's natural enough.

Two seemed plenty, she confided. Or if my little girls could have had more time... it's not that I wasn't willing to have a third, only not so very soon. Am I dreadful?

Not at all, Mrs. Garrett.

Now I think I'm being punished.

None of that! Rest and breathe.

And Bridie was by her side, gripping her other hand. Doctor's coming.

Oh, oh! A wave took Delia Garrett.

In the next respite, I got the woman on her side and had Bridie cup her right hand around Delia Garrett's right hip and set her left flat on the small of the back. I started the rotation. Like pedaling a bicycle, see?

Bridie asked, Is it?

It baffled me that this young woman seemed to lack experience of the most ordinary things—bicycles and thermometers and unborn babies. Still, she was so grateful for everything from skin lotion to ashy tea. And how quickly she got the knack of whatever I taught her.

Delia Garrett ordered, Don't stop.

I left Bridie to continue the pelvic tilts and went to check on the other two.

Fiery-faced, Ita Noonan was tossing and turning. I was at a loss as to how to quench this fever without our usual standbys, aspirin and quinine.

Mrs. O'Rahilly, how're you doing?

The young woman shivered and shrugged.

Her pangs were still twenty minutes apart, according to my notes. I suggested, Have a sleep if you think you could drop off.

I doubt it.

Maybe walk a bit more, then?

Mary O'Rahilly turned her face to the pillow to muffle her cough. She clambered out and started pacing around the bed again, a lioness in a too-small cage.

Delia Garrett let out a long groan. Can I start the bloody pushing?

Panic flapped in my chest. Do you feel the urge to bear down?

She snapped, I just want to get this over with.

Then please wait a little longer, till the doctor comes.

A mutinous silence. Delia Garrett said, I believe I'm leaking.

I checked. Hard to tell amniotic fluid from the water that had dripped from the compress, but I took her word for it.

Just then a boyish stranger in a black suit swept in and introduced himself as Dr. MacAuliffe, a general surgeon.

My heart sank. He looked no more than twenty-five. These inexperienced doctors rarely knew one end of a woman from the other.

He wanted to do an internal, of course. At least he wasn't slapdash about hygiene; he asked for boiled rubber gloves. He had a brief conversation with Delia Garrett while I fetched a paper packet and then unwrapped it for him. He soaped and nailbrushed his hands and snapped on the gloves.

I got Delia Garrett's thighs up at a right angle to her back, her bottom sticking out over the edge of the bed, to give the doctor more room to work.

When he began, she yowled.

MacAuliffe said, Well, now, madam—

(He'd clearly judged from her southside accent that she should be addressed that way rather than as *missus*.)

You're coming along very nicely indeed.

That was vague.

He tugged the gloves off.

I gestured to Bridie to put them in the bucket of items to be sterilised.

Fully dilated, Doctor? I murmured.

Ah, so it seems.

I gritted my teeth. Couldn't he tell? If he was wrong and the rim of the cervix was still in the way, and Delia Garrett pushed hard enough to make it swell up and block the passage...

MacAuliffe told her, Just take your ease and let Nurse Power look after you.

Her cough was a harsh bark.

I asked, May I give Mrs. Garrett something to make her more comfortable, Doctor?

Really, at this late point in the proceedings, it seems hardly—

And to calm her down, I urged. Dr. Prendergast's been worried about her elevated pulse force.

That had a visible effect, because Prendergast was his senior. MacAuliffe said, Chloroform, then, I suppose, the usual dose.

I should have asked him about Mary O'Rahilly next, but I was reluctant, somehow. Young doctors had a tendency to treat nature the way one would a lazy horse—with a crack of the whip. They particularly distrusted primigravidae, who had no record of being able to give birth unaided. Especially if the strain on a labouring woman was exacerbated by an illness such as the flu, a young general surgeon such as MacAuliffe might well panic at the delay, order a manual dilation, then go in with forceps. Despite how long the seventeen-year-old had been enduring her pains, the last thing I wanted was for this pup to start brandishing tools that could harm as easily as help.

Instead, I drew his attention back to Delia Garrett. When may she start pushing?

Oh, whenever she likes. As soon as you glimpse the head, call me down to deliver her, he added on his way to the door.

I doubt it'll be very long now—can't you stay, Doctor?

We're all stretched madly thin, he threw over his shoulder.

The ward was silent when the door had shut.

Acting ward sister, I reminded myself. I straightened my spine. I was a little wobbly, light-headed. It had been a long time since my bread and cocoa.

My helper was watching.

I summoned up a smile. Bridie, sorry, I never did send you down for lunch.

Sure I'm grand.

At least I had permission to give Delia Garrett some relief now. I went to the medicine cabinet for an inhaler and measured chloroform onto its stained cotton pad. Roll back onto your left side, Mrs. Garrett. Put this over your mouth and breathe it in whenever you like.

She sucked hard on the mouthpiece. I felt her pulse; it didn't seem much more bounding than before. Oh, why hadn't I remembered to remind MacAuliffe to check the foetal pulse with his stethoscope? Maybe Delia Garrett would let me try with the wooden horn if I asked now.

But here came another contraction already.

I pressed hard on the small of her back with both fists. How long a full minute of pain lasted, even for someone who was only observing it. I pushed and pulled her pelvis as if I were working some heavy machine. Waiting for the pang's grip on Delia Garrett to loosen, I realised I couldn't imagine enduring such sensations, and yet this was something most women all over the world did. Was there something uncanny about me that I only ever hovered over the scene, a stone angel?

Back to the here and now, Julia.

Delia Garrett had said her first two babies popped out. Best to be ready for it to happen any minute now and try to reduce any tearing when the head came down like a rocket. Impossible to offer her any privacy, but at least I could have supplies laid out and a crib standing by.

Bridie, could you nip back up to Maternity and ask for one of those foldout cribs on wheels that go at the end of a cot?

She dashed away.

Nurse Julia!

That was Delia Garrett. Breathe in more chloroform, I told her as I pressed the inhaler to her mouth. You're going great guns.

In the next lull, I washed my hands again and laid out what might be needed for delivery: gloves in a basin of biniodide of mercury, swabs, scissors, a hypo full of chloroform and another of morphine, needle-holder and needles, sutures.

Delia Garrett made a new sound, a low growl.

I asked, Ready to bear down next time?

She nodded furiously.

I took the inhaler out of her hand; I needed her alert.

It only struck me now that, unlike the proper hospital beds up in Maternity, these camp cots had no rails at the bottom. Nothing for it but to have Delia Garrett lie the other way.

Could you spin around, dear, and put your head at the end of the bed for me?

How's that going to help?

I stood her pillow up against the headrest. When the pang comes, jam your left foot against this and push, all right?

I wrenched blankets and sheets out of the way so she could rotate herself. I looped a long roller towel around a bottom corner of the metal cot and set it in her hand. Pull hard on this too.

Delia Garrett gripped the towel, her breathing harsh.

I pulled up her nightdress and bent her right leg up in my lap to get a good look.

I hadn't noticed when Bridie wheeled in the crib I'd asked for. She was looking white; faintness, fatigue, or just excitement? Of all the wards for her to have walked into this morning—had the young woman had any idea where Sister Luke was sending her?

Thanks, Bridie. Hurry for Dr. MacAuliffe now.

She shot off again.

The young surgeon might be irked if he had to stand around and wait through more than a few pushes, but I'd rather chance that than have him stay away too long.

The next pang made Delia Garrett screech.

I reminded her, Low sounds, they have the most heft to them.

I knelt over Delia Garrett and set my thigh into the small of her back for her to brace herself against as she pushed. The towel was so tight around her hands, it striped them with white. That silence as she held her breath and bore down; there was nothing like it. I realised something then: no other job would ever satisfy me.

Urghhhhhhh!

I said, And rest a minute now, catch your breath.

I felt her pulse to make sure its force wasn't too high.

Lunch. (A voice I didn't recognise.) Sorry it's so late.

I whipped down Delia Garrett's nightdress for decency and turned my head to the door, where that kitchen maid with a purple birthmark held three stacked trays. Not just now, please!

Thrown, she gazed around. There wasn't enough room on the counters or desk. Maybe if I set them down on the floor?

I knew one of us would be sure to stumble over them. I told her, *Out*side the door.

The kitchen maid disappeared.

I shook off my irritation and focused on Delia Garrett again. I could see the next pain in her eyes, an oncoming train. Chin down, now, Mrs. Garrett. Curl into the push. Kick with that heel and haul on the towel.

She moaned.

I thought of something Ita Noonan had said when she was admitted last week, back when she was still compos mentis.

She hadn't wanted to let me near her at first because she said she'd always had a neighbour called Granny in when she was having her babies, and Granny had lucky hands—did I have lucky hands? I'd been tempted to point out that I had three diplomas instead. But half the battle with patients was persuading them out of their fear, so I'd looked Ita Noonan in her red-rimmed eyes and sworn that I did indeed have lucky hands.

I pulled up Delia Garrett's nightdress again for a better look. I wrapped my left arm around her right leg and held it up out of the way. She went quite silent as she heaved this time. Her face was a dull crimson.

Between her thighs, at the heart of her purplish flesh, a darker tuft. I can see the head, Mrs. Garrett!

She sobbed, and it disappeared again.

Don't push this time, just nice little breaths, I urged her. As if you're blowing out candles.

Her perineum was bulging redly. If the head crowned too fast, during a contraction, it could tear her open. I could press on the perineum, but that would further strain the delicate skin. Instead I did what Sister Finnigan had taught me: set the heel of my right hand behind Delia Garrett's anus, pushing the unseen head forward, and snaked my left arm over her thigh and through her legs so I'd be ready at her soft parts. Now!

She pushed, heaving in my arms so hard, I thought she might snap my wrist.

I glimpsed the head again, just inches from my face, and with three fingers of my left hand I tried to get a purchase on the slickly furred scalp and draw it forward...

Delia Garrett made sounds like she was being eaten by wolves. She kicked at the cot rails.

Thudding steps behind me. Just Bridie. Seeing Delia Garrett with her head almost hanging off the end of the bed, she gasped.

The dark tuft disappeared again, swallowed up in purple. I kept my voice steady: Where's Dr. MacAuliffe?

Men's Fever, sorry. They wouldn't let me up there, but they've sent him a message.

I shut my eyes just for a second. I reminded myself that I knew how to deliver this infant. *Lucky hands.*

Again I waited for a gap between contractions. Heel of right hand, fingers of left, straining for a grip on the slippery scalp like a climber on a rock face in the rain. Now, with all your strength, Mrs. Garrett—

Urghhhhhhhhhhhhh! A blue vein inflated at the woman's temple. Delia Garrett was a key in a lock, jammed, jammed, then suddenly turning—

She roared. She ripped, a wet parcel. Blood seeped through my knuckles. Not just a head but the whole baby shot out on the sheet.

I cried, Magnificent!

But the infant had dark cherry lips. Skin bruised in places, peeling as if after sunburn though it had never seen the light. A girl. A tiny, still girl.

I picked her up in an infant blanket. A big head for such a meagre body. Just in case by some chance I was wrong, I smacked her on the back.

I waited.

I hated to do it, but I slapped Delia Garrett's baby one more time.

Nothing.

I smoothed the flaking skin. The wide face, exquisitely moulded eyelids.

Bridie goggled at the limp creature in my hands. Why's it all—

Dead, I mouthed.

Her face shut like a book.

On the middle cot, Mary O'Rahilly was propped up on one elbow, watching with appalled eyes. She read our expressions and turned away, contracting around her cough.

Give Mrs. Garrett back that inhaler, would you, Bridie?

Finding it in her mouth, Delia Garrett drew on it with a hiss.

My fingertips rested on the small, cooling limbs. Silently moving my lips: *Mother of God, take home this sleeping child.*

Then I shrouded her and asked Bridie to fetch me a basin.

I set the swaddled still into it. A clean cloth now, please.

I stretched it over the top. My eyes swam. I knuckled them dry.

It was so hushed in that close little room. Delia Garrett was slumped with her eyes shut, worn out from her work. I felt her pulse. Not bounding at all; that was good, at least.

The woman stirred. A girl?

I summoned all my strength. I'm afraid I have to tell you, Mrs. Garrett...she was born sleeping.

She didn't seem to understand.

I spelled it out: A dead birth. I'm awfully sorry for your loss.

Delia Garrett coughed as if she were choking on a rock and began to sob.

Bridie was rubbing the woman's shoulder, stroking her damp head, murmuring to her: Shush, now, shush.

It wasn't protocol, but there was such instinctive gentleness in it, I didn't say a word.

I made a reef knot around the bright blue cord two inches from the still's belly as if this were a live child. The second ligature I tied just past Delia Garrett's swollen parts. My fingers slid on the cord's jelly. Half an inch above the baby's knot, I cut through its rubbery toughness.

I picked up the basin.

Bridie whispered, Mrs. Garrett, do you want to see your daughter?

I stopped in my tracks. I'd been taught to take away a still as soon as possible and encourage the mother to start putting the loss out of her mind.

Delia Garrett squeezed her eyes shut and shook her head. Water leaked down her cheeks.

Only then did I carry the draped basin across the ward and set it down on the desk.

Bridie, could you get her right way round in the bed now?

In the silence, I remembered to check on my other patients. Mary O'Rahilly, in the next cot, was lying as rigid as a statue, but I could tell by the way she'd wrapped her arms around herself that she was mid-pang.

Mrs. O'Rahilly, are you all right?

She nodded with her eyes averted, as if embarrassed to be intruding on the other woman's tragedy. But wasn't a maternity ward like that, a random tin of buttons, one thing always jostling the next?

Over by the wall, Ita Noonan seemed asleep again.

Mrs. Garrett, we're just waiting for the afterbirth now, so I need you on your back.

Bridie's face showed me she'd never heard of it.

I explained under my breath: A big organ at the end of this cord that was keeping the baby alive.

(Until it failed to do that.)

The cord dangling out of Delia Garrett resembled a length of bladder wrack washed up on the shore. I kept up a very light traction on it while pressing a sterile cloth to her laceration.

Bridie stroked and murmured as if the mother were an injured dog.

Fifteen minutes passed by my watch. Fifteen minutes of the cloth reddening, and Delia Garrett crying. Fifteen minutes of holding the top of her belly to encourage the uterus to contract and expel its useless load. Not a word spoken in the small room. The cord wasn't lengthening at all; the uterus wasn't rising or firming or getting more mobile. And Delia Garrett was bleeding more than before.

But our policy was to give the placenta an hour to come out on its own. Up to two if the patient had been given chloroform, which could slow down this stage.

A whisper from Bridie: Can't you give the cord a yank?

I shook my head. I didn't say that it might break off or I might rip out the whole womb. I'd seen the latter happen to a worn-out grandmother, forty-seven years old, even though Sister Finnigan had been scrupulously careful, and whenever I recalled the moment, I thought I'd throw up.

Delia Garrett's curls were flattened on the pillow. I put the sticky back of my hand to her throat to be sure she had no fever. Give nature an hour, I reminded myself.

But I had a bad feeling. The placenta might be stuck to the inner wall, and if so, the longer it clung on, the more likely she'd get an infection.

I should wait for Dr. MacAuliffe. Or send Bridie again and tell her not to come back without him. Except what did that youngster know about this woman's insides?

A warm scarlet wave brimmed and flowed onto the sheet. Oh, Christ. The afterbirth must have ripped partly away. This was how so many mothers began to die.

I rubbed the uterus hard to help expel it, squeezed her like a lemon. Here you go, Mrs. Garrett, one more push now—

The cord's burden slithered out, a dark-maroon side of meat. There!

But relief drained away as I spotted what I was dreading: half the afterbirth was missing. The red tide was rising, soaking the bedding.

I remembered the rule: *A midwife should never risk manual removal of the placenta unless all other methods for controlling haemorrhage have failed and no doctor is available to perform the procedure.* But there was no time, and if I dithered any longer, Delia Garrett was going to bleed to death.

At the sink, I scoured my hands so hard, the nailbrush left red lines on my skin and the carbolic burnt. I sensed the bone man just outside the door. He'd claimed one small life already before any of us had realised, and now he was hovering close by, doing his rattling dance, swinging his smirking skull like a turnip in his bony fingers. I soaped my hands and tugged on a pair of rubber gloves.

I parted Delia Garrett's legs with my elbows and poured dilute disinfectant over the torn parts.

She whimpered.

I said, I'll be as quick as I can. Hold her knees open, Bridie, while I get the rest of it out.

Until now, I'd done this procedure only on an orange. In my third year of training, Sister Finnigan had talked me through a manual removal on a big loose-peeled Spanish one.

I put my left hand on her softened belly and grasped the ball of the uterus through the abdominal wall. I pressed it down to bring it within my reach and held it as steady as I could while I closed my right hand into a cone. I pushed in.

Delia Garrett howled.

A cave behind a waterfall; hot red past the gloves, all the way up my arm. I found the cervix. I went through it as slowly as I could while she wept and thrashed from side to side.

Bridie had her by the shoulders, pinning her. She crooned, Brave girl yourself!

I was in. Immediately I curled my fingertips back so as not to damage the uterine walls. I was a fearful burglar, creeping around a lightless chamber.

Delia Garrett tried to clamp her thighs around my arm but Bridie pulled them back and urged her, Let Nurse Julia fix you, it'll take only a minute.

How could she promise that? I was lost in here. I couldn't tell what I was touching through these rubber fingertips.

There, a shape under the heel of my cramped hand—unmistakeable.

Delia Garrett sobbed, Stop, stop.

Just a second.

I ran my little finger behind the afterbirth and raked its strings, sawing it free. I got two fingers behind it, then three, peeled the awful fruit with my awkward gloved hands. *Come away*, I found myself begging the thing. *Release your grip on her.*

Please, Nurse!

But I couldn't show mercy, not yet.

Bridie held Delia Garrett down, soothing her like a mother.

I worked on till I had it. All of it? I twisted the messy bundle and rolled up its membranes in my palm, a slippery tangle of flesh. Coming out now!

(Incongruously cheerful.)

Through the hard round lock I pulled my hand and my treasure. Stuck for a moment—

Then slipped free. The bloody fistful was on the sheet.

Delia Garrett wept on.

Another basin, please, Bridie?

I studied the afterbirth in the dish. This looked like the whole missing section, but to be sure, I needed to do a final sweep for any fragments or clots. I'm just going to have one more quick feel inside, Mrs. Garrett—

Her knees banged together so hard, I heard bone on bone.

I said sternly, It has to be done to make sure you won't get infected.

I changed to fresh gloves and tore open a packaged ball of antiseptic-soaked gauze. At a nod from me, Bridie got hold of Delia Garrett's knees. I went back in as gently as I could.

She cried harder but didn't fight.

I rubbed the whole concavity with the gauze, feeling for any trailing membranes on which bacteria could grow. All right, then, all right, all finished.

I lurched to the sink and stripped off the gloves. I prepared carbolic solution for douching her, to kill any germs I might have introduced, and heated it up over the spirit lamp because hot was better for stopping a haemorrhage. I blinked over my shoulder in case she was going to up and die on me after all that.

Bridie was crouched on the cot, holding the woman's hand, whispering.

I took down a sterile bulb syringe. The rubbery bulge, with its limp tubes, always reminded me of a red spider that had lost all but two legs. I tested the temperature of the solution by dripping it on the inside of my wrist, then filled a large jar. Fresh gloves.

The bleeding seemed to have slowed. Now, Mrs. Garrett, this will wash you out nicely.

I dropped the syringe's sinker into the jar and fed the glass nozzle inside her cervix. I squeezed the bulb to pump the liquid in while I massaged her rumpled belly with my other hand. Pinkish water flooded back out of her, across the sheets, soaking my apron and Bridie's.

At last, the unmistakeable feel of the womb contracting under my palm. The bleeding was stopping. I wouldn't need to dose her with ergot or plug her with a tin's worth of gauze. This was over, and I hadn't lost the mother.

Who's in charge here?

I jerked around guiltily.

A stranger all in black. This had to be the infamous Dr. Lynn. Collar and tie, like a man's, but a plain skirt and no apron. In her forties? Long hair (slightly greying) coiled up in plaits behind; this was the lady in furs I'd glimpsed from the window earlier.

She took in the sight of me and Bridie daubed with blood, standing over the shambles of Delia Garrett's cot. The empty crib. She turned her head to find the draped basin.

II

BROWN

As I WOUND UP my report over the small sound of Delia Garrett weeping, I realised it was dim; the autumn sun had started slipping down without my noticing. I stepped over to the switch and turned on the harsh overhead light.

Thank you, Nurse.

Dr. Lynn had uttered no word of blame yet.

I was embarrassed by the gory state of my cuffs, browning already; I unbuttoned them, dropped them in the laundry bucket, washed my forearms, and found another pair of cuffs.

Bridie stood in the corner, looking dazed by the havoc of the past hour.

Dr. Lynn pushed her little glasses up on the bridge of her nose, scanned Delia Garrett's chart, and wrote something on the bottom.

I knew I should be dealing with the mess of the birth, but I didn't want to step between doctor and patient. The empty crib—at least I could get that away from Delia Garrett's bed where it stood like a reproach. I wheeled it, one wheel squeaking, over to the ward sister's desk. (My desk today. My responsibility, all of it.)

Dr. Lynn said, I'm very sorry for your loss, Mrs. Garrett.

A whimper.

(Had I failed the woman? How I longed to get out of this airless room.)

From the look of your daughter, said Dr. Lynn, I suspect her heart stopped quite a few hours ago, most likely due to your influenza.

What the doctor meant was that the stillbirth wasn't my doing. But my spirits sank none the less; to think that this morning, while Delia Garrett had been griping, flicking through her magazines, snoozing, eating a stolen sausage, her passenger had departed already.

Delia Garrett said, But the other doctor—Prendergast—told me I wasn't a bad case.

Dr. Lynn nodded gravely. We're finding that even a mild dose can endanger a child in utero or jolt it out before its time.

Fresh sobs.

In her quiet voice: I couldn't have saved your daughter even if I'd been right here, Mrs. Garrett, but still, I'm terribly sorry I was delayed. Now, you have a little sleep while we tidy you up.

No answer from the weeping mother.

Dr. Lynn turned to me, but I was already going for the chloroform.

While the doctor disinfected her knobbly fingers, I tied the thick mask at the back of Delia Garrett's matted head and dripped on the anesthetic. In seconds the woman was under.

The doctor murmured, Apologies to you too, Nurse—the wire from the office took hours to reach me this morning, as I was away from home at a free flu clinic I've set up.

So was the fur-wearing physician some sort of benevolent Lady Bountiful? She seemed serious and able, and if she had her own practice and ran a charity clinic on the side, she had to be coming into the hospital today out of civic duty rather than for a locum's measly wages.

But I'd almost forgotten that she was a rebel combatant too—actually deported for taking part in a violent uprising, unlikely as that seemed. I couldn't make her out, this Dr. Lynn.

I cleaned my own hands, took down an instrument tray from the shelf, fitted a long curved needle into a holder, and threaded it with a length of catgut.

Dr. Lynn had Delia Garrett's knees open and was delicately fingering the damage. Oh dear—ripped up by that great head, and for nothing.

I couldn't help wondering how much experience she had at what she was about to tackle. You're in general practice, Doctor?

Shrewd eyes lifted to mine; that thin mouth had a hint of mirth. Are you asking how qualified I am to repair a lacerated vulva, Nurse Power?

I swallowed hard.

Obstetrics happens to be one of my areas of special interest, along with ophthalmology and insanity.

I blinked; that was quite a range of interests.

It may comfort you to know that I've a licentiate in mid-wifery and I've worked in several lying-in clinics.

Bridie, standing by the wall, seemed amused by my mor-tification.

I poured carbolic solution between the unconscious woman's legs and dabbed her with some flax-tow swabs.

No cotton?

Shortages, I explained.

Dr. Lynn nodded. This tear goes all the way back to the anus, which is rare bad luck in a multigravida.

I did try to support the perineum, I told her.

Oh, no criticism implied, she muttered without glancing up. I never like to spell out to a patient that she's had a close call, but frankly, she'd have been a goner if you hadn't stopped that haemorrhage.

Now Bridie was grinning at me.

My cheeks scorched. God knew I hadn't been fishing for a compliment.

Dr. Lynn took the needle-holder from me. No silk? I find it holds tighter.

I'm afraid we've been out of that for weeks too.

She put in the first suture. How long have you been on shift, Nurse?

Ah...since seven this morning.

No break?

I'm perfectly all right.

Dr. Lynn's stitching was meticulous, but Delia Garrett had such a ragged laceration, I wondered if she would ever feel right in herself again.

Bridie, I asked, could you go back to the refrigerator—you remember, in the supply room—and get a frozen cotton pad?

She shot off.

Dr. Lynn snipped the last thread. There, now. At least catgut dissolves so Mrs. Garrett won't have to come back to have her stitches out and be reminded of today.

I trickled more disinfectant and drew a sheet up to her waist for now.

After washing her hands, Dr. Lynn winched the top window all the way open. Don't let it get stuffy in here. Fresh air!

Yes, Doctor.

I was dashing off a note asking the office to telephone Mr. Garrett right away; I finished it and tucked it into my bib.

Dr. Lynn took Mary O'Rahilly's hand as if they were meeting at a party. Now, then, who have we here?

Mrs. O'Rahilly, seventeen, primigravida. Pangs for a day or two, but twenty minutes apart.

That doesn't sound much fun.

The sympathy made a tear run out of Mary O'Rahilly's left eye, and she started coughing.

I lifted down her chart from the wall and the loose nail spun across the floor. Sorry!

I handed the doctor the chart and scurried to pick up the nail. Which reminded me about my watch and the fresh mark I'd have to make for Delia Garrett's little still.

While the doctor interviewed Mary O'Rahilly, I turned away and slid the heavy disk out of my apron. I found a space among its markings and gouged a small scratch on the silver back. Not a moon this time, just a short line.

Bridie was standing there studying me. I dropped the watch in my bib pocket and fitted the nail back into the wall.

She held out a lumpy thing—not the frozen cotton I'd asked for. It's wet moss in a muslin casing, she told me. A nurse said it'd do nicely.

Meaning it was all they had. I sighed and took it.

In case Delia Garrett's sleep was lightening and she could hear me, I said, We're going to put the binder on you now, Mrs. Garrett.

I set the chilled sausage shape between her legs and safety-pinned it to the under-loop of the foot-wide belt. I cinched the three straps tight.

What's that for? asked Bridie.

To support her poor stretched middle. Oh, could you bring this note to the office on the third floor?

Bridie almost snatched it from me in her eagerness to help.

Delia Garrett moaned a little in her sleep.

I needed to get the still out of her sight before she woke up. Over at the narrow counter, I took down an empty shoebox from the stack. I spread out wax paper, uncovered the basin, and lifted out the blanket-wrapped body. I set it down on the wax paper and made as neat a package of it as I could. My hands shook a little as I put the lid on. I parcelled it up in brown paper and tied it with string, like an unexpected gift.

No need for a certificate of birth or death; legally speaking, nothing had happened here. *Garrett,* I wrote on the shoebox, *October 31.*

I hoped Delia Garrett's husband would come to collect the box tomorrow. Though in these cases some fathers preferred not to, so Matron would wait until we had several shoeboxes, then send them to the cemetery.

Dr. Lynn was palpating Mary O'Rahilly's bump and listening to it with her stethoscope. Patience is what I recommend at this stage, Mrs. O'Rahilly. I'm going to have Nurse Power give you a sleeping draught to help pass the time and restore your forces.

She came over to the desk and told me, Chloral. It can incline the cervix to open too. But no chloroform, as we don't want to suppress these early contractions.

I nodded as I noted that down.

The doctor added under her breath, I'm somewhat concerned that it's taking so long. The mother's not fully grown yet, and poorly nourished. If I were in charge of the world, there'd be no whelping before twenty.

I liked Dr. Lynn for that bold comment.

Mary O'Rahilly took her medicine without a word.

Here was Bridie, back already.

I set the shoebox in her hands. Now take this down to the mortuary in the basement, would you?

The what?

I whispered: Where the dead go.

Bridie looked down, realising what she held.

I asked, All right?

Perhaps I was demanding too much of one so untried. *About twenty-two.* Had she some reason to be vague or was it possible in this day and age that she really didn't know how old she was?

All right, said Bridie.

She shoved back a nimbus of bronze fuzz and was gone.

Dr. Lynn remarked, An energetic runner you've got there.

Isn't she?

A probie?

No, just a volunteer for the day.

Mary O'Rahilly seemed to be dropping off already. But Ita Noonan was stirring, and there was a distinct creak to her breathing. Dr. Lynn took up her wrist and I hurried over with a thermometer.

How are you feeling, Mrs. Noonan?

Her coughs were a hail of bullets but she smiled. Lovely and shiny! Never mind the wax.

Six days of fever, Dr. Lynn muttered. Did she already have white leg when she came in?

I nodded. She said it's stayed that size, and cold and hard, since her last delivery.

Ita Noonan's temperature was down almost a degree, but Dr. Lynn reported that her pulse and respirations were higher. She put her stethoscope to the concave chest. Hm. Under ordinary circumstances, she said, I'd send her for a roentgenograph, but there are patients queuing halfway along the corridor up there.

I tried to remember when things had last been ordinary—late summer?

The doctor added, At any rate, X-rays would only draw us a picture of exactly how congested her lungs are, not tell us how to clear them.

Ita Noonan addressed her in a gracious gasp: Will you be staying for the hooley?

I will, of course, thank you, Mrs. Noonan.

Dr. Lynn murmured to me, I see her left arm is slightly palsied. That can happen with this flu. Has she seemed dizzy at all?

Yes, I thought perhaps she was when I was bringing her to the lavatory earlier.

Dr. Lynn wrote that on the chart. Tantalising not to be able to get precise answers out of the delirious, isn't it? Every symptom is a word in the language of disease, but sometimes we can't hear them properly.

And even if we do, we can't always make out the full sentence.

She nodded. So we just shush them, one word at a time.

I asked, More hot whiskey for Mrs. Noonan, then? Dr. Prendergast said—

She answered a little wearily: Mm, it's looking as if alcohol's the safest for grippe patients, all things considered.

There was a junior I didn't know at the door. Dr. Lynn? You're wanted in Women's Surgical.

The doctor adjusted her glasses and said, On my way. Over her shoulder she told me, I'll send up a chaplain for a word with Mrs. Garrett.

And may she have whiskey too, for her afterpains and cough?

Indeed. With any of these patients, use your good judgement.

That startled me. You mean—I should give medicine without a specific order?

That would be scorning protocol. If I'd misunderstood her, I could lose my job for overstepping.

Dr. Lynn nodded impatiently. They have me running between half a dozen wards today, Nurse Power, and you seem awfully capable, so I authorise you to dose any of your patients with alcohol or, for bad pain, chloroform or morphine.

I was filled with gratitude; she'd untied my hands.

Coming in, Bridie almost crashed into the doctor in the doorway. She was panting a little, with a sheen on her speckled cheekbones; had she taken the stairs three at a time?

Dr. Lynn said, Catch your breath, dear.

I'm grand, said Bridie. What do you need next, Nurse Power?

I sent her off to the incinerator chute with the bundled mess of Delia Garrett's delivery and then to the laundry one with the ball of bloodied sheets.

I scanned my narrow domain, and my eye fell on the pot the thermometer had cracked in. I poured the cooled water down the drain, leaving the small glitter of glass and the mercury droplets rolling around in the bottom. I formed a packet out of newspaper and tipped it all in.

Bridie came back in and saw. I'm such an eejit to have broke that.

Not your fault. I should have warned you that boiling water would make the mercury expand too much and crack the bulb.

She shook her head. I should have guessed.

If a lesson's not learnt, I said, blame the student. But if it's not taught right—or not taught at all—blame the teacher.

She grinned. So I'm a student now? There's posh.

I wrapped up the packet of newspaper and murmured, I'm afraid I'm not much of a teacher at the moment.

Ah, well, sure everything's arsewise right at the minute.

Bridie said that under her breath, as if worried her language might offend me.

I smiled to myself to hear her come out with Tim's phrase.

In her stupor, Delia Garrett shifted around on the pillows.

Bridie nodded at her. Your one would have bled to death if you hadn't dug that lump out of her, isn't that what the doctor meant?

I grimaced. Who knows?

Her eyes were starry blue. Never seen the like!

The girl's worship weighed on me. If I'd been even a little clumsy this afternoon, I might have ripped Delia Garrett apart, left her barren or dead. I didn't know any nurse without a few big mistakes on her conscience.

Bridie went on as if to herself: I suppose she's as well off.

Wealthy, did she mean? I wasn't sure what good that would do the Garretts now. I asked quietly, Well off in what sense?

As well off without it.

It took me a second to get it. I whispered: Without—the baby?

Bridie blew out her breath. Only more pain in the end, aren't they?

I was speechless. How could such a young woman have formed so warped a view of the main business of humankind?

Didn't Mrs. Garrett tell us herself that she didn't want a third?

I said shortly, That won't stop her heart breaking.

I looked at the package of mercury and glass, forcing my mind back to practical matters. I wondered whether incinerating it might send up dangerous fumes.

I asked Bridie to take the packet outside the hospital and throw it in the nearest bin. And then get yourself a bite of lunch—or more like dinner now, I suppose.

I was rarely aware of hunger on a busy shift; my own body's

needs were suspended. I'd sent away the maid with the birth-mark, I remembered. Those lunch trays, Bridie, are they still outside?

She shook her head. Someone must have took them.

I couldn't send a special request when the kitchen staff were so hard-pressed. Tell you what, could you go to the canteen and load a tray up for us all?

She set down the packet of glass and her hands went to her hair—frayed wire now. She whipped out the comb I'd given her and did her best to slick it back.

Go on, you'll do.

She sped off.

An odd creature, this Bridie Sweeney, but such a natural at ward work.

Silence spread.

My apron was stained and spattered with blood; I changed it for a new one. I smoothed it down over my flat belly, which let out a gurgle. The shift went on, and so did I.

Delia Garrett blinked, coming back to consciousness. She heaved onto her side—

I grabbed a basin and a cloth from the shelf and ran over in time to catch most of what dribbled out.

When she'd stopped retching, I wiped her mouth. That's common after chloroform, Mrs. Garrett. You're just cleaning yourself out.

I could see the memory hit her like a fist. Eyes roaming. Where's she—what have you done with her?

Was she wishing she'd looked at her daughter's face? I felt bad that I hadn't urged it. But what if she'd been even more upset by the sight of those blackening lips?

I told her, She's gone to the Angels' Plot.

Hoarsely: What?

That's what they call the special place in the cemetery.

(How to describe a mass grave?)

I improvised: It's lovely. Grass and flowers.

Delia Garrett's round cheeks were carved with salty lines. What am I going to tell Bill?

Someone will have phoned your husband and explained.

(As if such a thing admitted of explanation.)

I used the cloth to wipe up the spatters of sick. Let's get you sitting up. Come on, now, Mrs. Garrett, it's better for you.

I didn't want to spell out that sitting up was necessary for her uterus to drain. I had to almost drag her up against the pillows.

Her heart rate and pulse force were down to normal; her blood was moving as it should now that her body had shed its small burden. I checked her pad; the bleeding was very light. All Delia Garrett had wrong with her was a cough and privates torn by her baby's head. And no baby. Empty-handed.

I feared whiskey might be too hard on her stomach, so I made her a cup of tea, stronger than usual and with three sugars for the shock, and put two biscuits in the saucer.

Delia Garrett sipped the tea, tears running into the corners of her mouth.

I prompted her to eat.

Unseeing, she fumbled for a biscuit.

The ward was quite calm, like a subdued tea party where the conversation had died away.

In the left-hand cot, Ita Noonan kicked out her legs, making me jump. She sat up staring and smacked her lips, wrinkled her nose as if there were a foul smell. Delirium could do that—cause hallucinations of odour as well as of sound and sight.

Thirsty, Mrs. Noonan?

I held out her lidded cup but she didn't seem to know what it was. When I put it to her lips, she turned her crimson face away. I tried wet cloths on her neck to cool her down; she threw them on the floor and dived down into the bedding. I reached for her wrist to check her pulse, but she withdrew her arm and hid it under her.

A clatter behind as Bridie walked through the door backwards with a loaded tray.

I rushed to clear her a space on the desk.

Two dishes of muddy stew with pale lumps like capsized boats. A mound of defeated cabbage and a mash that smelled like turnip. Marge spread on war bread. Two slices of pie I suspected was rabbit, and a bowl of prunes.

Bridie said, See, there's even sliced chicken.

It looked jellylike to me, tinned.

Fried fish too!

Then Bridie's face fell. Though one of the cooks was saying that's how this flu might have got started.

Through . . . fish?

She nodded. Ones that ate dead soldiers.

That's nonsense, Bridie.

Is it, for sure?

I'm one hundred per cent certain, I told her.

The young woman chuckled at that.

What?

You can't be one hundred per cent certain. Because nobody actually knows where the sickness comes from, do they?

I said in exasperation, Ninety-five per cent, then.

There was a printed sheet underneath the plates, still smeary.

STAY CLEAN, WARM, AND WELL NOURISHED,
BUT FORBEAR TO
USE MORE THAN A FAIR SHARE
OF FUEL AND FOOD.

THE PULL OF THE STARS

EARLY TO SLEEP AND KEEP WINDOWS WIDE,
WHILE TAKING CARE TO AVOID DRAUGHTS.
VENTILATION AND SANITATION
WILL BE OUR NATION'S SALVATION.

That paradoxical prescription made my mouth purse; it seemed intended to discomfit either way, whether one turned the gas a little up for health or a little down for economy. Already I felt ashamed every time I caught myself resenting small privations when others had it so much worse. Guilt was the sooty air we breathed these days.

But look at Bridie, on her feet, eating rabbit pie as appreciatively as if she were dining at the Ritz.

I made myself pick up a dish of stew. One spoonful. Another. The Ministry of Food claimed that levels of nutrition had actually improved since the war began because we were eating more vegetables, less sugar. But then I supposed they would say that.

I mentioned to Bridie that before this crisis, we nurses used to get an hour to ourselves in our own dining room.

She marvelled, The full hour?

We'd read the news aloud, knit, sing, even dance to the gramophone.

A hooley!

I said, Well, that's overstating the case. No drink, and no cigarettes ever, even off shift.

Still, it sounds jolly.

Call me Julia, if you like.

I surprised myself by saying that, very low.

I added, Only not in front of the patients.

Bridie nodded. Julia, she repeated softly.

Sorry if I'm snappish sometimes.

You aren't.

I admitted, under my breath, My temper's not the best since the flu. I've felt a little bit deadened.

You can't be a little bit dead. If you're not in the ground yet, you're *one hundred per cent* alive.

I grinned back at her.

Bridie glanced to make sure Mary O'Rahilly was asleep and Ita Noonan and Delia Garrett weren't listening before she whispered: Down in the canteen I heard talk about one fellow deranged with the flu who up and slaughtered his wife and kids.

I told her, That sounds like a story. (Hoping so.) But there've certainly been a few sufferers who've done away with themselves.

She sketched the sign of the cross on her chest.

One man went to buy medicine for himself and his family, I said. Cut through a park, went by a pond...and the constables found him facedown among the swans.

Bridie gasped. Drowned?

Though he mightn't have been thinking straight. Maybe he was burning up and the water looked so deliciously cool? Or he stumbled in by mistake?

She eyed Ita Noonan. We should keep an eye on your one with the bad fever, so.

Oh, I never leave any sharp instruments near a delirious patient, or bandages.

Bridie's smooth forehead creased. Where's the harm in bandages?

I mimed winding one around my neck.

Oh.

I didn't tell Bridie about a girl who'd managed to half throttle herself in the lavatory with a bandage before Sister

Finnigan had found her. No fever, in her case, but a reason for despair: twelve years old and seven months gone. From hints she let slip, we suspected her father.

Standing by the cot on the left, Bridie gazed down at Ita Noonan. Bluish, she remarked.

What's that?

Her fingernails. Is that from the thing you were telling me— red, brown, blue, black?

I hurried over. Ita Noonan's nailbeds had indeed darkened, which could be advancing cyanosis, but her face was still red and clammy. What alarmed me more was her wheeze, like air trapped in bagpipes, the leather stretching. I counted her pantings by my watch—thirty-six respirations a minute, heart and lungs working full tilt. She was a rower frantically oaring towards the bank. She was also shivering, so I swaddled her up in her shawl and another blanket. Her pulse was up to 104 beats per minute, but the force seemed much weaker to me.

Are you dizzy at all, Mrs. Noonan?

She muttered something I didn't catch.

For low blood pressure, I should elevate her feet on a square bedrest, but that would be the very worst position for her congested lungs. My mind went around and around in a panicky, defeated loop. So I did nothing; I watched and waited.

A tap at the door: Father Xavier.

The priest had the kind of lined, sweet face that made it impossible to guess his age; he could have been anywhere from fifty to a hundred years old. Nurse Power, he said in his wintry voice, do we have a Mrs. Garrett?

Dr. Lynn had sent the wrong chaplain. I pointed to her bed. But she's a Protestant, Father. Church of Ireland.

Ghost-faced, Delia Garrett had slid halfway down the

pillows, her tea cooling on the little cabinet beside her, a biscuit dissolving in the saucer.

The priest nodded. I'm afraid the reverend's been struck down. There's only me today, for right- and left-footers alike. Well, as they say, all cats are grey in the dark.

I explained to Bridie, Father Xavier used to be the Roman Catholic chaplain here till he retired and Father Dominic stepped in.

Only Father Dominic too went down with the flu last week, he said, so I've been summoned back.

I tucked a stool for him beside Delia Garrett's bed. Sorry there's so little room, Father.

No matter. I stiffen up when I sit for too long.

He positioned himself against the wall.

Mrs. Garrett, I'm standing in for my Church of Ireland colleague, as he's under the weather, if you've no objection?

Her closed eyelids didn't even flicker. Asleep, I wondered, or ignoring him?

He leaned over her. I'm very sorry for your trouble.

No response.

Father Xavier sighed. I believe Christians of all persuasions can agree on grounds to hope, at least, that in His infinite mercy, the Lord will provide some mechanism of salvation for those who pass away in the womb, unbaptised through no fault of their own.

A sob wracked Delia Garrett, then turned into a cough. I knew the fellow meant well, but I wished he'd leave her alone.

Didn't Jesus say to let the children come to Him? So you must entrust your little one to His loving care now, and to the guardian angels.

She must have heard that, because she turned her face away sharply.

The old man straightened up painfully and said, I'll let you rest.

Coming over to the desk, he asked, Have you a new junior, Nurse Power?

Just a skivvy, said Bridie before I could answer. A replacement, like yourself.

The priest looked back at me and jerked his head at her. I see she's a quick one.

I said: Don't I know it, Father.

He sneezed and wiped his great reddened nose. Excuse me, ladies.

I asked, Have you a cold brewing?

I'm just getting over a little dose of this flu.

If I may, Father—

I put the back of my hand to his forehead, which was warmish. Shouldn't you be in bed, then, to be on the safe side?

Ah, I'd rather walk it off, said Father Xavier. I might as well be useful on the fever wards.

But the strain—considering your...

He raised his tufted eyebrows. Considering my age, young lady, how much would it matter in the greater scheme of things if I were taken this very night?

Bridie let out a snort.

Father Xavier winked at her. I'll be grand. I hear the old are getting through this better than the young.

I qualified that: Well, as a general rule.

The priest said briskly, His ways are mysterious.

Delia Garrett's eyes were open now, her gaze following the old man out the door. She looked hollowed out.

I couldn't bear to see her this way. Hot whiskey, Mrs. Garrett?

As soon as I handed her the cup, she drained it. Then lay back on her pillows and closed her eyes.

Quiet again. A chance to catch one's breath after going like a juggler from minute to hectic minute.

I stared at the slumped figure of Ita Noonan. Head up, to ease her breathing, or feet up, for better pulse force? Or keep her flat—would that be the best compromise or no good for either problem? Every symptom was a word, yes, but I couldn't understand them, couldn't follow.

Bridie was mopping the floor, unasked. Such generous stamina this young woman had. I thanked her.

You're welcome, Julia.

She said my first name a little shyly, as if trying it on for size.

Outside the window, it was black; all the light had slipped away now.

Bridie remarked, I hate the old evenings.

Do you?

When the night draws in and you have to go to bed, but you can't get to sleep no matter how you try. Cursing yourself because you'll be sorry in the morning when you can't drag yourself up at the bell.

That sounded like a bleak life. I wondered whether the Sweeneys were in very straitened circumstances. Were Bridie's parents harsh with her?

A thump.

I looked at the cot on the left but it was empty, the sheets a risen wave. For half a stupid moment, I couldn't tell where Ita Noonan had gone.

I ran around Mary O'Rahilly's bed, barking my shin on the metal.

Against the skirting board, Ita Noonan thrashed like a fish, eyes rolled back. Her legs were trapped in the blankets, her arms lashing out. She banged her head on the corner of the little cabinet.

Bridie cried out, Jesus wept!

I couldn't tell if Ita Noonan was breathing. A stink went up from her bowels. I knelt over her, crammed a pillow behind her head. One hand whacked me on the breast.

Should we stick a spoon in her mouth? asked Bridie.

No, it'd smash her teeth. More pillows!

The thud of her feet, the slam as she ransacked the cupboard.

I stayed helplessly on my knees, trying to keep Ita Noonan from breaking any bones as she convulsed under me. Rose-streaked foam leaked out the side of her mouth. I needed to get her lying on her side so she wouldn't choke, but it was impossible, wedged as she was in this gap. Her feet were still up on the cot, knotted in the blankets.

The childhood prayer threaded through my head: *Holy Mary Mother of God, pray for us sinners now and at the hour—*

Bridie dropped three pillows into my arms.

But Ita Noonan was limp now. No writhing; no rise and fall of her chest.

I wiped her mouth with my apron, bent, and put my cheek to her lips.

What are you doing?

Shh!

I waited. No breath against my face, nothing at all. Help me turn her over, facedown.

Here on the floor? But even as she asked this, Bridie was wrenching the bed linen loose so Ita Noonan's lower legs came unstuck and slid and dropped down, the huge white one and then the skinny one.

We got her prone, one cheek to the floorboards. I should have been sitting at her head but there wasn't room. I pressed on her back as hard as I could, trying to pump the lungs. I straddled her and folded her arms with her yellowed fingers under her face, hauled her elbows back towards me to open the chest, as I'd been trained. I pushed on the back of her ribs, pulled up her elbows. Push, pull, push, pull. Kneading a vast lump of dough that was so dry, it would never make bread.

When at last I stopped, the room hung very still. I checked my watch: 5:31.

Is she...

I couldn't answer Bridie. This day was too much for me. I closed my eyes.

My hand was seized. I tried to jerk away.

But Bridie wouldn't let go; she only squeezed tighter.

So I gripped her hand. I held on to her fingers, hard enough to hurt.

Then I took my hand back so I could wipe my face. Just sweat; I couldn't afford to cry.

I was busy counting in my head. Sister Finnigan had measured the height of the uterus above the pubic bone and estimated that Ita Noonan was twenty-nine weeks on. In which case, all I should do right now was have a doctor certify her death. Theoretically, a foetus was viable from twenty-eight weeks on, but in practice, babies delivered before thirty weeks' gestation rarely survived, so if they were unresponsive, hospital policy was not to revive them.

Then again, because the uterus dropped in the final days of pregnancy, nine months could look more like eight, perhaps even seven. So there was a slim but awful chance that Sister Finnigan's estimate was wrong and that Ita Noonan—her belly sagging particularly low under its twelfth load—was actually at full term.

Bridie, fetch the doctor at once.

Will I not help you get her into bed first?

I roared: Go!

I couldn't put words to the terrible calculations I was making.
Right away, she said. Dr. Lynn?

I flapped my hand. Any surgeon.

For a posthumous caesarean section, an obstetrician wasn't absolutely necessary, since there was no mother to save, only her dead flesh to slice, a living baby to seize. The window of opportunity was twenty minutes, but the faster the better—less risk of damage to the brain.

Bridie's feet thudded off down the corridor.

I found I was as weak as water.

Delia Garrett sat bolt upright and stared at me accusingly as if this room were an antechamber of hell and I the attendant. Mrs. Noonan—is *she* gone now?

I nodded. I'm so sorry you—

Then why are you shouting, Nurse—what's so bloody urgent?

I couldn't tell her that sometimes a surgeon would harvest a woman's fruit while she was still warm.

I got my arms under Ita Noonan and heaved her onto the bed. My back spasmed. I laid her out flat. I closed her startled eyes and clasped her hands together. One of them slipped down and off the cot, so I retrieved it and tucked it back into the blanket. For lack of a priest, I murmured, *Eternal rest grant unto her, and let perpetual light shine upon her.*

I resisted the temptation to check my watch; the minutes were ticking by and I could do nothing to slow them. Maybe it would take Bridie more than twenty minutes to find a doctor, in which case we'd all be spared this awful decision.

I rolled up my apron and threw it in the laundry basket, tied on another to be ready for whatever came next. What more could I do than keep putting one foot in front of the other?

Dr. Lynn glided in, Bridie on her heels. She checked for a

pulse in Ita Noonan's neck while she listened to my rapid-fire report.

In the back of my mind, I was thinking, *What have I done? Why did I have to send Bridie so bloody fast?* If my qualms persuaded the doctor to haul out a stunted, suffering infant at twenty-nine weeks, or twenty-eight, or even twenty-seven, for all we knew...

I saw the moment Dr. Lynn decided not to cut. A slight shake of her braided head; no layperson would have understood what she was communicating.

I felt groggy with relief.

Death from febrile convulsions consequent on influenza, she scrawled at the bottom of Ita Noonan's chart, then signed *K. Lynn*.

I wondered what the *K.* stood for.

I'll inform the office myself, Nurse Power.

I wondered if this was the first patient Dr. Lynn had lost today.

I tried back pressure on Mrs. Noonan, I told her, and arm lifts.

Resuscitation's always worth attempting, she confirmed flatly. It sets one's mind at rest to have done all one can.

(But my mind was not at rest.)

If I'd realised how fast she was slipping away, I asked, should I have tried a stimulant—smelling salts or a hypo of strychnine?

Dr. Lynn shook her head. That might have bought her a few more minutes of pain but wouldn't have saved her. No, some flu patients are dropping like flies while others sail through, and we can't solve the puzzle or do a blasted thing about it.

Mary O'Rahilly coughed in her drugged sleep.

Dr. Lynn went over and put the back of her hand to the girl's pink cheek to check for fever. Then she turned on the spot and looked at the grieving woman.

How's your cough, Mrs. Garrett?

A shrug as if to say, *What does it matter.*

The doctor asked me, No signs of puerperal infection?

I shook my head.

Once Dr. Lynn had gone, Bridie sidled up to me at the counter where I was counting packets of swabs. What was all that about twenty-nine weeks?

I hesitated, then said very quietly, If the foetus had been farther on—more ready—the doctor would've taken it out.

How on earth—

By opening up the belly.

I gestured, using my finger as the scalpel.

Her light blue eyes widened. That's disgusting.

I managed a small shrug. To save one life out of the two...

And send it home with no mammy?

I know.

It was now 5:53 by my watch. I wondered when exactly the scampering heartbeat of the last Noonan child had stilled. What did it mean to die before ever being born?

Bridie, could you go for a couple of orderlies to collect Mrs. Noonan?

Certainly.

In her absence I cleaned the dead woman, working gently, as if Ita Noonan could still feel everything. I had time on my hands, and somehow I couldn't bear to leave the preparation to the mortuary attendants.

Delia Garrett had turned towards the wall as if to give her fallen comrade a bit of privacy.

I got Ita Noonan into a fresh nightdress, and I unclasped

the miniature tin crucifix from around her neck and tucked it under her thumbs. I put a white cloth over her face.

I packed up her few things. A paper bag I found turned out to hold her shorn hair—that almost broke me. Those Noonans waiting for her to come home, the barrel-organ man (when would he hear that he'd been widowed?) and the seven children, would receive instead of her this bag of limp curls.

Groyne followed Bridie in, serenading her:

When I leave you, dear, give me words of cheer,
To recall in times of pain.
They will comfort me, and will seem to be
Like the sunshine after rain...

I snapped: I asked for *two* men.

Sorry, I could only find Mr. Groyne.

He glanced at the cot on the left. Ah, now, don't tell me the mad shawlie's croaked?

I spoke through my teeth. Mrs. Noonan was only delirious.

He was unperturbed. So she's joined the choir invisible, then, the heavenly chorus. Answered the great call, poor biddy. Crossed the border. She's—

Shut up!

That was Delia Garrett, growling from her bed.

For once, Groyne held his tongue.

I pushed the crib towards him, and one wheel squeaked. Could you please get this out of here and come back with one of the other men and a stretcher?

Subdued, the orderly took the crib and rolled it out of the room.

I checked Delia Garrett's temperature, pulse, and respirations. Physically, she was making a perfect recovery.

Bridie wiped down the counter and desk with disinfectant, mopped the corner where it was daubed with Ita Noonan's fluids, then changed the water to clean the rest of the floor.

We all pretended a dead woman wasn't lying among us with a cloth draped over her face.

What seemed like hours later, Nichols and O'Shea carried in a stretcher tipped on its side, like a ladder or a pane of glass.

Mary O'Rahilly blinked at the men, one hand over her mouth, as if she'd woken to find herself in a bad dream. Mother of God!

Nichols kept his eyes down. Sorry, ladies.

I realised that she hadn't encountered his metal mask before. I was struck by the misery of the man's situation: to walk among his kind but with a copper half-face—better than the grotesque crater it hid, but still eerily unlike.

I spoke to the orderly in a kind tone: Carry on, Nichols.

Bridie was right by Mary O'Rahilly, arm around her, whispering in her ear. She had to be explaining what had happened to Ita Noonan.

The men got the body onto the stretcher easily enough; Shaky O'Shea was capable, for all his tremor. Was it his hands that had been damaged at the front or his brain? So many veterans, such as my brother, had come back damaged goods though they hadn't a scratch on their bodies, only invisible bruising of the mind.

We all crossed ourselves as the orderlies carried Ita Noonan out.

After a long silence, Bridie asked, What happened to his *face*?

I said, The war.

How much of it's left, though, underneath?

I couldn't tell you, Bridie.

I took down Mary O'Rahilly's chart to get the loose nail

because I hadn't recorded Ita Noonan yet. I pulled out my watch and looked for a space among the scratches crowding the silver disk. I'd reached the point of each woman's round moon having to overlap with that of one who'd gone before her or with the crescent or broken line of an infant lost after or before birth. I gouged Ita Noonan's small circle with the nail as neatly as I could, but it skidded and finished at a sharp point. I gripped the watch as if I were counting its ticks. The hieroglyphic tally of the dead floated past me, a stream of stardust.

Everything dimmed, and for a moment I thought there was something wrong with my eyes. Then I registered that it was the ward lights.

Mary O'Rahilly gasped.

Another brownout, I said mildly. Apologies, all.

This had come to be a regular occurrence in the early evenings as hour by hour more workers came home and got the tea on, huddling around the limited light we all had to ration out.

In the murk, Bridie stripped the cot on the left without being asked.

I asked, Did you have a nice sleep, Mrs. O'Rahilly?

She spoke confusedly: I suppose so.

I felt her bump to check the foetus was still in the right position; I took down the horn and found the faint, rapid heartbeat. And the pains now—are they different at all?

Not really, I don't think.

She shivered and coughed.

I made a hot whiskey and set it in her hands.

Mary O'Rahilly gulped it and spluttered; it nearly slopped over the rim.

Little sips, now, if you're not used to spirits, I told her. This should help with the pangs as well as your cough.

I was secretly concerned she mightn't have the strength to deliver when it finally came to it. Could you fancy an egg flip, Mrs. O'Rahilly? Beef tea?

She shook her head in revulsion.

A bit of dry bread?

Maybe.

As I got her half a slice from the packet on the shelf, Mary O'Rahilly fretted aloud: Himself would rather I'd stayed at home than come to hospital. They're not even letting him in to see me.

Delia Garrett spoke up hoarsely: Well, at least you've no other children at home to worry about.

Mary O'Rahilly nodded and nibbled her bread. Though I look in on my five brothers and sisters morning and night, she mentioned, so I don't know how Dadda's going to manage.

Bridie asked, Can't your husband keep an eye on your brothers and sisters for you?

The young woman shook her head. Mr. O'Rahilly used to be a stevedore, but the port's at a standstill right now, so he's started as a conductor. Only a spare man, though, not a permanent, she added breathlessly. He's obliged to turn up at the tram depot every morning, rain or shine, and if they've no work for him, he's had the trip for nothing.

It was probably the whiskey loosening her tongue. I said, That must be inconvenient.

When she answered, her voice was small, as if she were on the verge of a cough. It maddens him! And now I'm getting behind on my work too.

Bridie asked, What kind of work?

I used to work on the slob lands, cinder-picking, but Mr. O'Rahilly didn't like that.

(I was taking against the man without ever having met him.)

122

The young woman went on, So now I draw threads at home. A boy delivers a bundle of handkerchiefs and I pull threads out of them to make a pattern with what's not there, see?

Delia Garrett said, I have a set like that.

Maybe I did them!

Then Mary O'Rahilly went ramrod stiff as a pain seized her. She coughed hard into her hand, four times.

I checked my watch in the faint lamplight; a quarter of an hour since the last.

When she flopped back, I suggested, Maybe walk around some more, Mrs. O'Rahilly, if you're able?

Obedient as a puppet, she got out of bed.

Here, let me help you with your shawl.

I wrapped it around her shoulders and over her head.

Her face contorted. She whispered, Nurse, why won't my baby come out? Might it be ... like hers?

A slight tip of the head towards Delia Garrett, just feet away.

I took the girl's warm hand, the skin a little scaly. I told her, I heard its heartbeat loud and clear with the ear trumpet, remember? It's just not quite ready yet.

She nodded, trying to believe it.

I said, Nature works to her own clock, but she knows what she's doing.

Mary O'Rahilly stared back at me, one motherless daughter to another. She knew as well as I did what a lie I was telling, but she took what comfort she could.

To think, she'd come in here this morning expecting her navel to open. Practically a child herself, but soon she'd be transformed; she'd have to be the mother.

Knock-knock! A man's voice at the door.

In walked Groyne with a girl in his arms, like a bride he was carrying over the threshold.

Groyne, what do you think you're—

He plonked her down on the left-hand cot and said, Shortage of wheelchairs.

(What, had I expected Ita Noonan's bed to stay empty?)

The new patient doubled over, spluttering. Only when she straightened up could I see, squinting in the brownish light, that she wasn't as young as Mary O'Rahilly, just similarly under-grown. Wide eyes under straw-coloured hair, and a vast belly.

I put a hand on the knob of her shoulder. I'm Nurse Power.

She tried to answer me but she was coughing too hard.

Wait till you have a sip of water.

Bridie rushed to fill a glass.

The new patient persisted in speaking, but I couldn't make out a word. She had rosary beads wound twice around her arm, imprinting the skin.

It's all right, Mrs....

I held my hand out to Groyne for the chart. I tilted it towards the dim bulb: *Honor White, second pregnancy, twenty-nine years old.* (Same as me.) Due at the end of November, which put her at thirty-six weeks right now. She'd caught the flu a full month ago, but as so often happened, there'd been complications.

Can't shift this nasty cough, then, Mrs. White?

She hacked on, eyes streaming. Anaemic, I guessed from that paper-pale skin.

I noticed a little red Sacred Heart on the lapel of her thin coat when I hung it up and an odd bulge in the pocket. The dry layers fragmented and shed in my hand. Is this...garlic?

Mrs. White gasped out, very low: For warding off the grippe.

Groyne let out a yelp of laughter. Much good that did you.

The new patient's accent was from the far west, I thought. I couldn't change her clothes until the orderly left.

He was dawdling. So, Nurse Power, how're you getting along with the diehard?

The word confused me for a moment. Oh, Dr. Lynn? She seems highly experienced.

Groyne snorted. Experienced at agitation and anarchy!

Come, now.

Bridie put in, I heard she was nearly executed.

I stared at her thrilled face. Was my runner taking the orderly's side now? I asked: Heard where?

On the stairs.

That's a fact, Groyne assured us. After the Rising, they handed down ninety death sentences—but they spared all the ladies, he added discontentedly, and called off the firing squads after the sixteenth go!

Well. (I was uneasy that my patients were hearing all this.) At least we have a doctor with some obstetrical expertise in today.

Sure Miss Lynn's probably only here to dodge the peelers, he told me.

I frowned, not following. Why would the police still be after her at this point? Didn't the government let the rebels out of prison last year?

Groyne snorted. Don't you read the papers, Nurse Power? They tried to round up the whole traitorous crew again in May for gunrunning with the Germans. I don't know how Her Nibs slipped through the net, but I tell you, she's on the run as we speak, she—

He froze.

I turned to see Dr. Lynn sweeping in. Behind her glasses, her face gave no indication that she'd heard a word, but mine burnt.

She scanned the low-lit ward. Good evening Mrs. Garrett, Mrs. O'Rahilly...and who's this?

I introduced Honor White.

The doctor's coiled plaits were so sedate, her collar so prim, I told myself it couldn't be true what Groyne had claimed about her conspiring with a foreign power.

Stay alive, ladies, said Groyne. He sauntered out, singing:

Oh, death, where is thy stingalingaling,
Oh, grave, thy victory?
The bells of hell go tingalingaling
For you but not for me...

With Bridie's help I got Honor White into a nightdress while Dr. Lynn examined her. No fever, but her pulse and respirations were rather fast. Straining for breath, the woman denied being hungry, wanted only to rest.

Dr. Lynn told me to give her a spoonful of ipecac to loosen her chest.

Does it hurt when you cough, Mrs. White?

She rubbed her sternum and whispered: Like a knife.

You're not due till the end of November?

Honor White nodded. A doctor said.

And this was how long ago?

A while back. A couple of months.

I don't suppose you remember when were the first movements?

I knew Dr. Lynn was asking because the quickening usually happened by the eighteenth week. But Honor White only shrugged.

She started coughing again, so I passed her a sputum cup with carbolic sloshing in the bottom. She brought up greenish stuff with dark streaks.

Start her on daily iron for her anaemia, Nurse, said the doctor, but do watch to see if it upsets her stomach.

I went to the jar in the cupboard to fetch a pill.

Dr. Lynn said, I believe you've got a pneumoniac infection, which means the flu's lodged right down deep in your lungs.

The patient's eyes glistened. She tugged on her holy beads.

But don't worry yourself, Nurse Power will take great care of you.

(I thought, *As I did of Ita Noonan and Eileen Devine?*)

Honor White confided in a whisper, Doctor, I think I'm going to split.

She put her fingers to the centre of her bump.

When you cough, you mean?

She shook her head.

Dr. Lynn assured her, It's common to feel full to bursting this far along.

No, but—

Honor White tugged up her nightdress as modestly as she could, revealing the great pink shiny ball between hem and sheet. She pointed to the brown line that ran straight up past her navel to her ribs. It's darker every day.

Dr. Lynn managed not to smile. That's just the linea nigra, nothing but a streak of colour.

Some women get it under the eyes, I told Honor White, and on the upper lip too.

Truly, said the doctor, the brown skin's as strong as the white.

But I didn't have it...

Last time, I guessed Honor White must mean.

Delia Garrett spoke up suddenly: My streak stops at the belly button.

Honor White twisted to her left to see her neighbour.

Bill's mother said that meant I was going to have a girl.

Then Delia Garrett's eyes flooded with tears.

I couldn't think of anything to do for what ailed her. No medicine for that grief.

I gave Honor White her iron pill with a hot whiskey for her cough.

But she recoiled from the alcoholic waft, wheezing, I'm a Pioneer.

I remembered the little Sacred Heart on her coat. Oh, it's medicinal.

She shook her head and crossed herself.

Dr. Lynn said, Quinine for Mrs. White, then, with a hot lemonade. Now, how's our primigravida progressing?

I looked at Mary O'Rahilly, who was lying back with her eyes shut. Her pangs are still about fifteen minutes apart, I'm afraid.

No sign of her membranes rupturing yet?

I shook my head.

The doctor pursed her lips and went to scrub her hands at the sink.

Ah; that meant it was time to risk an internal.

I said, Mrs. O'Rahilly? The doctor's going to check you're coming along nicely.

The seventeen-year-old was meek, doll-like. But when I got her into the examining position—on her side, with her bottom right out over the edge of the bed—and lifted her nightdress, she cried, I'll fall!

No, you're grand. Bridie will hold you steady.

Bridie perched on the other side of the bed and took the young woman's hands in hers.

I told her, I'm making you ready now...

I disinfected her vulva with Lysol solution, scrubbed it with soap, and then douched her vagina with a syringe to make sure the doctor wouldn't pass any germs from outside to inside.

Dr. Lynn murmured, Relax your muscles, dear, I won't be long.

Mary O'Rahilly made no protest, but I could hear her breathing quicken. She coughed convulsively.

I knew the doctor was feeling with one finger for the edge of the cervix, hoping not to find it; only when the tissue thinned so much it was undetectable would the woman be ready to start pushing.

Dr. Lynn pulled out her gloved hand. I believe I'll break your waters now to move things along.

She turned her head to me and murmured, Given the circumstances.

Clearly Mary O'Rahilly wasn't much further on than when she'd come in this morning. A few months ago, we'd have let her take as much time as she needed, but the doctor wanted to spare the young woman the double burden of the grippe and days of exhausting labour in this makeshift ward.

So I went and got the tray with the long sterilised hook.

She burst into tears at the sight.

Oh, the doctor won't be poking *you* with that, Mrs. O'Rahilly. It's just to make a little opening in the bag of fluid the baby's swimming in.

She'd probably never heard of the amniotic sac either.

Two towels, please, Bridie?

I folded them under Mary O'Rahilly, who let out a *rat-a-tat-tat* of nervous coughs. I douched her again. This wretched brownout; I took out my small battery-powered torch and aimed it so Dr. Lynn could see what she was doing. (German manufacture, of course. A miracle it had lasted four years; I never let it out of my sight.)

The doctor deftly opened Mary O'Rahilly with her left hand and slid the hook in, guarded by the fingers of her right, then stared into the distance as if navigating a mountain pass by night.

Amniotic fluid leaked out. It was clear, in the sharp beam of my torch; no greenish, yellowish, or brownish traces of meconium, which would be a strong hint that we should get the baby out fast.

Excellent, said the doctor.

I pulled down Mary O'Rahilly's nightdress and helped her to sit up.

She shivered and sucked on her cooling whiskey. Will it stop hurting now, Nurse?

Her innocence bruised my heart. Ought I to break it to her that we were trying to make her pangs come faster and harder, powerful enough to squeeze out her baby?

Instead I said, That should have made some room in there and hurried things along a bit.

Bridie took away the wet towels and I straightened up the bed.

I went over to the doctor, who was stripping off her gloves. I said quietly, There'll be no midwife here once I go home tonight, only a general nurse.

Dr. Lynn nodded tiredly. Then I'll be sure to check up on Mrs. O'Rahilly before I go off duty, and I'll ask—who is it, Prendergast?—to look in on her in the small hours.

After she'd gone, Honor White coughed up more sputum. I gave the cup to Bridie to empty and rinse out with carbolic.

The lamps turned back up just then, which was a relief.

I took a fuller look at the newcomer's chart and noticed that all it said after *Husband's name* was *White*, with no Christian name, and below *Husband's occupation*, only a blank. So there wasn't actually a husband; *Mrs.* must be a courtesy title. One of those things that had been very shocking before the war but were rather less so now; were there more illegitimate births or did it just seem to matter less when so many men weren't making it home? A fervent Catholic, though, in a temperance league, and pregnant out of wedlock, perhaps for the second time; that combination did intrigue me. At any rate, I never gave an unmarried patient any grief for her situation—though the same couldn't be said for some prigs of the old school such as Sister Luke.

At the side, under *Transferred from*, I recognised the name of an institution just a few streets away, a large mother-and-baby home where women went to bear unwanted children. Or were sent, perhaps; I was hazy on the details. The whole phenomenon was so shrouded in shame. It was known that if a woman got into trouble she'd be taken in by the nuns; these institutions dotted the country, but nobody ever said much about what they were like inside. What had happened to that first child of Honor White's, I wondered—had it lived?

Over at the sink, where Bridie was washing up, I said in her ear: I know you have a way of chatting to the patients—

Sorry, I'm an awful blabbermouth.

No, no, it sets them at ease. But Mrs. White...please don't ask anything about her circumstances.

Bridie's eyebrows contracted.

She, ah, went to school before the bell rang.

The young woman showed no sign of knowing that phrase.

Unwed. (I barely whispered the word.) From one of those mother-and-baby homes.

Oh.

I wonder what'll happen after the birth, I murmured. It'll be adopted, I suppose.

Bridie's face closed up. Go into the pipe, more likely.

I stared; what could she mean?

Nurse Julia, I need the lavatory.

I lifted down a bedpan and brought it over to Delia Garrett.

Not that. Let me go—

Sorry, you're still on bed rest for at least a few days.

(It was actually supposed to be the full week after a birth, but I couldn't spare the cot for that long.)

I tell you, I can walk!

I was glad to hear Delia Garrett sounding more like her snappish self. Come on, let me slip this pan under you and you'll be all set.

With a huff of breath, she heaved up one hip to make room for the cold steel.

I took her pulse. No fever, I could tell from her skin, but I leaned in to take a covert inhalation. I prided myself on having a nose for the first hint of childbed fever, and all I was getting was sweat, blood, and whiskey—but I'd stay vigilant.

I heard the urine let down at last, and Delia Garrett gasped.

Two beds over, the new patient let out a ravaging cough as if her lungs were being torn to pieces. I went around Mary O'Rahilly's cot and got Honor White propped up against a wedge-shaped bedrest.

Her pulse and respirations were still scudding along. She crossed herself and murmured, It's just deserts.

Your flu? Don't be thinking that way, I said soothingly. There's no rhyme or reason to who's getting struck down.

Honor White shook her head. I don't mean just me.

I felt foolish for having jumped to conclusions.

All of us. (She heaved a crackling breath.) Serves us right.

All of us sinners? I wondered. This might be religious mania. She gasped: For the war.

Ah, now I caught her drift. Human beings had killed so many at this point, some said nature was rebelling against us.

Honor White breathed, God save us.

It was a prayer of hope, but I all I could hear in this woman's husky voice was mortification and loneliness.

Delia Garrett demanded, Do you mean to leave me on this thing all evening?

I lifted the bedpan out from under her, wiped her clean, then fetched antiseptic gauze and dabbed her stitches ever so gently.

Bridie, could you empty and rinse this in the lavatory? And get me another chilled pad for Mrs. Garrett.

Good evening, Nurse Power.

I turned to see Sister Luke addressing me through her mask, looking as starched as ever.

Where had the hours gone? I glanced at the clock and saw it was nine o'clock on the dot. I supposed I'd feel bone-weary if I let myself think about it. But I didn't want to leave.

I noticed that both Mary O'Rahilly and Honor White were rigid, laying eyes on the night nurse for the first time—she was an Egyptian mummy come to life.

Sister Luke snapped the string of her eye patch as she tightened it. How did you get on today?

I couldn't think how to sum up all that had been packed into these fourteen hours. I pictured their faces: Ita Noonan taken off in convulsions, despite all I did; the unnamed Garrett girl born dead before I could do anything for her at all. Her mother might have bled out, though, but hadn't. Such an arbitrariness to all their fates.

In a low voice, I brought Sister Luke up to date. Mrs. White's pneumonia needs watching, I told her, and so does Mrs. Garrett's wound. The only one in labour is Mrs. O'Rahilly, who hasn't been making much headway, so Dr. Lynn's just broken her waters.

Sister Luke nodded as she hung up her apron. Having a long old time of it, are you, Mrs. O'Rahilly?

The girl managed a nod and a wet cough.

The nun quoted philosophically, Well, *Woe unto them that are with child.*

Irritation stiffened my spine. Some older nurses seemed to think every woman who'd had relations with a man—even her husband—should expect the punishment that followed. I hardly liked to leave this weary and frightened girl in the nun's hands.

I said, Mrs. O'Rahilly may have more chloral to help her sleep through her pangs, if need be.

But what would the night nurse consider *need*?

I warned her, If the pangs get much stronger or start speeding up, step into Women's Fever and have them call a midwife down from Maternity, right?

Sister Luke nodded.

And as there are so few physicians on duty, Dr. Lynn's given permission for any of these patients to have whiskey, chloroform, or morphine.

Above the mask, the nun's eyebrows arched at this breach of protocol.

Bridie dashed in with the chilled moss pad.

Sweeney, have you been making yourself useful?

It seemed a curt form of address, but Bridie only shrugged.

I took the pad from her hand and said, Indispensable, in fact.

That made the corners of Bridie's mouth turn up.

The nun was unpacking an apron. The queue I passed outside the picture house! Grown men, women, and children, all gasping to get into the great germ box.

Well, the small pleasures of the poor, I murmured as I got my coat on. Can you blame them?

Sister Luke jerked a fresh pair of mackintosh sleeves up past her elbows. Courting death, so they are. Off you go now, Sweeney.

Her rudeness took me aback.

But Bridie grabbed her coat and left the room.

I said a quick good night to my three patients and put my cape and bag over my arm.

I thought I might have lost her, but I spotted her below me. Bridie!

I caught up to her and we headed down the noisy staircase together. You shouldn't let Sister Luke boss you about that way.

Bridie only smiled.

And she's very harsh on cinemagoers, I added. In depressing times, doesn't one need a cheap escape?

I saw a picture once.

Oh, yes? Which one?

I don't know what it was called, she admitted. By the time I managed to slip off and sneak into the cinema by the side door, the story was half told.

Slip off from where? I wondered. And why sneak in by the side door—hadn't she the price of a ticket?

Bridie said, But I do remember the heroine was only gorgeous, a wee slip of a thing. She was marooned, and this fellow showed up, and next thing, they had a baby!

She laughed a little bashfully.

Then wouldn't you know, another ship turned up with his wife on it…

I asked, This was a couple of years ago?

The title came back to me. *Hearts Adrift,* I told her. Mary Pickford and…I forget.

Mary Pickford? echoed Bridie. I didn't think she'd have an ordinary name like Mary.

She's quite something, isn't she? Nothing ordinary about her.

Hearts Adrift; Bridie brought out the phrase with a slow savor. Oh, I'm getting it now, *adrift* because they're shipwrecked.

Didn't you love her in *Rebecca of Sunnybrook Farm?*

I've only seen the one picture.

Sympathy stopped me in my tracks. Once, in her roughly twenty-two years? I'd been going to the cinema ever since I'd come up from the country, and Tim came along with me after he moved to Dublin. Did Bridie's parents not let her out in the evenings or hadn't they two pennies to rub together? But I couldn't shame her by asking.

I continued down the steps. Then it's as well it was a good one, I suppose.

Bridie nodded with one of her gleaming grins.

The plot of *Hearts Adrift* was coming back to me. At the end, when Mary Pickford leaps into the volcano...

I thought I'd die with her!

(Bridie's eyes as wet as shore pebbles.)

I said, I can't remember what happens to the baby, though. Do the married couple take it away with them?

No, no, she has it in her arms when she jumps.

Bridie mimed that, protective arms caging the invisible infant on her chest, her face lit up with ecstasy.

It was such a pleasure to be able to chat for a minute without worrying about patients. But at the base of the stairs, staff pushed past us in the hullabaloo of shift changeover.

Are you all right walking home in the dark, Bridie?

I'm grand. Where do nurses sleep?

Well, big lodging houses, most of them, but I rent with my little brother. I take a tram and then cycle the rest of the way. Tim's twenty-six.

I added that belatedly, in case I'd made him sound like a boy.
Bridie nodded.

He enlisted in '14, I surprised myself by telling her.

Did he? How long was he gone?

Nineteen months at first. Then he sent word from Macedonia
that he'd been made second lieutenant, and I should expect him
home on leave. But he never turned up, and it took me three
days to discover that he was in hospital with trench fever. No
sooner did he get over that than they told him it had counted
as his leave, and he was being posted back.

Bridie groaned.

Well, I said, one has to laugh.

(What I didn't mention was that when Tim had finally been
shipped back to me from Egypt fourteen months after that, he
wasn't speaking.)

Good night, then, Julia.

I was still oddly unwilling to let the conversation end. Have
you far to go?

Bridie jerked her thumb left. Only down the street.

Her eyes dropped briefly.

She added, To the motherhouse.

Oh, now I understood why Sister Luke took such a propri-
etorial tone. Bridie's shabby clothes, too, the lack of free
evenings and spending money...

The moment was awkward. I tried to make a joke: Rather
funny that *motherhouse* is the word for an order's main
premises when there's not a mother in the place.

She chuckled.

So you're a—a novice, Bridie? Or is *postulant* the term?

A dark laugh now. I wouldn't be a nun for a hundred pounds.

Oh, my mistake, I thought—

I just board there.

THE PULL OF THE STARS

Her voice went very low.

I come from one of their homes, she added, down the country.

I registered that. It suddenly struck me as perverse that someone was said to have grown up in a home only if she had no real home.

Awfully sorry, Bridie, I didn't mean to pry.

That's all right.

A stiff kind of silence.

She muttered, I'd rather you knew why I'm so stupid.

Stupid?

They only sent me up to Dublin at nineteen, see, and it's all still new to me.

Bridie, you're the opposite of stupid!

Ah, you wouldn't believe the mistakes I still make, she said bitterly. Handling change, reading signs, getting around on the trams, losing my way or losing my hat—

You're a traveller in a strange land, I told her. Clever *and* brave.

That made Bridie beam.

Nurse Power?

Dr. Lynn, coming up from the basement, almost barged into us. I know it's a lot to ask, but could you possibly help me with Mrs. Noonan?

I blinked, wondering what could be done for Ita Noonan now.

With the p.m.

A discreet abbreviation for *postmortem*.

Oh, of course, Doctor.

Frankly I'd have preferred to go home, but how could I say no to her?

The flare of Bridie's head had already disappeared in the throng. I felt nettled that the doctor had broken up our chat.

I followed her down the stairs.

She told me, It has to be tonight, since the body will be released to the husband first thing in the morning.

Families were rarely told in so many words about autopsies; it was hard for them to understand the benefit to medicine of our hacking their loved ones about.

Then it occurred to me that I might be in real trouble. I asked, You're not thinking Mrs. Noonan's cause of death is in doubt?

Not at all, the doctor assured me. Since the outbreak began, I've been seizing any chance to do a p.m. on a flu case, especially a pregnant one.

Just my luck to run into a true scientist; I could have been on my way to bed by now. Still, Dr. Lynn's zeal impressed me, especially considering she was living under the shadow of arrest, if the gossip was true; how did she manage to rise above her own sea of troubles and concentrate on the common good?

The mortuary was deserted. I'd been down to its white chill before, but I'd never seen it so eerily full of coffins. Six high against all four walls, like firewood stacked ready for the furnace. I wondered how the attendants remembered who was who—did they pencil the names on the sides?

So many!

Dr. Lynn murmured, This is nothing. Out at the cemetery there are hundreds of caskets piled up, waiting their turn. Hazardous to the living, I call it. The Germans—an eminently practical race— cremate their dead.

Really?

A shocking notion, but *fas est ab hoste doceri,* you know.

My face was blank, so she glossed that: Learn even from enemies. It wouldn't surprise me if this flu turned out to be caused by a miasma of rot blowing over from the battlefields...

I followed her into the autopsy room, where the table was a gleaming altar: white porcelain with a central drain and deep grooves like the veins in a leaf. I put down my things as Dr. Lynn slid out one of the laden shelves and lifted off the sheet.

Ita Noonan, paled to grey already, in a few hours. Those fingers, incongruously bright from the TNT she'd packed into shells. The mound of her belly under the nightdress. *There's a baby*, she'd whispered in my ear. With pride, dread, bewilderment?

In the ordinary way of things, she'd have shed her burden sometime in January, then some weeks later gone to be blessed and sprinkled with holy water. Only now did churching strike me as a peculiar tradition, as if giving birth left a faint taint on a woman that needed wiping away. Did Ita Noonan's death do away with the need to be churched? I wondered—was it enough to purify her in the priests' eyes?

Dr. Lynn set a rubber block on the ceramic table. This improves access to the abdominal cavity. Can we manage her between us or will I go fetch an attendant?

She had the far ends of the sheet gripped in her hands.

Childishly, I couldn't bear to stand there alone in the underlit vault while she stepped out. So I said, No bother.

I seized the near corners and braced myself. The small woman was heavier than I'd expected. My back tightened; I arched it a little to relieve it. The two of us got Ita Noonan onto the ceramic and rolled her to one side, then the other, to remove the browned sheet and set the rubber block along her spine.

A little pink leaked out of her nose. I dabbed it away.

The doctor was already rolling the surgical lamp across the floor. She trained its light on the body and clicked it up to its very brightest.

I began to undo the tapes of the nightdress; I lifted and tugged. Rather ashamed to bare Ita Noonan so to the air.

I stationed myself across from Dr. Lynn with my fountain pen and paper.

She murmured, Livor mortis, the blue of death.

She put her fingertip to Ita Noonan's livid arm, which went white at the spot. After twelve hours, she remarked, it'll stay blue even when pressed.

I pointed out, The body doesn't seem stiff yet.

That's due to the cold down here, Nurse.

Really?

It may sound rather back-to-front, but it's the metabolic processes of decomposition that cause rigor mortis, whereas a low temperature slows down decay and keeps the cadaver soft.

Purple was pooling in patches on Ita Noonan's shoulders, arms, back, buttocks, the backs of her legs. Bruising above her elbows from where I'd tried to revive her. (So often we had to mete out indignity on a body in a vain attempt to keep it breathing.)

Dr. Lynn let out a breath. What a wreck. Practically toothless at thirty-three, and that huge leg must have given her constant pain.

I considered the devastated terrain of Ita Noonan's belly, which had been pushed up from plain to mountain a dozen times.

Did you know, said the doctor, we lose half again as many lying-in cases here as they do in England?

I didn't.

Mostly because Irish mothers have too many babies, she added as she unrolled her blades. I rather wish your Holy Father would let them off after their sixth.

I almost laughed at the image of Dr. Lynn—Protestant socialist, suffragette, republican firebrand, in her mannish collar and bluestocking glasses—demanding an audience with Pope Benedict to press her point.

She glanced up as if to check I wasn't offended.

I said, Ready, Doctor.

Now, I don't think we'll chance a cranial cut, as they're hard to cover up.

I was relieved; I'd helped peel back a face before, and it was one of those sights I wished I could unsee.

Dr. Lynn's finger rested on Ita Noonan's hairline. This weird flu. I've seen it start with thirst, restlessness, sleeplessness, clumsiness, a touch of mania—then, afterwards, a blurring or dulling of one or more senses...but alas, none of this shows up under the microscope.

I volunteered: For a few weeks after my own dose, all colours looked a little grey to me.

Then you got off lightly. Amnesia, aphasia, lethargy...I've seen survivors with shakes and others frozen to living statues. Also suicides, far more than the papers will admit.

I asked, They do it in the delirious phase?

Or long after, even. Hadn't you a patient jump to his death last week?

Oh. (I felt gullible.) We were told he'd slipped from an open window.

Dr. Lynn set her scalpel by Ita Noonan's left shoulder. I'll start the trunk incision here and the family will never spot it. God bless the work.

I watched the skin part in a deep, clean arc under the limp breasts. Barely a trickle of blood.

She murmured, Never easy when it's one's own patient.

I wondered if by *one* she meant herself or me.

If you don't mind my asking, Doctor, with your interest in research, why aren't you on staff at one of the big hospitals?

Her thin lips twisted wryly. None of them would have me.

She cut straight down from breastbone through navel to pubis, finishing the capital Y.

I was offered a position some years ago, she added, but their medical men shied away from the prospect of a petticoated colleague.

I knew it wasn't my place to comment, but...Their loss!

Dr. Lynn nodded to acknowledge that. She added crisply, And on the whole, my gain. Shifting my tent has let me encounter and study *all the ills that flesh is heir to.*

She snipped on, adding, Besides, I'd have been cashiered by now anyway for my commitment to the cause.

My face was suddenly hot. I'd assumed the doctor would keep a veil drawn over her other, underground life. Since she'd brought it up, I made myself ask, So it's true, then, that you were with the rebels on the roof of City Hall?

She corrected me: With the Irish Citizen Army. I took over as commanding officer when Sean Connolly was shot putting up the green flag.

A silence.

I said unevenly, I got some experience with gunshot wounds during that week.

I'm sure you did, said Dr. Lynn.

A woman who was with child, a civilian, was brought in on a stretcher and bled out before I could stop it.

Her tone was sad: I heard about her. I'm sorry. One of almost five hundred killed that week, and thousands injured, mostly by British artillery.

I saw red, because that was Tim's army. I said, My brother served. The king, I mean.

(I added that awkwardly, in case I hadn't been clear.)

Dr. Lynn nodded. So many Irishmen have sacrificed themselves in the cause of empire and capital.

But it was you terrorists who began the shooting in Dublin, and treacherously, in the middle of a world war!

My hands froze. Berating a physician—what had I done? I thought Dr. Lynn might order me out of the mortuary.

Instead she set down her blade and said civilly, I saw the national question much the same way as you until five years ago, Nurse Power.

I was taken aback.

I took up the cause of women in earnest first, she added, then the labour movement. I pinned my hopes on a peaceful transition to a self-governing Ireland that would treat its workers and mothers and children more kindly. But in the end I realised that despite four decades of paying lip service to the principle of home rule, the British meant to keep fobbing us off. Only then, after much soul-searching, I assure you, did I become what you call a terrorist.

I said nothing.

Dr. Lynn picked up the big shears and worked it along each side of Ita Noonan. Then she lifted the breastbone and frontal ribs in one go, the raising of a portcullis.

That made me tremble. How frail my own rib cage; how breakable we all were.

I needed to get us off politics. So I asked, Did your own dose of flu leave you with any odd symptoms, Doctor?

She didn't look up as she said, I haven't had it.

Christ Almighty, the woman was up to her elbows in microbes. My voice came out shrill: Would you not put on a mask, even?

Interestingly, there's very little evidence that they have any protective effect. I scrub my hands, and gargle with brandy, and leave the rest to Providence. Retractor, please?

I handed the doctor what she asked for; I measured and

weighed. I didn't want to disappoint her, for all the gulf between our beliefs.

Dr. Lynn went on, As for the authorities, I believe the
pandemic will have run its course before they've agreed on
any but the most feeble action. Recommending onions and
eucalyptus oil! Like sending beetles to stop a steamroller. No,
as a wise old Greek once said, we all live in an unwalled
city.

She must have sensed she'd lost me, because she spelled it
out: When it comes to death.

Oh, yes. Quite.

She lifted Ita Noonan's lungs—two black bags—and dropped
them wetly into my waiting dish. Dear me, what a mess. Take a
specimen, please, though I expect the engorgement will obscure
the image.

I shaved a thin layer; I labelled the slide.

You know there's a brand-new expensive oxygen machine
upstairs?

I shook my head.

Dr. Lynn said, I tried it out on two men with pneumonia this
afternoon, quite uselessly. We trickle the pure gas right up their
noses, but it can't get through their gummed-up passages.

She dictated now, more formally: *Swelling of the pleura. Puru-
lent material leaking from the alveoli, bronchioles, bronchi.*

I wrote it all down.

If something attacks the lungs, she murmured, they fill up,
so one drowns in one's own inner sea. I had a comrade go like
that last year.

From the flu?

No, no, he'd been force-fed, Tom Ashe had, and it went
down the wrong way.

I'd heard of suffragettes mounting hunger strikes, but—Sinn

Féin prisoners too? My voice wobbled as I asked, This man actually...died of it?

Dr. Lynn nodded. As I stood there taking his pulse.

I felt terribly sorry for him, and for her, but that did not change my disapproval of their cause.

One dark braid was coming loose at the back of Dr. Lynn's head; it bobbed as she worked her instruments. I wondered how long she'd spent in prison and how she'd stayed so sturdy, so lively.

She dictated: *Vocal cords eroded. Thyroid three times normal size. Heart dilated.*

Isn't it always bigger in expectant women, though?

She held up the heart for me to study. But Mrs. Noonan's is flabby on both sides, do you see? Whereas the normal enlargement in pregnancy is only on the left—to supply the foetus with more blood.

I supposed the foetus demanded more of everything. A mother's lungs, circulation, every part had to boost capacity, like a factory gearing up for war.

I asked, Could that be why this flu is hitting them so hard—because their systems are overworked already?

The doctor nodded. Sky-high morbidity, even for weeks *after* birth, which suggests their defences have been weakened somehow.

I thought of the old tale of Troy, Greek soldiers dropping out of the wooden horse's belly under cover of night and throwing open the gates. Betrayed by one's own side. What was it Dr. Lynn had quoted about an unwalled city?

She cut, she scooped; I labelled, I bagged.

She grumbled: So many autopsies being industriously performed all over the world, and just about all we've learnt about this strain of flu is that it takes around two days to incubate.

Aren't they any closer to a vaccine, then?

She shook her head and her loose braid leapt. No one's even managed to isolate the bacterium on a slide yet. Perhaps the little bugger's too small for us to see and we'll have to wait for the instrument makers to come up with a stronger microscope, or possibly it's some new form of microbe altogether.

I was bewildered and daunted.

All rather humbling, she added ruefully. Here we are in the golden age of medicine—making such great strides against rabies, typhoid fever, diphtheria—and a common or garden influenza is beating us hollow. No, you're the ones who matter right now. Attentive nurses, I mean—*tender loving care,* that seems to be all that's saving lives.

Dr. Lynn peered into the abdominal cavity, which was pulpy with dark juice. She dictated: *Liver swollen, signs of internal bleeding. Kidney inflamed and oozing. Colon ulcerated.*

I followed her scalpel with my own, taking samples.

She murmured, We could always blame the stars.

I beg your pardon, Doctor?

That's what *influenza* means, she said. *Influenza delle stelle*—the influence of the stars. Medieval Italians thought the illness proved that the heavens were governing their fates, that people were quite literally star-crossed.

I pictured that, the celestial bodies trying to fly us like upside-down kites. Or perhaps just yanking on us for their obscure amusement.

Dr. Lynn freed Ita Noonan's small intestine with her scissors and lifted it in the way of a snake charmer. Now, *autopsy* comes from the Greek word meaning *to see with one's own eyes.* You and I are lucky, Nurse Power.

I frowned. Lucky? To be alive and well, you mean?

To be here, in the middle of this. We'll never learn more or faster.

Dr. Lynn put down her scalpel and flexed her fingers as if they were cramped. Then she picked the blade up again and slit Ita Noonan's uterus with delicacy. We all do our bit to increase the sum of human knowledge, including Mrs. Noonan.

She lifted the flap, peeled back the amniotic sac. Added under her breath, Even her last little Noonan.

She scooped the foetus out of the red cavity, cupped it in her hands.

Not it—*him*. I saw that it was a boy.

Dr. Lynn said, No sign the flu did him any harm. Measure, please?

She stretched him lengthways in the dish as if he were standing up for the first and only time in his life.

I set the tape at the crown of the skull, went down to the big toe. I said, barely audibly, Just under fifteen inches.

I placed the dish on the scales and added, A little under three pounds.

About twenty-eight weeks, then, said Dr. Lynn with relief. And underweight.

I understood; she'd been right not to do a caesarean.

The tiny, alien face. I let myself look too long and all at once was gasping, blinded by salt water.

Nurse Power. Julia. The doctor's voice was kind.

How did she know my first name? I wondered as I choked on my tears. Excuse me, I—

It's quite all right.

I sobbed, He's perfect.

He is.

I wept for him, and his mother on the slab, and his four brothers and sisters gone before him, and the seven orphaned ones, and their bereft father. Would Mr. Noonan raise them somehow or would they be carted off to grandparents, aunts, strangers? Scattered to the winds? To a home, so called, like Bridie Sweeney was?

I wiped my eyes as Dr. Lynn started putting the organs back.

Her hands slowed to lay the infant inside his mother. I offered her a box of flax-tow swabs. She put in three handfuls as padding, then set the rib cage into place. She pulled the edges of skin together as if drawing bedroom curtains to shut out the night. I was ready with the threaded needle, and she began to stitch.

After she finished, Dr. Lynn thanked me briskly and went off to conduct night rounds.

I washed Ita Noonan one last time before putting her in a fresh nightdress to be buried.

Outside the hospital gates, I took a deep breath of the chill, dark air and felt my exhaustion.

Buttoning my coat as I headed for the tram stop, I almost stepped into a pothole two feet deep. I wondered if I'd be secretly glad to break a leg if it meant a month off work.

Let them go, I told myself as I did at the end of every long shift. Eileen Devine, and Ita Noonan with her never-to-be-born son; Delia Garrett's stillbirth. Secretive Honor White gripping her prayer beads; Mary O'Rahilly trapped in a labour that seemed like it would never end. I had to let it all fall from me so I could eat and sleep and be fit to pick it up again tomorrow morning.

The three nearest streetlamps had burnt out; no doubt the carbon electrodes were German and couldn't be replaced. Dublin was sinking into dilapidation, its cracks yawning. Were all its lights going to blink out one by one?

I spotted a waning crescent moon speared on a spire and

draped in clouds. A red-eyed paper boy, his cap upended on the pavement in hopes of coins, was singing that rebel song in a squeaky soprano: *Tonight we man the gap of danger...*

I thought of Dr. Lynn and her comrades clambering onto the roof of City Hall; they'd *manned the gap of danger,* and for what? So strange to think of a physician taking up the gun, blasting bodies apart instead of mending them.

But then, army doctors did the same, it struck me. War was such a muddle.

A goods tram went by freighted with spuds. The next held pigs, shrieking in their darkness. Then a locomotive hauling wagons of rubbish; I held my breath till the stench had cleared.

The paper boy repeated his chorus, the battle cry sounding innocent in his sweet voice. Of course, he might not give a fig for king or freedom; he'd pick whatever songs pleased the customers. Street traders were supposed to be at least eleven, but this fellow looked more like eight. I wondered what kind of home he'd go back to at the end of the night. I'd made enough follow-up visits to patients to be able to guess. Cracks rived the walls of what had once been mansions; families now lay five to a mattress under crumbling plaster vines and dripping washing lines. All the Dubliners who could had escaped to the suburbs, leaving the rest to live like squatters in the capital's rotting heart.

Perhaps the paper boy had nowhere to live at all. I supposed one could survive a chill night on these streets at the end of October, but how many nights, over how many years? I thought of Dr. Lynn's dream of an Ireland that would treat its least citizens kindly.

I wondered about the orphanage that Bridie had grown up in and about what she'd said of an unwelcomed baby such as the one Honor White was expecting, that it would go *into the pipe*. A rather extraordinary young woman, this Bridie Sweeney. Such zest and vim. Where had she learnt all she seemed to understand? No comb of her own; a single stolen visit to a cinema. Had she ever been in a motorcar, I wondered, or listened to a gramophone?

"Faith of Our Fathers" tolled from the church behind, drowning out the singing boy. The stained glass glimmered with candlelight. A notice on the door under the heading *Allhallowtide* said, *During of this time of crisis, TWO special masses will be offered each evening at six and ten to entreat divine protection.*

That jogged my memory—tomorrow was a holy day, so I supposed I should attend the vigil mass. But I didn't have it in me; I was dead on my feet.

That flip phrase made me wince. My aching awareness of every muscle was so entirely unlike the blankness of death. I should be glad to have sore feet and a back that grumbled and fingers that stung at the tips.

Finally a passenger tram stopped; it was full but I pressed onto it with the others. People glared at us for crowding them further and some squirmed away in case we were contagious.

On the top deck I stood holding on to the balcony rail. The same small notice had been pasted to the floor every two feet, I saw: SPIT SPREADS DEATH. One of them was already marked, derisively, with a spatter of smoky brown.

Strangers' bodies weighed against mine. I pictured trams grinding along their lines across Dublin like blood through veins. *We all live in an unwalled city,* that was it. I saw lines scored across the map of Ireland; carved all over the globe. Train tracks, roads, shipping channels, a web of human traffic that connected all nations into one great suffering body.

A light in a druggist's window below us illuminated a handwritten apology: *Have Run Out of Carbolic.* Passing shopfronts and houses, I glimpsed hollowed-out turnips with penny candles that wavered with flame. I was happy that the old beat of festivity still sounded. On Halloween when Tim and I were small, we had barmbrack, the moist fruit bread, toasted at the fire and buttered till the raisins shone. I always hoped to get the lucky ring in my slice, but I never did. My stomach growled now. How long it had been since that bowl of stew this afternoon.

I wondered what Bridie got to eat with the boarders at the motherhouse.

The tram rattled on, past a dark maze of streets where many of my patients lived—rickety stairways, toppling walls, filthy courts, red brick browned by coal smoke; smashed fanlights over doors were eyes put out. A Negro man sat slumped against a wall.

No, a white man, metamorphosed. *Red to brown to blue to black.* This poor fellow was at the end of that terrible rainbow. Had anyone run to a telephone exchange to ring for an ambulance? But the tram trundled past before I could make a note of the street.

Nothing I could do now. I tried to put him out of my mind.

Alighting at my stop, I caught a whiff from a communal kitchen for the needy. Corned beef, cabbage? Rather nasty, but it made me even hungrier for my supper.

John Brown's baby has a pimple on his arse, a drunk sang.

John Brown's baby has a pimple on his arse,
John Brown's baby has a pimple on his arse,
And the poor child can't sit down.

In the alley I found my cycle locked safely. I drew up the sides of my skirt in preparation, knotting the tapes for safety.

Light blinded me. A high-pitched call: All right there?

Two of the Women's Patrol shone their beams all the way to the back wall. To ensure my protection or, put another way, to check if I was reeling drunk or up to no good with a soldier.

I snapped, Perfectly all right.

Very well, carry on.

I wheeled my cycle up the alley, towards the street.

A bell sounded in the factory ahead. Munitionettes began spilling out, calling to each other, their fingers dyed so yellow I could see it by streetlight; were these women from Ita Noonan's Canary Crew? One of them coughed whoopingly, laughed, coughed again as I pedaled past.

At the top of my lane, boys skittered by in motley gear—a bright scarf around a forehead, a checkered tie worn over the nose, men's jackets on backwards, the smallest boy wearing the paper face of a ghost. I only wished they had shoes on their knobbly feet. It surprised me that they'd been let out to go house to house at such a time; I'd have thought all doors would be shut. I tried to remember what it was the old ones used to sprinkle on us children at Halloween in the part of the country where Tim and I had grown up.

A tall boy blared at me. His bugle was dented, scarred with solder, plating all worn away at the mouthpiece. Was his father a returned veteran, perhaps? Or a dead one, of course, his bugle sent home in his place. Or perhaps I was being sentimental, and the boy had won it off another in a bet.

The younger lads clashed saucepan lids. Apples and nuts, missus!

The miniature ghost cried, Go on, would you ever have an old apple or a nut for the party?

He sounded drunk to me. (Quite plausible, since many people believed alcohol could keep the flu at bay.) I dug into my purse for a halfpenny even though he'd called me *missus* instead of *miss*.

He blew me a phantom kiss over his shoulder.

Clearly to a child I looked well past thirty. I thought of Delia Garrett calling me *spinster*. Nursing was like being under a spell: you went in very young and came out older than any span of years could make you.

I asked myself whether I minded about tomorrow's birthday. The real question was whether I was going to regret it if I never got married. But how could I possibly know for sure until it was too late? Which wasn't reason enough to do it, to throw myself headlong at every half-viable prospect the way some women did. Regret seemed all too likely either way.

When I let myself into the narrow terraced house, it smelled cold. Candle stubs burnt in jam jars.

My brother was scratching his magpie's glossy head at the table.

I thought of the old rhyme for counting magpies. *One for sorrow, two for joy.*

Evening, Tim.

He nodded.

Odd how one took conversation for granted. A ribbon held taut between two people—until it was cut.

I mentioned too perkily: Rather a red-letter day. Sister Finnigan was needed up in Maternity, so yours truly found herself promoted to acting ward sister.

Tim's eyebrows jogged up and down.

I had an awful habit of making up for my brother's lack of chatter by doubling my own. I put my bag down and peeled off my coat and cape. The trick was not to ask questions,

or only safe ones to which I could guess the answers. How's
your bird?

(I didn't know if he'd given it a name in his head.)

Tim didn't meet my eyes very often, but he could manage a
half smile.

In the summer he'd found the enormous creature in the alley,
grounded by a banjaxed leg. He'd bought it a rusty rabbit
hutch to roost in and kept the door tied open with a piece of
string so it could come and go as it pleased. Its sheeny green
tail was always knocking things over. The magpie also did its
business wherever it liked, and whenever I complained it was a
menace, Tim pretended not to hear.

I'd been looking forward to something hot tonight, but
clearly the gas was off. What about the water? I tried the
tap—only a dribble. Damn and blast it!

It was a luxury to let myself curse off shift. To shed the guise
of Nurse Power and be Julia.

Tim had a saucepan still hot on the Primus stove; he lit
the kerosene flame to bring the water back to the boil for tea.
I pushed aside the notebook that was always on the kitchen
table for writing notes. Mine were frequent and chatty; Tim's
rare and sparse. (Whatever was locking his throat had the same
grip on his writing hand.)

I remarked into the silence, Awfully busy today. I lost one
patient, from convulsions.

Tim shook his head in sympathy. He tugged at the touchwood
charm on its chain around his neck as if wishing protection
for me.

The week he'd joined up I'd given him the creepy charm half
in jest—an imp with a swollen head of oak and an attenuated
brass body. Some soldiers called it a *fumsup* because of the two
thumbs perpetually turned up, for luck, on the tiny arms that

went up and down. The only features left on Tim's touchwood were two staring eyes; I supposed the rest of its face had been rubbed away by his fretful thumb. I thought of Honor White with her holy beads doubled around her wrist; it wasn't just servicemen who clung to amulets.

I added, But it could have gone very much worse, really.

I'd have liked to tell Tim about the odd redhead who'd helped me today. But an uneducated girl with cracked shoes, raised in a home, lodging at a convent—Bridie might sound as if she were the opening line of a joke. I couldn't seem to find words for her.

Tim took saucepan lids off two plates and set them down at our places.

He'd waited all this long dark evening to eat tepid food with his big sister. But he didn't care for gush, so all I said was Oh, Tim, you've outdone yourself. Runner beans!

Another faint smile.

Before the war my brother had been rather more quick-witted and chipper than I. Like Bridie, actually—a real spark to him.

So you must have been at the allotment today.

(We had only an eighth of an acre, but Tim worked wonders.)

Potatoes were as scarce as gold nuggets. Tonight's ones were perfect dimpled globes, the size of acorns. Barely boiled, skin still crisp to the teeth.

I had a qualm. It's wasteful not to leave them in the ground till they're bigger, though, isn't it?

My brother shrugged grandly.

There were onions too, of course; we had them coming out our ears. (The government would approve.) The lettuce was holed with a few slug bites but tasted ever so alive.

And look at this, celery! They've started selling it as a nerve cure, would you believe?

I thought that might amuse Tim. But his face stayed blank. Maybe the notion of shattered nerves hit too close to the bone.

At the military hospital, they'd called it *war neurosis*. It could take a bewildering variety of forms, and even civilians got it; there was that Englishwoman who'd lost her mind in an air raid and decapitated her child.

They'd dosed Tim with chloral to prevent the nightmares, or at least to make him forget the details when he woke up groggy; it gave him a perpetually queasy stomach. Massages to soothe, walks to invigorate, hypnosis to get my brother's mind back on track; lessons in brush-making, carpentry, boot repair to make him useful.

Tim had been discharged after a few months since he was fairly able compared to so many others. The psychologist had admitted he could do nothing for the speechlessness, and they needed the bed. The prescription was *rest, nourishment, and congenial occupation.*

I'd weaned Tim very gradually off the sedative. These days he was less jumpy, though he still couldn't stand crowds. Rather more able to eat, especially if I ate with him. I just had to trust that quiet and pottering about—gardening, shopping, cooking, cleaning, tending his magpie—would mend him in time.

Anything come in the post this morning?

My brother shook his head and made a gesture with his hands.

I didn't follow.

Pointing into the hall, he shook his head again, almost crossly.

Never mind, Tim.

He was scraping back his chair and tugging out the table's shallow drawer, the one that always stuck.

It doesn't matter, really.

I couldn't bear it when Tim had to grab the notebook to make himself understood to me, the nearest thing to a mammy he'd ever had; it made me feel we were thousands of miles apart.

He slid his jagged handwriting over so I could read: *Temporary suspension.*

Of the post? Oh, of delivery, I see. I suppose they've too many off sick at the sorting office. I added ruefully, At the hospital we'd never be allowed a *suspension* of service, not even for a day. Ours are the gates that can't close.

I wondered how long it would take me to remember not to ask Tim whether any post had come that day. How many weeks before I stopped missing it? This was how civilization might grind to a halt, one rusted-up cog at a time.

I remarked: I ran into some lads dressed up and going around the houses. I've been wracking my brains—what was it the old ones used to sprinkle on us at Halloween to ward off the spells of the little people?

Tim held up the little glass cruet.

Salt! That was it.

I took it from him, reminiscent. I shook a little into my hand and half solemnly touched a pinch to my forehead and another to Tim's.

He flinched at my touch, but bore it.

I was so glad Tim had had the flu already—the week before me, and just as mildly. Otherwise I'd be watching him every morning, every night. I'd feared losing my brother for years on end, and then he'd been returned to me, changed utterly; I couldn't endure the idea of having what was left taken now.

The jam-jar candles were guttering in their puddles. Tim rolled a meagre, meticulous cigarette.

Can I've one?

He slid it over and started another for himself.

We took our time smoking them. I thought of the lore veterans brought back from the front with their fags: *Never be the third to light up from a single match.* Was that simply good sense, because of the likelihood of the flare catching a sniper's eye in the dark if it shone out for more than a second? Or was the rule really about preserving the magic circle of friendship, two chums hunkered over a brief flame?

I remembered the photograph that hung a little askew over Tim's bureau upstairs, him and his pal Liam with arms slung around each other's neck; laughing boys showing off their battalion's smart kit the day they'd first put it on. His uniform with its solitary pip on the shoulder hung in the wardrobe now. His character certificate in the back of a drawer, a printed form with his specifics filled in by hand:

The ex-soldier named above has served with the Colours for two years, three hundred and forty-seven days, *and his character during this period has been* good.

My brother stubbed out his cigarette and went into the pantry.

His shillelagh was leaning against the wall, stains on its thick knob. Tim used the club to cudgel the occasional rat that ventured into our pantry; he'd had no mercy on them ever since the trenches.

He came back with a barmbrack, dark brown and glossy.

Where did you get hold of this?

My question was rhetorical, mock outraged. No doubt it was from the old one up the lane, known for her apple pies.

Shall I be mother?

I cut into the brack's still faintly warm middle. I set out thick slices on Tim's plate and on mine, the dried fruits pebbling the pale bread. So fresh it didn't need toasting or buttering. Bet I get the coin, for riches.

Tim nodded seriously, as if taking my wager.

I bit into it. White wheat flour, not eked out with anything. The tang of fresh tea plumping up each sultana. I mumbled, That's only gorgeous.

I wondered what it had cost. Still, Tim took care we never ran short before the end of the week.

My brother's eyes were on the kitchen wall, or something past it. What could he not help but see?

I bit into a hard lump. Oh!

I unwrapped its waxed paper. (Reminded, for a split second, of parcelling up the stillborn Garrett.) It was the ring, its gold paint rubbing off already.

I boasted, very blasé: Married within the year, so.

Tim gave me a slow clap.

You haven't found a charm in your slice yet?

He shook his head and nibbled on. As if it were a duty, that was how he ate now, with a hint of dread, as if the food might turn to ashes in his mouth.

There was a time I'd have been thrilled by winning the tin ring, would've half believed its promise, even.

Enjoy your brack, I told myself.

The second time I bit into a minute packet, I nearly swallowed it. Another charm!

Even before I got the paper off I could tell by the shape. The thimble. I put it on my little finger and held it up, forcing a grin. What do you make of that, then, Tim? Bride and spinster in the one year, according to the brack. Just goes to show it's all a pack of nonsense.

Thinking that maybe we were indeed the sport of the stars. With their invisible silks, they tugged us this way and that.

One candle was drowning now. Tim snuffed it between finger and thumb, blew, snuffed it again to be sure.

I was suddenly so overcome with tiredness, my head swam.

Good night, Tim.

I left my brother in the kitchen with the other candle, stroking his bird. I didn't know when he slept these days. He was always up later than me, and earlier. Did he still have nightmares? If he got no sleep at all, surely he'd have collapsed by now. So if he kept getting up every morning, I supposed that was a good sign and should be enough for me.

I went up in the dark, bewildered with drowsiness.

Morbidly I dwelled on what might have happened if Bridie Sweeney hadn't been sent to my aid today, arriving out of nowhere, like a visitation. At some point, would I have thrown down my apron and howled that this job was beyond my powers? More likely, would I have failed to save Delia Garrett from the red tide?

I stumbled on the loose runner and almost fell, had to brace myself against the seam of the wallpaper.

Enough, Julia, I told myself. *Time for bed.*

III

BLUE

I SLEPT AND DREAMT that life was beauty. Stuck in my head, a tag from an old song. *I slept and dreamt that life was beauty. And then I woke—*

Then I woke—

The jangling alarm clock had roused me from sleep. I slapped down its knob and chivvied myself: *Up you get.*

My legs paid no attention. Those strings that connected handler to puppet seemed cut, or at least tangled.

I tried persuasion, telling myself that Tim would have the tea wetted for us already.

I tried castigation. Mary O'Rahilly, Honor White, Delia Garrett—they all needed me. As Sister Finnigan had drilled into us: *Patient first, hospital next, self last.*

The song was still bothering me. *I slept and dreamt that life was beauty. Then I woke up and—*

I was thinking about Bridie with the fuzzy bronze halo. I'd never thought to ask last night whether she meant to come back again. It could be that her first day had scared her off hospitals for life.

Snagged in my head: *And then I woke—*

Then I woke up—

I woke, and found that life was duty. That was it.

I winched my limbs out of bed in the dark. Sponged myself all over with cold water and brushed my teeth.

Tim's botch-legged magpie was hopping around on the kitchen table, its ratcheting screech like a policeman's rattle. Its eye had an awful intelligence. *Two for joy,* I thought. Was this one lonely despite my brother's silent company?

Morning, Tim.

He gave me both pieces of toast.

What's that on your cheek?

Tim shrugged as if it were a smear of jam or smut.

Come here so I can see.

My brother's hand shot out to keep me at bay.

I told him, Let me do my job.

I held his head steady, turned it to see better. It was a graze with a small blue bruise purpling behind it. Did you knock your face on something, Tim?

He nodded slightly.

Or was it another one of those yobbos who attacked you in the lane?

He shrank back into himself.

Strange times to be an invalided veteran in Dublin. An old fella might shake Tim's hand to thank him for his service, and the same day a widow might sneer at him for a shirker because he still had all his limbs. A passer-by might shout that it was filthy Tommies who'd brought the plague home to these shores in the first place. But my guess was that yesterday, some young green-wearing, would-be rebel had called him a pawn of the empire and pelted him with rubbish, because that's what had happened before.

Tell me, Tim. Otherwise I'll just have to imagine. Write it down if you'd rather.

I shoved the notebook towards him, and the pencil rolled in a circle.

He ignored it.

Being a mother must be like this, a constant struggle to interpret a baby's distress. But at least a child would be learning a little every day, whereas my brother...

I risked putting my hand over his.

Tim let it rest there briefly. Then with his other hand he pulled open the drawer of the kitchen table, and retrieved two packages tied with coils of old ribbon.

I said, My birthday. It went right out of my mind.

My brother loved me. A tear dropped onto my skirt now.

Tim reached past me for the pencil and notebook. He wrote, *Only thirty!*

I whooped with laughter and wiped my eyes. It's not that, truly.

Instead of trying to explain, I unwrapped the first box. Four Belgian truffles.

Tim! Have you been hoarding these since the war broke out?

He smirked.

The second package was quite round; under its skins of tissue paper I found a fat shiny orange. All the way from Spain?

Tim shook his head.

I played the guessing game. Italy?

A satisfied nod.

I put the fruit to my nose and drew in the citrus tang. I thought of its arduous journey through the Mediterranean, past Gibraltar, and up the North Atlantic. Or overland through France—was that even possible anymore? I just hoped nobody had been killed shipping this precious freight.

I tucked the orange and chocolates into my bag for a birthday lunch while Tim packed up his tools for the allotment. I stood in the lane; the slice of dark sky was streaked with pink. He got his motorcycle started on the third try. I'd bought it for him at a widow's auction of an officer's goods, though I'd never told him so in case the thought of riding a dead man's machine bothered him.

I waved as he rumbled slowly away, then went to fetch my coat and cape. I lined up my hooks and eyes. Standing beside my cycle, I drew up my skirts on their strings. It was mild, for the first morning of November.

Bridie had probably never ridden a bike. Her having been in a home made sense of so many things: ringworm marks; melted arm from a kitchen accident; outsize gratitude for canteen grub, skin lotion, and hot water. No wonder she'd had no understanding of how a foetus lived and moved inside its mother—she'd grown up in a house of orphans and ended up boarding with nuns she couldn't stand for want of anywhere else to go.

I pedaled past the shackled gates of a school where a fresh-painted notice said CLOSED FOR FORESEEABLE FUTURE BY ORDER OF BOARD OF HEALTH. I thought of the young Noonans; if slum children weren't going to school these days, they couldn't be getting their free dinners there.

Clouds hissed and billowed from the high windows of the shell factory, which meant the fumigators were steaming the workrooms; maybe they'd been toiling in their sulphurous fog all night. Outside, in a line that snaked from the door, munitions girls shifted from foot to foot as they chatted, stained hands pocketed against the dawn chill, impatient to get in and get at it.

In my head, I told Ita Noonan: *Your work's done.*

I pedaled faster. Thirty years old. Where would I be at thirty-five? If the war was over by then, what would have taken its place?

Back to this moment—what would be asked of me this morning? Delia Garrett, weeping into her sheets. The gasping, husbandless one, Honor White: *Let her lungs be winning the fight.* Mary O'Rahilly: *Please, her travails over and a baby in her arms.*

I locked my cycle in the alley.

Passing the shrine to the fallen soldiers, I noticed that a rebel had daubed NOT OUR WAR across the paving stone at its base. I wondered if he could possibly be the same lout who'd attacked Tim.

But wasn't it the whole world's war now? Hadn't we caught it from each other, as helpless against it as against other infections? No way to keep one's distance; no island to hide on. Like the poor, maybe, the war would always be with us. Across the world, one lasting state of noise and terror under the bone man's reign.

I joined a knot of people waiting at the stop; they were far enough apart to be out of coughing range of each other but not too far to reach the door of the tram when it drew up. A drunk sang, surprisingly tuneful, oblivious to the scowlers:

I don't want to join the bloody army,
I don't want to go to bloody war.
I'd rather stay at home,
Around the streets to roam,
Living on the earnings of a—

We all braced ourselves for the dirty rhyme.

...lady typist, he warbled.

The tram came and I managed to squeeze on.

From the lower level, I counted three ambulances and five hearses. Church bells rang ceaselessly. On a newspaper inches from me, I tried not to see a headline about a torpedoed liner: *Search Continues for Survivors*. Below, the words *Likelihood of Armistice* snagged me. Twice already, the papers had declared the war over; I refused to pay any attention until I had proof it was true.

It was a relief to get down outside the hospital in the dawn light and breathe a little before I went through the gates. Nailed up under a streetlamp, a new notice, longer than usual:

THE PUBLIC IS URGED
TO STAY OUT OF PUBLIC PLACES
SUCH AS CAFÉS, THEATRES, CINEMAS,
AND PUBLIC HOUSES.
SEE ONLY THOSE PERSONS ONE NEEDS TO SEE.
REFRAIN FROM SHAKING HANDS, LAUGHING,
OR CHATTING CLOSELY TOGETHER.
IF ONE MUST KISS,
DO SO THROUGH A HANDKERCHIEF.
SPRINKLE SULPHUR IN THE SHOES.
IF IN DOUBT, DON'T STIR OUT.

In I went, in my sulphurless shoes, through the gates that said *Vita gloriosa vita*.

I wanted to go straight up to Maternity/Fever, but I made myself get some more breakfast first in case today was even half as hectic as yesterday.

In the basement, I took my place in the queue. I had reservations about what they might be bulking out the sausages with these days, so I decided on porridge.

I listened in on speculations about the kaiser being on the verge of surrender; the imminence of peace. It occurred to me that in the case of this flu there could be no signing a pact with it; what we waged in hospitals was a war of attrition, a battle over each and every body.

A student doctor was telling a story about a man who'd presented himself at Admitting, convinced he had the grippe because his throat was closing up. The chap turned out to be sound as a bell—it was just fright.

The others sniggered tiredly.

But wasn't panic as real as any symptom? I thought about the unseen force blocking my brother's throat.

Our queue shuffled forward past the latest sign, which said, in strident capitals, IF I FAIL, HE DIES.

I ate my porridge standing up in the corner and couldn't manage more than half the bowl.

No russet head when I hurried into Maternity/Fever; no Bridie Sweeney.

Indefatigable in pristine white, Sister Luke moved towards me, a broad ship. Good morning, Nurse.

I found I couldn't bear to ask about Bridie, as if she were the young woman's keeper.

On the stairs last night, I'd wasted time chattering about film stars, and Bridie had never actually said anything about coming back, had she? I'd jumped to conclusions simply because I wanted her help so much. It shook me to realise that I'd been irrationally counting on her being here today; she was what the poster called a person *one needs to see*.

Over on the right, Delia Garrett seemed to be asleep.

Mary O'Rahilly, in the middle, was a snail curved around her own bump. Dr. Lynn had pierced the sac and let the girl's waters out, so it really wasn't safe for delivery to be delayed too long; there was a higher risk of infection. I murmured, Any progress there?

Sister Luke grimaced. Pangs every eight minutes. Stronger than before, but the doctors aren't happy with the pace.

I doubted Mary O'Rahilly was either. Her eyes were squeezed shut, her black hair limp with sweat; even her cough sounded weary.

It occurred to me that Bridie might in fact be here this morning but on a different ward. The office would assign every volunteer to where she was most needed, of course.

Honor White was telling her beads with bloodless hands, mouthing the words.

That one makes a great show of piety, said the nun in my ear.

My temper flared. I answered, very low: I thought you'd approve of prayer.

Well, *if* it's sincere. But a year of praying did nothing to reclaim Her Nibs.

I turned to stare. Mrs. White? I whispered. How can you possibly know that?

Sister Luke tapped her nose through the gauze mask. A sister at our convent serves at that mother-and-baby home, and I asked her all about *Mrs.* over there. It's her second time there. Not six months after release, didn't she show up in the exact same condition again?

I gritted my teeth. And then a question occurred to me: She stayed on for a whole year after the first birth?

Well, that's their term, if the infant lives.

I didn't follow.

Sister Luke spelled it out: How long a woman has to do housework and mind the little ones to work off the costs if she hasn't been able to pay.

I puzzled it through. So for the crime of falling pregnant, Honor White was lodging in a charitable institution where tending her baby and those of other women was the punishment; she owed the nuns a full year of her life to repay what they were spending on imprisoning her for that year. It had a bizarre, circular logic.

I asked, Does the mother keep...can she take her child away when the year is up?

Sister Luke's one eye bulged. Take it away and do what with it? Sure most of these lassies want nothing more than to be freed from the shame and nuisance.

Perhaps my question had been naive; I knew unwed mother-hood couldn't be an easy life. I wondered whether such a woman might pretend to be widowed.

Sister Luke conceded, The occasional first offender, if she's truly reformed and very fond of the child *and* if a married sister or her own mother is willing to call it theirs, she might be allowed to bring it home to her family. But a hardened sinner? (Narrowing her eyes at Honor White.) That one will have to stay two years this time. Some are kept on after that, even, if they're incorrigible—if it's the only way to prevent another lapse.

That left me speechless.

When I saw the red curls coming in the door, the relief staggered me. Morning, Bridie!

She pivoted towards me with her mile-wide smile.

But I shouldn't have used her first name, not in front of Sister Luke. Bridie didn't call me anything, I noticed—just bobbed her head.

I asked, Have you breakfasted?

She nodded appreciatively. Black pudding and lashings of sausages.

The nun said, Sweeney, sprinkle this floor with disinfectant and rub it all over with a cloth tied around that broom.

The day shift was mine, so why was the nun giving orders? I pointedly waited for Sister Luke to leave.

She shed her apron and put on her cloak. Have you heard mass yet, Nurse Power?

That confused me for a second, because it wasn't Sunday. Oh, for All Souls, yes. (God forgive me the lie; I couldn't bear a scolding from her.)

All *Saints*, you mean.

I could hear the pleasure Sister Luke took in correcting me.

On the first of November, she reminded the whole room, we celebrate the church triumphant in heaven, watching over us poor sinners on earth. Whereas tomorrow, the Feast of All Souls, we honour the church penitent—the holy souls in purgatory.

Could she really imagine I wanted a lecture on the finer points of the liturgical calendar? Bridie was cleaning the floor already. I got on with putting my coat and bag away and scrubbing my hands.

Honor White let out a wet cough.

Sister Luke said, You could try a poultice on Mrs. White.

I reminded myself that the night nurse wasn't in authority over me. Actually, Sister, in my experience poulticing isn't much help in these chest cases.

Her visible eyebrow—the one not covered by the patch—disappeared into her coif. In my much longer experience, it will help if you do it correctly.

I could tell by Bridie's shoulder blades that she was attentive to every word of this.

So tempting to point out that much of Sister Luke's experience and all of her training was from the last century. Instead I said mildly, Well, as we're so short-staffed, I believe I'll use my good judgement.

A faint sniff.

I told her, Sleep well.

The nun buttoned up her cloak as if she had no intention of doing anything so feeble.

Sweeney, she said, don't get under anyone's feet today.

The minute Sister Luke had swept out, Bridie leaned on her mop and let out a snort. You told the old crow, all right. You told her something fierce.

But it would do this young woman no good if I stirred up trouble between her and the nun, given that they lived under the same roof. And besides, patients shouldn't be made uneasy by dissent in the ranks. So I shook my head at Bridie. But I added, I'm glad you came back today.

A grin. Sure why wouldn't I?

I said, poker-faced, Oh, I don't know. Hard work, nasty pongs, and horrors?

The work's even harder for us at the motherhouse, and there's all the praying on top.

Us meaning you and the nuns?

Bridie corrected me. Us *boarders*, about twenty girls. Anyway, of course I came back. A change is as good as a rest. And it's all go here—something new every minute!

Her cheer was infectious. I remembered the cut she'd got from the broken thermometer yesterday. How's your finger?

She held it up and said, Not a mark. That pencil of yours is magic.

Actually, it's science.

Delia Garrett was half awake, struggling to sit up in her cot. I checked that her stitches were healing nicely.

She was limp, monosyllabic.

Tell me, is your chest tender today?

Tears spilled.

A chest binder should help, Mrs. Garrett.

Somehow, flattening the breasts told them to give up making

unwanted milk. I fetched a roll of clean bandage. Working blind under her nightdress, I wound the stuff four times around her. Tell me if that's too tight or if it constricts your breathing at all.

Delia Garrett nodded as if she barely cared. A hot whiskey? All right.

She probably didn't need it for her flu, but if I were her, I'd want to sleep these days away.

Honor White was propped up in the right position for a pneumoniac, but her breathing was loud and her pallor was greenish. I checked her chart to make sure Sister Luke had remembered her strengthening pill. She had, and she'd written *Sore stomach* beside it; iron often had that effect. Pulse, respirations, temperature—no worse, but no better.

When I asked, Honor White was still obdurate on the subject of strong drink, so I gave her a low dose of aspirin to bring down her fever and a spoonful of ipecac for her cough. I undid the neck of her nightdress and applied a camphorated rub to her chest.

Incorrigible; the word stung me on her behalf. All Honor White had endured, and now she was facing a further two-year incarceration. Could the law really allow the nuns to hold her against her will?

I rebuked myself—for all I knew, Honor White might be choosing to stay at the mother-and-baby home, might have no other shelter. What could I say for sure about this silent woman, about what she'd been through, what she wanted?

Mary O'Rahilly was shifting around in the middle cot, so I turned to her and checked my notes. Seven minutes between contractions now.

I waited till I could tell by her face that it was over, then asked, How are you doing, Mrs. O'Rahilly? Did you catch a few winks last night?

I suppose so.

Do you need the lavatory?

Sister Luke's only after taking me. Will it be much longer, do you think?

Her voice was so softly desperate, I could barely catch the words.

All I could say was Hopefully not.

(Trying to remember how long after the waters broke before the risk of infection skyrocketed; was it twenty-four hours? If a doctor didn't come by soon, I'd send for one.)

Let's get you a hot whiskey. And one for Mrs. Garrett. And a hot lemonade for Mrs. White.

Bridie started mixing up the drinks at the spirit lamp before I could get there. She brought the cups over and set them into each patient's grasp.

Those graceful, swollen knuckles of hers; I wondered how much her chilblains were bothering her. Don't forget to put more of that lotion on, Bridie, every time you wash your hands.

May I really?

Help yourself.

Bridie took down the jar now and rubbed a dab of balm into her reddened fingers. She put them to her face. I adore this stuff.

That amused me. Eucalyptus? My tram reeks of it every morning. You know it's a vapour given off by trees?

Bridie scoffed: No trees I've ever smelled.

Tall ones, with their bark peeling off, in the Blue Mountains of Australia. On warm days, I've heard, they give off a perfumed haze of the stuff, a blue sort of fog—that's where the mountains get their name.

She murmured: Imagine!

Honor White had her head back and her eyes closed. Praying again? I wondered. Or just worn out by her clogged lungs?

Mary O'Rahilly let out a whimper.

I asked, Where do you feel the pang most?

Her small hands clawed her back, her hips, her belly—everywhere.

Is it getting stronger?

She nodded, pressing her lips between her teeth.

I wondered if she had that craving to push yet, but I didn't ask in case I put the idea in her head; she was the meek kind who'd tell one whatever she thought one wanted to hear.

Up, dear. Let's see if we can ease that a bit.

I got Mary O'Rahilly into a chair against the wall and pushed just under her knees, shoving her legs back in their sockets.

Ah!

Does that help?

I...I think so.

I told Bridie to crouch down and fit her hands on the same spot at the top of Mary O'Rahilly's knees. Keep that pressure up. If you get tired, sit down on the floor and lean back on her.

I won't get tired, Bridie assured me.

Honor White was whispering the Rosary, gripping each bead the way a drowning woman might a life preserver.

I found myself saying, It just so happens it's my birthday, ladies.

Bridie said, Many happy returns!

Well, now.

That was a man's voice. I turned around to see Groyne's head in the door.

He added, I suppose it'd be a shocking breach to ask which birthday?

I didn't smile. Can I help you, Groyne?

The orderly pushed a metal crib into the ward on squealing wheels. Sister Luke said this might be wanted today for Mrs. O'Rahilly.

Delia Garrett made a small sound of pain and turned her back.

Was it the same crib that had stood ready for her baby yesterday? But there was no way to spare her such sights.

Ignoring my question, then, Nurse Power? Groyne sniggered. That's an answer in itself. I find girls are happy to give the figure till they hit twenty-five.

I said, I'm thirty years old, and I don't mind who knows it.

Ooh, a grown woman!

Groyne leaned one elbow on the door frame, settling in. I suppose you'll be picking our next members of Parliament and all that. If you're a female householder, that is, he added mockingly, or an occupier of a premises rated at five pounds?

My name had been down as the householder ever since Tim had enlisted, but I'd no intention of discussing my domestic arrangements with this fellow.

Bridie asked, Aren't you in favour of votes for women, Mr. Groyne?

He let out a scornful plume of air.

I couldn't make myself stay out of it. Haven't we proved our worth to your satisfaction yet?

The orderly grimaced. Well, you don't serve, do you?

I was taken aback. In the war? Many of us most certainly are serving, as nurses and drivers and—

The orderly waved that away. Don't pay the blood tax, though, do you? Not like we fellows do. Ought you really get a say in the affairs of the United Kingdom unless you're prepared to lay down your lives for the king?

I saw red. Look around you, Mr. Groyne. This is where every nation draws its first breath. Women have been paying the *blood tax* since time began.

He snickered on his way out.

Bridie was watching me with a one-sided grin.

Mary O'Rahilly moaned quietly.

Unprompted, Bridie pushed on the young woman's shins to ease the pain.

When that one was over, I said, Only five minutes between them now.

Mary O'Rahilly asked faintly: Is that good?

Very good.

Over her shoulder, Delia Garrett was watching Mary O'Rahilly with resentful, drunken eyes.

That crib; I didn't want to set it at the end of the girl's cot in case it would make her feel hustled. But over by the sink, it would only get in our way. Besides, it might keep her spirits up by reminding her what all this pain was in aid of. So I trundled it to the end of the middle cot, close to Mary O'Rahilly's feet. Just getting everything ready, dear.

Her eyes closed and she let out a groan as her head tipped back.

I went over to the supply cupboard to lay out the things that might be required for a delivery. Bridie was already boiling gloves and instruments in a bag. You never seem to need telling, Bridie.

She liked hearing that.

I asked, So when's your birthday?

Haven't got one.

I waved that off. Everyone has a birthday, Bridie.

Well, I suppose it's a secret.

I said, a little huffily, Don't tell me if you prefer not—

Bridie spoke in a low voice. I mean that no one ever told me.

Just then Honor White coughed so hard I went over to check the sputum cup to be sure she hadn't brought up a piece of lung. I reapplied the camphor rub to her chest.

Then Mary O'Rahilly asked if she might lie down for a while, so I got her into bed on her left side.

When I next had a chance for a word with Bridie, we were by the sink. I murmured, Didn't you ever know your people?

Not that I remember.

Are they still alive?

She shrugged in her oddly playful way. They were when I was given over to the home, or taken. They weren't able, that's what the nuns said.

What age were you then?

Don't know. From then till I was four, I was a nurse-child.

My face must have shown I didn't know the term.

Bridie specified: Boarded out. With a foster mother, see? If I got to four years old with the use of all my limbs, she must have minded me well enough.

Her calm tone made me feel sick for her—or, rather, for the small, bewildered girl she'd been.

She went on: Maybe it was her called me Bridie, for Saint Bridget? I'd had another name before. They wouldn't tell me what it was except that it wasn't a saint's.

I was trying to follow this bleak narrative. By *they*, you mean the nuns?

And the teachers and the minders at the home. It was called an industrial school, though it wasn't really any kind of school, Bridie said with scorn. Two nuns were the managers but they went back to the convent every night and left a couple of lay staff in charge.

I remembered my question about her birthday that had

prompted all this. So none of these people ever told you what day you were born?

Nor what year, even.

It hurt my throat to swallow. I said diffidently, Share my birthday if you like. Say yours is today too—it might very well be.

Bridie grinned. All right. Why not?

We worked on in silence at the counter.

She said out of nowhere, You're lucky your dadda kept you after your mammy died.

I was taken aback. Why wouldn't he have?

Well, these three sisters I knew—they were sent to the home because the parish priest wouldn't let their widowed father have them living with him in the house. Said it wasn't *proper,* given their age, she added satirically.

I didn't get it. What, were they awfully young for a man to raise?

No, the two older ones were thirteen and fourteen, and the youngest eleven.

I flushed as I understood. For a priest to make such a comment—somehow both prudish and filthy-minded...Do you think they'd have been better off staying at home, Bridie?

Her nod came fast and unequivocal. No matter what happened.

Surely she couldn't mean even if their father had ended up interfering with them? Bridie!

They'd have had each other, at least. At the home, they weren't allowed to talk.

I was confused again; some kind of vow of silence? I said, The three girls?

Bridie explained: To each other, I mean. They were told they weren't sisters anymore.

The arbitrary cruelty of that shocked me.

She changed the subject. So you and your brother...

I was only four, so I don't know if anyone objected to Dadda rearing us on the farm, I told her. When I was seven and Tim was three, our father married again, a woman with older children. But I was still Tim's little mammy.

Then something occurred to me.

Though I suppose the shoe's on the other foot now, since I'm out at work like a mister and Tim's at home planning the dinner!

Bridie let out a laugh. Nice for you.

I thought of this morning's poster: *refrain from laughing or chatting closely together.* I said, Oh, believe me, I'm grateful.

Nice for the both of you, I mean. Having and minding each other.

Delia Garrett asked sharply, If you chums aren't too busy, could I ever trouble you for another hot whiskey?

Of course, Mrs. Garrett.

Mary O'Rahilly was weeping silently, I noticed. Was it the pain or the waiting?

I fetched a cold cloth and wiped her face. Will we try you upright in the chair again, with more pressing on your hips?

But in swept Dr. Lynn, in the same collar and tie and skirt as yesterday. She said in greeting, Well, another day of battle, bless us all.

I hurried to collect the three patients' charts, placing Mary O'Rahilly's on top.

Delia Garrett cut in before I could say anything, her voice thunderous: I want to go home.

The doctor said, Of course you do, you poor creature. But the hard fact is, the week after delivery is actually *more* perilous to the health than the week before.

(I thought of my mother holding Tim for the first time. Thought of all the mothers on these wards I'd seen smiling over their newborns before they got the shivers on the second day and died on the sixth.)

Delia Garrett pressed the heels of her hands to her puffy eyes. I didn't even have a bloody baby.

Dr. Lynn nodded. Your daughter's in God's arms now, and we must make sure Mr. Garrett and your little girls don't lose you too.

Delia Garrett sniffed and subsided.

Next, the doctor listened to Honor White's chest and ordered heroin syrup.

Breathlessly: I don't take intoxicants.

My dear woman, it's medicinal. We use it to calm a cough in bad bronchial cases.

Still.

I murmured, Mrs. White's a Pioneer.

Dr. Lynn said, So's my uncle, but he takes what he's prescribed.

Honor White wheezed, No intoxicants.

A sharp sigh. Aspirin again, then, Nurse Power, but no more than fifteen grains, and hot lemonade, I suppose.

Finally the doctor scrubbed and gloved up and went to the middle cot to examine Mary O'Rahilly. I got the girl into position, on her side with her bottom hanging over the edge.

Ah, now we're getting somewhere!

Dr. Lynn stripped off her gloves.

I helped Mary O'Rahilly onto her back. She stared down at the thrusting prow of her belly.

The doctor told me, She's reached the pushing stage, so she may have chloroform now that there's no risk of it slowing things down.

Mary O'Rahilly shut her eyes and made a low hum of protest as the pain came back.

On her way out, Dr. Lynn added, But do hold off near the end, won't you?

I nodded; I knew the drug could get into the infant and impair its breathing.

I took the chloroform down from the shelf, dripped a spoonful onto an inhaler's little pad, and handed it to Mary O'Rahilly. Breathe in some of this whenever you feel the need.

She drew hard on the inhaler.

I told her, You're open wide inside, at last.

I am?

On your left is the best position, now, with your feet at the top of the bed so you can jam them against this pillow here.

I was moving bedding, tugging it out of the way.

Awkwardly, Mary O'Rahilly reversed herself on the mattress.

I'm going to tie this long towel just by your head so you can pull on it, I told her. Wait for the next pang, and be ready to push.

I had such long acquaintance with other women's pain, I could almost smell it coming. I said, Look down at your chest, Mrs. O'Rahilly. You're going to hold your breath and haul on the towel with all your might, like you're ringing a church bell. Here we go. Push!

She did, the weary girl; she set her teeth and gave it a good go, considering that she'd never done it before in her life.

Afterwards, I said, That's a start. Now rest for a minute.

She suddenly wailed, Mr. O'Rahilly won't like me staying away all this time.

My eyes met Bridie's across the bed and a bubble of laughter rose up in the back of my mouth.

Don't worry about him, Mrs. O'Rahilly. Sure how can you get his baby out any faster than it comes?

I know, but...

Bridie set her hands around the labouring woman's on the looped towel.

I said, Put all that out of your mind. You've nothing else to do today but this.

Sweat broke out on Mary O'Rahilly's forehead and she lashed about in the sheets. I can't.

Sure you can. Here it comes. Push!

But she'd lost control of that pang; the wave crashed over her head. She writhed and sobbed and coughed. I really don't know how, Nurse, I'm awful stupid.

My eyes slid to Bridie. Not a bit, Mrs. O'Rahilly. Nature knows how.

(*Knows how to serve her own ends,* I didn't say. I'd seen nature crack a woman like a walnut shell.)

I'll be right here to help, I'm not going anywhere, I swore.

Mary O'Rahilly gasped out, And Bridie.

Bridie said, Too right.

I gave the girl the chloroform inhaler to suck on.

Oh, oh—

The next pain seized her.

Push!

She held her breath till she was purple in the face, humming through gritted teeth.

I crooned into her ear, Save your strength. Go limp as much as you can in between the pangs.

But there was only a couple of minutes' grace.

Bridie and I moved Mary O'Rahilly's legs in their sockets while she coughed and panted. I rotated her pelvis and did hip squeezes, but none of it seemed to be easing the pain.

She gasped, The breathy thing?

I gave her back the inhaler with more chloroform sprinkled on. I checked her pulse, temperature, respiratory rate.

The waves kept coming, bigger every time. I tried all my tricks. I massaged Mary O'Rahilly's locked jaw. When her right calf went into spasm, I set Bridie to kneading it.

Forty minutes had passed like this, I saw by the clock.

Bridie whispered in my ear, How many pushes does it take?

I admitted, There's no rule.

Mary O'Rahilly's voice was almost inaudible: I'm afraid I'm going to be sick.

Bridie ran for a basin.

Over the next quarter of an hour, I began to let myself worry. The foetus didn't seem to be budging. Mary O'Rahilly's drawn face told me that this prolonged labour was wringing her out—and of course she had the flu to fight off too.

I took Bridie aside. Go find Dr. Lynn, would you? Say Mrs. O'Rahilly's been pushing an hour. Or, no, hang on—

A first birth often took two hours of pushing. How to put my finger on what was bothering me? I wondered if it might be a case of uterine inertia—did the tired girl's contractions just not have enough power to move the foetus down the passage? Or was something blocking the way? The ticker tape of dangers ran through my head: swelling, rupture, haemorrhage, infection.

I added in Bridie's ear, Tell the doctor I'm concerned she may be obstructed. Will you remember the word?

She repeated, *Obstructed*.

And dashed off.

I was in a blue funk now, but I couldn't let my patients see it. Not that the other women were paying more attention to me than they could help; Honor White was praying with her eyes tight shut, and Delia Garrett lay in a spiritous doze, her bound chest as barrel-shaped as a man's.

I put my knee against Mary O'Rahilly's back and braced her as her feet shoved against the pillows.

When Bridie came back there were two men on her heels, each tightly buttoned in a navy jacket and wearing a tall egglike helmet marked with a star.

I stared, then stood and whipped a sheet up and over Mary O'Rahilly. How dare you barge in here? Out, out! This is a women's ward.

The Dublin Metropolitan Police retreated only as far as the door. The smaller constable said, We're looking for—

The taller butted in. It's the woman doctor we want. Lynn. We've a warrant. (Patting his breast pocket.) War crimes.

The first fellow asked uncertainly, This is the lying-in ward?

I was on the point of telling him that the main one was upstairs. But if they were stupid enough to believe that a hospital this size might have only three women in its maternity ward, why should I correct them? I flung out my hand at the waiting baby crib. What do you think?

The taller one frowned and adjusted his chin strap. Then where would we find this Mrs. Lynn?

How should I know?

The fact was, I couldn't do without the doctor, not right now, when there wasn't an obstetrician in the building. If they arrested her—locked her up or deported her to England again—what would happen to Mary O'Rahilly? My patients' welfare came first, and politics would just have to wait.

I demanded, What's this warrant?

The constable fished out his piece of paper. *Defence of the Realm Regulation Fourteen (b)*, he read a little stumblingly, *being suspected of acting or having acted or being about to act in a manner prejudicial to the public safety.*

What on earth does that mean?

Bridie took a breath to speak.

I threw her a look.

She said, I was upstairs just now, and I couldn't find Dr. Lynn.

The first policeman's shoulders sagged. Well. When she comes in next, tell her she's obliged to present herself—to turn herself in at Dublin Castle, as a matter of urgency.

I said, Certainly, Constable.

Head skewed around at the end of the mattress, Mary O'Rahilly had been watching this scene play out with fearful eyes. But now a pang seized her; she hauled on her looped towel and let out a long groan.

The policemen fled.

This time I lifted up her right foot and set it against my hip as she pushed. No sign of any progress.

When I got a chance, again over by the sink, I asked Bridie in a whisper: Did you make that up, about not being able to find Dr. Lynn?

Bridie's mouth was mischievous. Not exactly. They said she was in surgery and they'd get a message to her.

Mary O'Rahilly cried out again.

I hurried back. I palpated her abdomen and used the ear trumpet to check that the foetal heartbeat was still pattering away. She'd been working for—I checked my watch—more than an hour and a quarter now, and the head didn't feel to my hands as if it had descended an inch. What could be blocking the way?

Such confidence in Bridie's light blue eyes, turned towards me as if I knew everything, as if all things were possible to me and my lucky hands.

The bladder. Mary O'Rahilly hadn't emptied it on my shift.

Bridie, a bedpan, right away, please.

I persuaded the girl to lean up on one hip and got the thing under her. You need to pass water to make room in there, Mrs. O'Rahilly. Try to release it. Even a drop.

She sobbed and coughed. There's nothing there.

I wondered if the foetus's head was blocking the urethra, preventing liquid from flowing.

I told her, I'm going to let it out for you.

(Such a simple description of a tricky procedure. Yet in the absence of a doctor, I had to try it.)

I got Mary O'Rahilly lying down on her left again. Then I dashed to the sink to scrub my hands and find a sterile catheter as well as a bottle of carbolic solution.

Mary O'Rahilly had her chin on her chest, her teeth bared. She heaved, eyes bulging.

When the pang was over, I told her, You're doing grand.

She gasped when I poured the cold disinfectant over her privates.

I mouthed at Bridie: *Hold her.*

Bridie set her hands on the young woman's ankles.

Mrs. O'Rahilly, stay very still for a minute, please…

I'd inserted a catheter before, but not often, and never into a woman being wracked by labour.

This will sting, I told her, but only for a moment.

Her face screwed up. Somehow I found the opening and slid the greased end in, half an inch. She let out a sharp cry.

But what if everything was pressed out of shape by the small skull—what if I punctured the bladder? I closed my eyes, took a breath. I fed the catheter up into—

Urine the colour of weak tea shot all over my apron. Quickly I aimed my end of the catheter into the dry bedpan.

Bridie cried, You did it!

Mary O'Rahilly was pissing like a soldier now, like a horse, like a mountain spring. When the flow trailed off, I pulled out the tube and Bridie carried the bedpan to the sink.

I swiped the dark hair out of Mary O'Rahilly's eyes and told her with more conviction than I felt, That should help.

She nodded weakly.

Time went by, and it didn't help. Nothing helped.

I considered an enema but decided that she'd been eating so little, there was probably nothing in her bowels. The pangs kept coming every three minutes, a clockwork torture. For all Mary O'Rahilly's efforts, nothing in her great taut bump seemed to be descending. Could the head be stuck at the pelvic brim? Nothing was changing except that the young woman was getting limper and paler.

I tried to clear my muddy mind and remember exactly what I'd been taught about obstructed labour. The cause could be *passage, passenger, or powers*—maybe Mary O'Rahilly's pelvis was too small or misshapen, or the foetus's head was too big or had a bad angle of presentation, or the mother was too worn out to expel the foetus on her own.

Please let this not be a case for forceps. They saved lives, but the mothers and babies I'd seen mangled...

I felt Mary O'Rahilly's forehead—no fever. But when I took her pulse, it was over a hundred, and thready.

Panic rose in me. Between the flu and the strain of labour, she was going into shock.

Intravenous saline.

I told Bridie, Stay with her.

From the sterile trays on the high shelf I snatched a long needle, a tube, and rubber bulb syringe. I filled a bowl to the two-pint mark with hot water from the pan, measured the salt in, then brought it down to blood temperature by adding some cold.

When I tied a catgut ligature above Mary O'Rahilly's right elbow and tightened it until a sky-blue vein stood out, she barely seemed to notice. Obedient to the next contraction, she gripped the roller towel and pushed her stockinged feet against the bare rails. (The pillow had fallen to the floor, but I couldn't reach it.)

I injected the warm saline and pumped it into her as fast as I could.

Holding her wrist, I counted for fifteen seconds and multiplied by four. Pulse dropping towards ninety already; good. Was the force any stronger, though?

What are you doing, Nurse Power?

It was Dr. MacAuliffe in his smart black suit.

Blast it. I needed Dr. Lynn, with all her experience in lying-in wards. Unless she'd been arrested already—could she have walked right into the men in blue?

I said, I've given Mrs. O'Rahilly saline for shock.

I yanked the cannula out of her arm and put a clean bandage over the site. Press just there, would you, Bridie?

Why is she the wrong way around? MacAuliffe wanted to know.

So she can push against the rails with her feet.

He was soaping and scrubbing at the sink already. I gave him a pair of sterile gloves.

With his right hand inside Mary O'Rahilly, MacAuliffe waited for her next pang and pressed hard with his left on the top of the uterus.

She let out a long groan.

I gnawed my lip. One couldn't simply pop a baby out of its mother, and it might damage them both if one tried. I'd seen wombs perforated or turned inside out by rough handling. But to say so would be insubordination.

You say she's been trying for a full hour and three-quarters, Nurse? The head should be much lower than this.

I resisted the urge to say, *That's why I called for a doctor.*

Hm, said MacAuliffe. Clearly some disproportion.

The word I always dreaded to hear—a mismatch between a narrow woman and a big-skulled foetus.

He went on: I estimate the occipitofrontal diameter to be four to five inches and the pelvic outlet rather less than four, but I can't be sure without taking thorough measurements with a Skutsch's pelvimeter, and that would probably require general anesthesia.

This girl might pass out at any minute, and he wanted to put her to sleep so he could fiddle with instruments and formulas to determine the exact ratio of the problem?

MacAuliffe went on, But all in all, I believe it's time to intervene surgically.

I stared, thinking, *What, here, in a makeshift fever ward with barely inches to spare between the cots?*

He murmured, The mortality rate for caesareans is so high, I'd rather try a symphysiotomy. Or actually, better still, a pubiotomy.

My heart sank. These operations to widen the pelvis were common in Irish hospitals because they didn't scar the uterus and limit future childbearing. Pubiotomy did have one advantage over a caesarean: it was less likely to kill Mary O'Rahilly even if it was performed under local anesthetic only on a camp cot by a young general surgeon who'd learnt it from a diagram. But it would mean two and a half weeks of her lying here with her legs bound together afterwards, and it could very well do her damage; I'd heard stories of patients left limping, leaking, or in pain permanently.

I tried to think of how to phrase my objections.

Mary O'Rahilly pushed and groaned, but quietly, as if trying not to draw attention to herself.

MacAuliffe leaned into the girl's sight line and said, I'm going to numb the area and deliver you now, Mrs. Rahilly. A simple little procedure that means you'll have no further trouble having this baby or his little brothers and sisters to come.

She blinked up at him in fright.

Shouldn't the man warn her that he was about to saw her pubic bone in half?

Shouldn't I?

I pleaded, Dr. MacAuliffe—

Message for you, Nurse Power.

I spun around to find that junior nurse from before panting in the doorway. What is it?

Dr. Lynn says, have you tried Walcher's?

Vol-curse? I didn't understand the nonsense syllables. Then they resolved into German and made sense.

I asked MacAuliffe, almost stuttering in my rush, What about Walcher's position, Doctor—can't that open the pelvis a little and draw the head down?

He pursed his lips, irritated. Perhaps, but at this point—

The junior added, Oh, and you're wanted urgently in Men's Fever, Dr. MacAuliffe.

I seized my chance. I said in my humblest tone, Why don't I try her in Walcher's while you're gone just to see if it might help at all before the surgery?

Mary O'Rahilly's eyes shifted between us.

The young surgeon sighed. Well, I'll need to get hold of a hand-cranked wire saw, anyway. But do get her prepared, won't you?

The moment he was gone, instead of shaving, washing, and disinfecting Mary O'Rahilly for a pubiotomy, I pulled *Jellett's*

Midwifery from the shelf. I thumbed through the book, but my hands were shaking so much I couldn't find the page describing Walcher's position; I had to look under W in the index.

Rarely used supine dorsal recumbent... it could encourage the pelvis to widen by half an inch, I read. *Employ for no more than two to four uterine contractions or a quarter of an hour.* Because it hurt the woman so much? Dr. Jellett didn't say.

The instructions for positioning called for a surgical table or at least a hospital bed that could be winched up at either end. I had a cheap, low cot.

But it was open at the foot and there was room for her legs to dangle, so all I had to do was raise it.

Let's get you standing up for a minute, Mrs. O'Rahilly.

She resisted; she sagged; she wailed in my arms.

I said in a level voice, Bridie, could you look in that bottom cupboard and get out the bedrests—

Which of them?

(She was already there.)

All of them. Stick them under the end of this mattress to make it as high as you can.

Bridie couldn't possibly have understood what I was up to, but she didn't ask anything else, only wrenched up the mattress and fitted the wedges on top of each other on the bed frame like a puzzle.

Another pang seized Mary O'Rahilly. I held her under the armpits as she cried, crouched, and sagged. I knew I should take her pulse to see if she was going into shock again, but I didn't have a hand free.

I told Bridie, That's it.

Or, rather, it would have to be, since there were no more bedrests.

She let the mattress fall. It was tilted up now, as if there'd been an earthquake. The sheets were loose but she pulled them straight.

Lucky that Mary O'Rahilly was so tiny; this mad arrangement would never have worked with a tall woman. I said, Let's get her bottom on the end of the bed and her legs hanging right off.

Bridie stared but then helped me move the young woman into place.

Finding her hips lifted higher than her head, her back arched, helpless as a pinned insect under her huge bump, Mary O'Rahilly wailed, No!

Trust me, I told her. The weight of your own legs will help open you up to let the baby down, to let it out.

(That made it sound as if Mary O'Rahilly was the captor, but wasn't she a prisoner too?)

Oh, oh, but the pain's coming—

She let out a scream loud enough to be heard all down the passage. She sobbed, couldn't catch her breath. I'll snap in two!

I was a torturer, breaking this girl on the wheel. *No more than two to four uterine contractions.* Did that mean I should give up after two? Three? Four? Wait for MacAuliffe to arrive with his saw to do his necessary butchery?

You'll be all right, Mrs. O'Rahilly.

But there was no relief for this girl, no respite. She was a canoeist shooting the rapids; nothing stood between her and her fate. The air in the narrow ward seemed to prickle with static.

Hold her so she doesn't slip, Bridie.

I ducked and squatted between Mary O'Rahilly's dangling feet. I fixed my eyes on the violent red flower of her privates. Your strongest push this time, Mrs. O'Rahilly. Now!

As she growled and heaved, a dark disk revealed itself just for a moment.

I told her, I saw the head! One more big effort. Third time's the charm.

Collapsed, she barely breathed the words: I can't.

You can, you're splendid.

Then I had a wild idea and stood up. Your baby's head's right there. If you felt it...

Red in the face, Mary O'Rahilly writhed and panted.

I seized her right hand, to be ready.

Her pain stalked around her, doubled back, waited, hit.

Push!

But this time I pulled her hand around her bump, between her splayed thighs. Not hygienic, but maybe just what she needed. As soon as I glimpsed the black circle I pressed her fingers to it.

Mary O'Rahilly's face went stark with surprise.

In the brief lull, I straightened up. A shilling-size bit of the head was still visible.

She gasped. I felt hair.

I said, The same black hair as yours.

Now the baby was crowning, I could free Mary O'Rahilly from Walcher's position. I lifted her right leg up and set the flat of her foot against my belly.

Bedrests out, Bridie.

She tugged them away.

The mattress jerked back down and Mary O'Rahilly with it. I thrust one of the wedges behind her head and helped her up until she was semi-inclined.

Will I put them back—

Leave them, Bridie! Just hold her other leg for me.

She ran around the bed and lifted Mary O'Rahilly's left foot.

Shrinking back against the wall, in the cot on the left, Honor White was transfixed.

Here it comes, Mrs. O'Rahilly.

She held her breath and shoved so hard with her feet, I staggered backwards.

A conical head, gummy with blood, facing sideways, straight across the room.

Bridie cried, Janey mac!

Half in, half out; always a weird moment, between worlds. The colour was good but I couldn't tell anything more. I said, The head's here. Nearly over, Mrs. O'Rahilly.

As I spoke I was checking for the cord. So as not to introduce germs, I didn't use a finger, only tipped the tiny face towards the mother's spine and...yes, there was the cord, wound around the neck. In this position, the cord might keep the body roped inside, or it might get compressed, which would starve the baby of blood; either way, I had to free it. At least it was only looped around once. I hauled on the cord till it was long enough to pull over the small skull.

A hasty physician would grab the head now and deliver the body himself, but I'd been taught better. *Watch and wait.*

On the next pang, I said: Come on, now, bring out your baby!

Mary O'Rahilly went quite purple.

The most extraordinary thing, one that I'd seen so many times and never tired of seeing: the pointed head turned down like a swimmer's and the infant dived out into my hands. Alive.

Bridie laughed as if she were at a magic show.

As I wiped its nose and mouth, it was mewing already, breath animating the wet flesh. A girl. Her legs were skinny, her privates dark and swollen.

Well done yourself, Mrs. O'Rahilly. You have a fine girl.

Mary O'Rahilly let out something between a cough and a

laugh. Maybe she couldn't believe the impossible job was done. Or that *girl* was the word for her minute daughter now, never again for her seventeen-year-old self.

While I waited for the thick blue cord to stop pulsing, I checked the baby for the basics—all her fingers and toes, no tongue-tie or sunken fontanelle, no imperforate anus or clicky hips. (Almost every infant did come out perfect, even from women who bore all the stigmata of poverty, as if nature designed babies to take as much as they needed, no matter the cost to the mothers.) No signs of asphyxia despite those hours jammed against the pelvic bone. No sign that the mother's illness had done the baby any harm.

The cord delivered its last blood and was still now. I laid the tiny girl facedown on her mother's softened belly so I'd have my hands free. Mary O'Rahilly's fingers crept down to touch the sticky skin.

I tied ligatures around the cord in two places, then scissored through it. I wrapped the baby in a clean cloth and gave her to Bridie to hold.

The redhead was flushed, exuberant. Oh, but that was something, Julia.

Mary O'Rahilly begged: Show me?

Bridie held the girl low enough for Mary O'Rahilly to get a good look.

Before the mother could ask, I said, They come out with slightly pointy skulls if they've had a long journey, but it rounds out in a few days.

Mary O'Rahilly nodded blissfully. She had a splash of red in her left eye where she'd burst a blood vessel by pushing, I saw now.

Honor White spoke up in an asthmatic voice from the bed on the left: The one that gives most trouble, the mother loves double.

I stared.

She added, 'Tis a saying.

Maybe from her part of the country; I'd never heard it. I thought of the trouble, in several senses, that Honor White's first baby must have brought her, and all the further trouble ahead of her.

Mary O'Rahilly stroked the top of her newborn's rounded-cone head. The delicately coiled ear. So small!

Oh, she's just brand-new, I told her.

I had no scales down here, but the infant looked a good size to me.

Five minutes later the placenta slid out of Mary O'Rahilly on its own, whole and healthy-looking. No bleeding, even. And after all this first-timer had been through, she was barely torn; I disinfected the short rip, but it was nothing that couldn't heal itself. Her pulse was safely down in the low eighties now.

I put the baby in the crib and sent Bridie for another of those chilled moss packets. Oh, and have them tell Dr. MacAuliffe that Mrs. O'Rahilly's delivered on her own, I said with satisfaction.

I got her sitting propped up in Fowler's position to let all her fluids trickle out and fastened her into an abdominal binder as well a nursing one for the breasts, with flaps of gauze over her great brown nipples. I put her in a fresh nightdress and wrapped a shawl around her shoulders.

Honor White was coughing hard, the sound of a hammer on sheet metal. I dosed her with ipecac and more hot lemonade.

Mrs. Garrett? Anything you need?

But Delia Garrett had turned her face to the wall. A living baby, that was what she needed.

I went back to the O'Rahilly child and cleaned her face and the inside of her mouth with a sterile cloth. I put two drops of silver nitrate into each eye. No sign of fever, runny nose, congestion, or lethargy; it seemed she'd slipped free of her mother without picking up her flu. With Bridie's help I gave the infant her first bath in the sink—I took off that cheesy coating with olive oil and a flannel, lathered on soap with a soft sponge, dipped her in warm water, then dried her with dabs from a soft towel.

Bridie gestured at the tied stump. Aren't you going to take this thingy off?

No, in a few days it'll dry up and drop off by itself.

I powdered and bandaged it before drawing on the minute binder that would support the baby from hips to ribs. I pinned on a nappy, then added an adjustable shirt, petticoat, and warm dress as well as knitted socks.

I went back to the mother. Now, Mrs. O'Rahilly, you deserve a nice long sleep.

The young mother struggled higher in the bed. Can I see her again first?

I held the baby close enough for her to examine every feature.

Mary O'Rahilly reached out to seize the bundle from my hands.

In ordinary times, we might isolate a newborn from a sick mother and send it straight up to the nursery, but I had to assume they were short-staffed up there, and bottle-fed babies generally didn't thrive as well as those nursed by their mothers. All in all, I thought this one would do best if she roomed in, even in a chockablock fever ward. All right, I said, but be careful not to cough or sneeze on her.

I won't, I swear.

I waited to be sure the young mother had a safe hold on the girl. She did seem to know what she was doing by instinct.

I asked, Mr. O'Rahilly will be delighted, won't he?

A tear sparkled down and hung on the young woman's jaw, and I wished I hadn't mentioned the husband. Had he wanted a boy, was that it?

The baby let out a faint plaint.

Would you like to try putting her to the didi right away?

Mary O'Rahilly plucked at her laces.

I helped her undo her nightdress. I lifted the gauze lid over one huge nipple. Tickle her upper lip with it.

The young woman was abashed. Really?

Delia Garrett said, That's what makes them open their mouths.

She was up on one elbow, watching with an indecipherable expression.

Like this? Mary O'Rahilly looked past me at her neighbour.

Delia Garrett nodded. And the second she opens wide, mash her on.

When the moment came, Mary O'Rahilly pressed the small face to her breast, and I added more force with my cupped hand, saying, That's it, good and firm.

The young mother gasped.

Delia Garrett asked, Does it hurt? It can, the first weeks.

No, it's just...

Mary O'Rahilly was at a loss for words.

I'd never felt a baby latch on, myself, could only guess what that lock of gums felt like. A tired but urgent working, the rooting of a worm in the dark ground?

She asked, Won't I suffocate her?

Delia Garrett said, Not a chance.

Watching Mary O'Rahilly with her baby, Bridie wore a soft but uneasy expression.

I wondered if she'd been nursed by her mother, the one she'd been told hadn't been able to raise her. Would Bridie ever even have seen this done, in fact, growing up in a strange little society of outcast children?

Things were beautifully quiet. The baby was soon asleep on the teat—there wasn't much to suck, the first few days—but Mary O'Rahilly wouldn't have her disturbed, not even to let us change her own sheets. I knew that letting the newborn spend so much time in her mother's arms might increase her risk of catching her flu, but then again, there was nothing so conducive to a baby's sleep and growth as breastfeeding. I tucked the shawl around her again to keep them both warm.

Bridie left, holding a tray of dirty things to be sterilised in one hand and a bucket of soiled linen for the laundry chute in the other.

I made tea all round. Delia Garrett wanted three biscuits, which I took as a sign of life.

When Bridie returned, she slurped her tea and sighed. Lovely.

I sipped mine and tried to appreciate the flavor of woodchip and ash. It's really not, Bridie. Before the war, people would have spat this stuff out.

Well, but you brewed it fresh for us, she pointed out. And three sugars.

I wondered how many spoonfuls the boarders at the motherhouse were allowed—one each?

And a biscuit.

You're a tonic, I told Bridie. Just what the doctor ordered. Have another biscuit, if you like—you must be half dead.

She grinned. Not even one per cent, remember?

I stand corrected. We're all one hundred per cent alive.

I drank my tea down, thinking, *Dust of the Indies.*

Out of the corner of my eye I saw that Mary O'Rahilly had dropped off. I went over, rescued the baby from the crook of her mother's elbow, and set her in the crib.

Bridie murmured, Like the story.

Which story?

About the mother who comes back.

From where?

You know, Julia. The other side.

I got it. She's *dead*, this mother in the story?

Bridie nodded. The babby won't stop crying, so the mammy comes all the way back to nurse it.

I knew some ghost stories but not that one. I watched the O'Rahilly baby. How long had the spectral mother stayed with her child? Not for good; that wouldn't be allowed. Maybe all night, till cockcrow.

It struck me that the newborn girl hadn't been registered yet. I found a blank certificate in the desk and began a chart for her. I wrote *O'Rahilly* under *Family name* and noted the time of birth.

Bridie, could you ever hold the fort while I go find a doctor to sign this?

I paused in the doorway.

I know that I know nothing, Bridie recited.

That made me smile. Well, I conceded, you know a bit more than you did yesterday morning.

Sister Finnigan would still be outraged, I thought as I headed for the stairs. So many rules I was getting used to breaking, bending to an unrecognizable degree, or interpreting in the spirit rather than the letter of the law. Only *for the duration,* of course, *for the foreseeable future,* as the posters said. Though I was having trouble foreseeing any future. How would we ever get back to normal after the pandemic? And would I find myself relieved to be demoted to mere nurse under Sister Finnigan again? Grateful for the familiar protocols or forever discontented?

Snatches of conversation were smoke winding around me.

Between the sixth and eleventh days.

(That was one black-suited doctor to another.)

Oh, yes?

Typically, with this flu. If they're going to go, that's when.

By *go*, he meant die, I realised. I thought of Groyne and all his colourful euphemisms for it.

I could have got any doctor to sign the newborn's certificate, but I kept asking after Dr. Lynn until a junior nurse directed me to the top floor of the hospital, a room at the very end of a corridor. I heard soft music coming from behind the door, but it was already dying away by the time I knocked.

A small, shabby box room. Dr. Lynn looked up from the table she was using as a desk. Nurse Power.

I found I was shy of mentioning the police. Instead I chanced asking, Did I interrupt you...singing, Doctor?

A half laugh. The gramophone. I like to restore my spirits with a little Wagner when I'm catching up on paperwork.

I couldn't see a gramophone.

She pointed it out, on a chair behind her. It's a hornless model, or, rather, the horn is hidden within, behind slats. Much easier on the eye.

So that was the wooden case I'd seen her lugging in yesterday morning. Oh, I just came to say that Mary O'Rahilly delivered her baby in Walcher's position without surgical intervention.

Good work!

Dr. Lynn put her hand out for the birth certificate. I gave it to her, and she signed it. Do you need me to come down and suture the mother? Give the infant the once-over?

No, no, they're both doing very well.

She gave me back the document and said, I'll tell the office to phone the husband with the news. Is there anything else?

I hovered uneasily. I wonder...should I have thought to try Walcher's much earlier? Might it have shortened her labour and kept her from going into shock?

Dr. Lynn shrugged. Not necessarily, if she wasn't ready. At any rate, let's not waste time on ruminations and regrets in the middle of a pandemic.

I blinked and nodded.

I noticed a brown smudge on her collar; I wondered if she knew it was there. There was that opulent fur coat slung over the back of the chair that held her gramophone. Also a folded hospital blanket and a pillow on the floor behind the desk; was the philanthropist locum kipping here like some tramp?

Dr. Lynn followed my gaze. Her voice was jocular: I can't get home much under the current circumstances.

The influenza, you mean?

That and the police.

Then she must have heard they'd barged into the hospital looking for her. Did she know I'd put them off the scent for now? It felt too awkward to ask.

Dr. Lynn said, When I have to go out, these days, I take cabs instead of riding my tricycle.

That image made my mouth turn up at the corners.

I've been trying to pass for an officer's widow in a coat borrowed from a comrade who's married to a count, she added with a derisory gesture at the fur. I affect to be a little lame in my left leg.

Now a yelp of laughter escaped me. The whole situation reminded me of a slapstick sequence in a picture.

Then I sobered and said, May I ask...is it true? Not your leg.

Is what true?

Was Dr. Lynn going to make me spell it out—what she was wanted for?

She shook her head and said, Not this time. All we Sinn Féiners were doing last spring was protesting against the plan to extend conscription to Ireland. This so-called German plot was a fiction to justify the police banging us up, with the result that almost all my comrades have been held without charge in British prisons since.

I wondered if that could really have happened, that the gun-running conspiracy was trumped up. Dr. Lynn hadn't denied her part in the Rising of '16, after all, so if she claimed innocence on this occasion, I was inclined to believe her.

Something else occurred to me. If she was in hiding at the moment, lying low at her flu clinic or seeing private patients, why on earth had she agreed to fill in at this big hospital, where we were all strangers to her and many of the staff, like Groyne, would be happy to see her dragged off in handcuffs? Except that...surely even Groyne would have to admit how much we needed competent doctors.

I said suddenly, I fobbed them off this afternoon. The peelers who came looking for you, I mean.

Did you, now? Well, thanks.

She held her hand out, surprising me. I shook it. Hard and warm.

My voice came out shrill: They could be back tomorrow. It's not safe for you here.

Oh, my dear girl, nowhere's *safe*. But *sufficient unto the day* and all that.

I should have been back on the ward by now, but I lingered. On the desk stood a silver framed photo, Dr. Lynn arm in arm with a smiling woman. I asked, Your sister?

Her smile was lopsided. No, I'm afraid my family tried to have me declared a lunatic when I was deported, and even now they won't let me come home for Christmas.

I'm so sorry.

That's Miss Ffrench-Mullen in the picture, the dear friend I live with—when I'm not camping in box rooms, that is. We met in the Belgian refugee relief effort, and she's funding my clinic.

Clearly Dr. Lynn did nothing in the conventional way. I was suddenly aware that I was being nosy; I muttered my thanks and turned towards the door.

Has the O'Rahilly infant tried the breast?

Oh, she's latched on well already.

Very good. Nourishment direct from above. Not that these slum women have much to spare, Dr. Lynn added with a sigh. That baby will suck the marrow from her mother's bones and still have less chance of surviving her first year than a man in the trenches.

That horrified me. Really?

She said sternly, Infant mortality in Dublin stands at fifteen per cent—that's what living in the dampest, most crowded housing in Europe will do. Such hypocrisy, the way the authorities preach hygiene to people forced to subsist like rats in a sack. Year after year newborns are sent out in their frail battalions, undefended against dysentery, bronchitis, syphilis, TB...and the death rate for illegitimates is several times higher again.

I thought of Honor White's babies. The difference between them and Mary O'Rahilly's could hardly be physiological; I supposed those born out of wedlock had so few on their side fighting to keep them alive.

Dr. Lynn rolled on furiously. *Ah, well, constitutional debility,* the cushioned classes sigh. But perhaps slum children wouldn't be so bloody debilitated if we tried the experiment of giving them clean milk and fresh air!

I felt rather hectored but also shaken by her fervour.

She put her head to one side, as if weighing me up. In our proclamation, there's one line that's very close to my heart: *cherishing all the children of the nation equally.*

I stiffened at the mention of the manifesto the rebels had pasted up all over the city two years ago announcing their imaginary republic; I remembered skimming a copy (bottom torn off) on a buckled lamppost. I said gruffly, But to found a nation on violence?

Now, Julia Power. Has any nation ever been founded otherwise?

Dr. Lynn held up her palms. And really, she added, would you call me a violent woman?

Tears prickled behind my eyes. I said, I just don't understand how a physician could have turned to the gun. Nearly five hundred people *died*.

She didn't take offence; she looked back at me. Here's the thing—they die anyway, from poverty rather than bullets. The way this godforsaken island's misgoverned, it's mass murder by degrees. If we continue to stand by, none of us will have clean hands.

My head was spinning. I said, faltering: I really have no time for politics.

Oh, but everything's politics, don't you know?

I swallowed. I'd better get back to the ward.

Dr. Lynn nodded. Tell me, though, your brother, the soldier—has he come home yet?

The question caught me off guard. Yes, Tim lives with me. Though he's . . . not what he was.

Dr. Lynn waited.

Mute, if you must know. For now. The psychologist said he should recover in time.

(Not quite a lie, just an overstatement.)

Dr. Lynn's mouth twisted.

I asked accusingly, What? You don't think he will?

I've never met your brother, Nurse Power. But if he's been to hell and back, how could he not be left altered?

Her words were gentle but they crushed me. I was the one who knew him, and I couldn't deny the truth of what she was saying. I should face it—the old Tim was not likely to come back.

I turned to go.

The doctor wound up the gramophone's crank.

The song hadn't a tune, exactly. One woman singing, very melancholy at first, with strings behind her. Then her voice blazed up, slow fireworks.

I didn't ask, but Dr. Lynn said, It's called *Liebestod*. That means *love death*.

The love of death?

She shook her head. Love and death at the same moment. She's singing over her beloved's body.

I'd never heard the like. The sound got huger and huger and then the voice descended gently; the instruments went on for a while before they stopped too.

On the stairs on the way down I found my knees were jerking under me. I supposed it had been a while since that half bowl of porridge. A few minutes more away from the ward was unlikely to make much difference, so I hurried all the way down to the canteen in the basement and loaded up a tray to carry back up to Maternity/Fever.

When I came in, Bridie cried, Look at that!

As if I'd laid out some banquet.

Everything all right while I was gone?

She said, No bother at all.

Good work, I told her, just as Dr. Lynn had told me.

None of the patients were hungry except Delia Garrett, who

took some bread and ham. Bridie had a plate of stew, and I managed some bacon and cabbage.

Don't eat that bread, Bridie, it has a spot of mould.

I've a cast-iron stomach, she assured me as she put it in her mouth.

I'm terribly sorry.

That was Honor White in a stiff voice, followed by a volley of coughs.

I stood up, wiping my mouth. What is it, Mrs. White?

I think I may have wet the bed.

Don't worry, it could happen to a bishop. Come on, Bridie, we'll change the sheets.

But the circle on Honor White's bottom sheet didn't have that sharp tang of urine. Mild, almost milky.

I checked her chart and confirmed that she wasn't due till the end of November. Damn and blast it; another premature labour. What I found myself thinking, selfishly and childishly, was *Could we not be let to sit still for five minutes?*

I think your waters have broken, Mrs. White.

She clamped her eyes shut and wrung her rosary beads.

Not another! Delia Garrett heaved onto her side and pulled the pillow over her head.

I wished we had anywhere else to put the grieving mother but this room.

I told Honor White, You're a few weeks earlier than expected, but don't worry.

I felt her abdomen. The foetus's bottom was at the top, as it should be. But instead of finding the hard arc of the spine, my fingers sank into a hollow before they reached the head. The foetus was faceup. This was common enough in late pregnancy, and the awkward positioning might explain why Honor White's amniotic sac had broken already. Hopefully it would revolve to facedown before it was time to push. Otherwise it could mean a long, painful back labour, a bad rip, maybe even (if worse came to worst) forceps...

I got out the ear trumpet and moved it around till I found the faint but lively beat low down on her right flank.

I told her, You're progressing nicely now the waters have broken. I'm just going to wash my hands and see what the story is before we change your bed.

I put Honor White on a bedpan first to make sure her bowels and bladder were empty. Then I got her to lie back in her soaked sheets. She opened her legs without a murmur.

I was feeling to make sure the cord hadn't prolapsed, because sometimes a loop came out first and could get pinched by the skull. But to my astonishment Honor White was wide open already; my gloved fingers could detect only a thin lip of cervix. I felt awful for not having checked her before.

Have you been having pangs, Mrs. White?

She nodded and coughed.

Where, in your back?

Another nod.

For how long?

A while.

You should have said.

Her face was stone.

So! You're well on the road now.

Nearly ready to push, I would have added if her foetus had been facing her spine.

Usually in this situation, the doctor would give the mother a draught of morphia and we'd cross our fingers that her contractions would turn the foetus while she was asleep, but Honor White would refuse the drug, and in any case, there just wasn't time.

For a breech birth (wrong way up), I might have tried to persuade the tiny passenger to flip over by pressing the abdomen, but for this presentation, it was best to use gravity. I got Honor White out of bed and sat her on a chair. Lean forward, please, Mrs. White. Hands on your knees.

Bridie helped me put a fresh nightdress on her and then we stripped and made the bed, working smoothly together.

Out of the corner of my eye, I saw Honor White hold her breath and redden.

No bearing down yet, Mrs. White!

She let out her breath in a splutter of coughing.

I told her, It's the angle your baby's at, the head's pressing so, it tricks you into thinking you're ready.

She stifled a groan.

Bridie bundled up the wet sheets for the laundry.

I asked, Once you've dropped that down the chute, could you find Dr. Lynn and tell her Mrs. White has a persistent posterior presentation and she's almost fully dilated?

I saw Bridie mutter the phrase to herself silently, trying to memorise it.

Just say *posterior*.

She nodded and rushed off.

Now that I was looking out for it, I could see the tightening in Honor White's face when the next pang came. She let out a cough so ragged, I passed her the sputum cup. She hawked up something dark.

Mary O'Rahilly spoke up, eyes shiny with concern: If you don't mind my saying, Mrs. White, I found the chloroform such a help.

No answer.

Would you not take an inhaler for a minute to soothe your cough, even? Save your strength for the pushing?

But the woman shook her head savagely.

She worried me, this one. I'd been assuming that Honor White was simply the stoic type, but perhaps she was putting herself through this labour in a spirit of grim penance for what the nuns called her *second lapse,* her *second offence.* I'd occasionally been called in to see a woman who'd been labouring away at home quite unsupported, and it often went badly, even after my arrival; it was as if the isolation had sapped her spirit. That wasn't only the unwed either. One wife near fifty was so embarrassed to find herself in that condition again at her age that she hadn't told a soul, not even her husband—she'd been wheeled into this hospital with a tiny live foot sticking out of her, and Sister Finnigan and I had spent a long hard night saving them both.

Now, Mrs. White, I said, stand up and lean on the bed and rock your hips, would you?

She blinked.

Come on, it's to get your baby into the right position.

She obeyed, facing the wall and swaying backwards and forwards in a slow, incongruous dance.

The O'Rahilly baby let out a goatish wail in her crib.

I picked her up and showed Mary O'Rahilly how to change the nappy.

Green slime!

That's how it comes out at first, I told her.

Disgusting, she said fondly.

What are you and Mr. O'Rahilly thinking of calling your daughter?

Maybe Eunice, for my aunt.

Lovely, I lied.

Afterward we got little Eunice on the breast again.

Bridie had come in silently and was rubbing Honor White's

214

back. The woman paid her no attention but didn't rebuff her either. Bridie reported, Her legs are shaking something awful.

Honor White grunted. Can't I just lie down and push?

Not quite yet, sorry.

(Feeling her bump for any hint of the foetus revolving yet.)

I told her, The doctor should be here very shortly.

(*Please, God, let Dr. Lynn arrive in time for this delivery.* What if the skull got jammed and everything swelled, and there was nothing I could do to rescue mother and child from each other, from their joint and private hell?)

Delia Garrett had her magazine out as a shield for her eyes.

Mrs. White, I said, let's try you on the bed on hands and knees.

Like a dog? Mary O'Rahilly asked, mildly outraged on her neighbour's behalf.

But Honor White climbed onto the mattress, leaning on Bridie's skinny arm. She rocked back and forth in a kind of fury. Oh, oh, I need to—

Let me check you again. Stay right where you are.

I scrubbed and gloved and lotioned. I felt inside her and there was no trace of the cervix at all.

Please!

Even if the foetus was still facing upwards, I couldn't say no to this overwhelming urge of hers. As long as the back of the skull was leading and the chin was well tucked in, it should be possible to deliver now, shouldn't it?

All right, time to lie down on your left and push.

(I was praying for one of those last-minute miracles that nature sometimes worked—the foetus finally, suddenly, gloriously corkscrewing into place, then into the light.)

Honor White dropped down heavily, head to the wall, a martyr of old.

I crooned, Good woman yourself.

Temperature no higher; pulse just a little too fast, and thready. I was about to listen to the foetal heartbeat for any sign of distress when her next pang made her start to groan.

Chin down, I said, hold your breath, and give a fine strong push.

I saw all her muscles harden and the strain move right through her.

Feel free to make noise, Mrs. White.

She stared past me.

I looped a towel around the top rail for her to pull on. She was the wrong way round to be able to brace her feet on anything but I didn't want to move her now. This primitive little storeroom!

A squeak as Bridie wheeled in a second baby crib. She murmured, For when it's needed.

Honor White hissed through her teeth, *God be with me, God help me, God save me.*

A red puddle was forming around her hip. Old brown blood coming out during labour was quite usual, but this was very bright.

Her eyes followed mine to the scarlet. She wheezed, Am I dying?

I said, Oh, birth's a messy business.

But by the time Dr. Lynn bustled in, Honor White's bleeding was distinctly heavier.

I gave a rapid report.

Thirty-six weeks, said the doctor, that's only a week from early term, so the lungs should be well developed, at least. And most stargazers do come out on their own.

Stargazers?

That was Bridie.

I explained over my shoulder: Born faceup, looking towards the sky.

Dr. Lynn muttered, No, it's the mother's pulse force that concerns me, and the haemorrhage. Most likely the afterbirth's come away already.

Honor White bore the internal exam wordlessly.

At the sink after, scouring her hands again, Dr. Lynn said, You've done splendidly, Mrs. White, but we're going to get your baby out without further delay. Forceps, please, Nurse.

My stomach clenched. I asked, French or English?

French.

The long ones. That told me the bad news: the head wasn't very far down the passage yet.

Bridie was all agog, but I hadn't time to explain.

I fetched a pair of long Andersons, with their handle grips and finger ring, as well as carbolic solution, a scalpel, ligatures, scissors, cloths, a needle, and thread. I filled a syringe with cocaine hydrochloride.

I'd seen women left botched by forceps, their infants with skulls dented or mashed, sometimes spastic for life. *Don't think about that.*

Dr. Lynn was asking Honor White to lie on her back.

She cried, Wait!

She gripped the towel and pushed, a vein standing out at her temple.

The doctor asked, Ready now?

Honor White nodded. Her cough sounded sharp enough to crack a rib.

Local anesthetic, Doctor, as she won't take chloroform?

Dr. Lynn accepted the syringe of cocaine hydrochloride and injected it into Honor White's soft parts while I held her legs.

Once the area was numbed, the doctor made the snip. Working fast, before the oncoming pang, she slid the first flat branch of the forceps all the way up and alongside the foetus's skull. Then the next.

Honor White cried out then.

Blood ran even faster; I wondered how the doctor could see what she was doing in this gaudy mess. That was the paradox of forceps—if they didn't get the baby out right away, they could worsen a haemorrhage.

Faster, faster.

Dr. Lynn clicked the handles together at the midpoint and locked them.

Honor White writhed and coughed as pain struck her like lightning.

I helped her up a little so she could catch her breath and wiped the catarrh from her lips.

Dr. Lynn murmured to herself, Easy does it.

Gripping the awful tongs, she worked on. I wedged myself behind Honor White, holding her as still as I could as she leaked more and more scarlet across the sheets.

Holy Jesus, Honor White said, gasping.

Dr. Lynn straightened up and gave me a preoccupied shake of the head. Ah, not quite within reach yet.

She slid the forceps out in one piece and rested them on the tray. Perhaps ergotoxine to strengthen the contractions? But it's so unpredictable...

I'd never heard Dr. Lynn dither. Awkward, I looked away and busied myself taking Honor White's pulse. Twenty-six in fifteen seconds, so a heart rate of one hundred and four. What worried me wasn't the speed but the lack of force, a feeble music under my fingers.

I bent lower to hear what the patient was whispering: *For*

though I should walk in the midst of the shadow of death, I will fear no evil, for thou art with me.

When I put the back of my hand to her grey cheek, it was clammy with sweat. Are you nauseated, Mrs. White?

I thought she nodded but I couldn't be sure. Her pressure's dropping, Doctor.

(She might lose consciousness at any moment.)

Dr. Lynn stared; for once she seemed at a loss. In that case, she said, I doubt saline will be enough. Mrs. White needs blood, but the hospital's stocks are awfully low. I wonder, would there be any walking donors in the building?

Donors on the hoof, that was the jocular phrase. My mind cleared and I told her, We nurses are all on the register. I'll do it.

Oh, but—

I'm right here. You wouldn't even need to do a cross match, my type is O.

The universal blood donor; that made the doctor's face brighten.

I hurried to get the sterile kit from the top shelf.

Behind me I heard Honor White cough shrilly as the next pang pulled her back into the eye of the storm.

The doctor told her, Keep pushing if you're able.

Honor White groaned as she bore down. The bed was a sea of red.

I readied my left arm by whirling it a dozen times.

Bridie watched as if witnessing some arcane ritual.

I checked the other patients. Mary O'Rahilly was somehow sleeping through all this, but Delia Garrett asked, What on earth—

Just transfusing some blood, I said as glibly as if it were something I did every day.

No room for a chair by her cot, so I perched on the edge and un-buttoned my cuff with my trembling right hand. I wasn't afraid, only thrilled at the prospect of giving exactly what was needed.

Dr. Lynn said loudly, Mrs. White, I'm going to put a pint of Nurse Power's blood into you.

No response. Was she sliding beyond our reach?

I took her pulse again. It's climbed to one hundred and fifteen, Doctor.

(Her heart was pumping faster to compensate for the fact that she was bleeding to death.)

Bridie, said the doctor, a glass of water for Nurse Power.

I almost barked, *Don't waste time.* But I was a patient now, so I held my tongue.

The doctor would need my artery for fresher blood and stronger flow to help her pump it faster into the sinking woman. So I offered her the thumb side of my wrist, hoping she had the knack of locating the deep radial pulse.

Dr. Lynn refused it. No, no, those little arteries hurt like the devil, and there's the risk of leakage and embolisms.

I really don't mind—

You're too necessary to risk your health, Nurse. Besides, I read an article that said vein to vein, assisted by gravity, will do in a pinch.

In a pinch; was that where we were now? And had the doctor never actually tried this vein-to-vein technique before?

She slid her warm hand into the crook of my elbow. When she found the best vein, she bounced on it a few times.

I looked away and drained the glass of water Bridie was holding out; oddly enough, I was squeamish when it came to anything piercing my own skin.

Dr. Lynn took only two goes to get the needle in, which wasn't half bad for a physician. A dark line of blood filled the tube, and she turned the stopcock before it could spill. Rapidly, she bandaged the apparatus onto my arm.

But Honor White's head was falling back; her eyelids closed. Were we too late? Another contraction seized her now, ghastly to watch—an unseen monster shaking her limp body on a crimson bier.

I said, Do it!

Dr. Lynn was calmly attaching my tubing to the other metal syringe. She tied Honor White's arm to make the veins stand out, but they were flat as string.

With my right hand I took the pulse on the woman's other wrist—up to a hundred and twenty now, and so faint.

The doctor still couldn't find a vein on the dying woman.

Heat? My voice came out almost angry. Bridie, dip a clean cloth in the pot of hot water, would you?

Dr. Lynn murmured, I almost have the bugger.

But for all the probing and prodding, Honor White's veins kept rolling under the doctor's fingers.

When Bridie brought over the hot cloth, I snatched it myself, despite my impediments. I flapped it in the air two or three times to release some steam so it wouldn't burn Honor White, then folded it over and pressed it along her inner arm.

Can you, Nurse Power? Dr. Lynn offered me the handle of the syringe.

Even in the hurry, I respected her for knowing that this was a moment when all her study and experience was no match for a nurse's.

I grabbed the syringe and pulled the hot cloth off Honor White's arm. There, on the pink-flushed skin, was a little blue line—a creek in a canyon. I beat out a rhythm on it with my fingertip: *Stay alive, Mrs. White.* The wary blood vessel rose a little, just enough, and I slid the needle in.

Dr. Lynn took over promptly, bandaging the tube onto the slumped patient so it wouldn't slip out.

Stand up, she urged me.

I leapt off the cot.

As soon as she opened the stopcock, my blood began to flow down the tube. The doctor seized my left hand and set it on her own shoulder to keep it high; my elbow locked. She pressed my flesh above the needle so hard I almost cried out. She squeezed my arm, milking me of life.

Hearing some commotion in the corridor, I jerked; could that be the police come back, still hunting Dr. Lynn?

Either she hadn't heard anything or she had nerves of steel. A captain in the rebel army, I remembered. Bullets whizzing past her like hail.

Dr. Lynn murmured, Now, I can't be sure how much I'm taking, Nurse Power, so do speak up at once if you feel faint.

With my other hand I gripped the head of the bed, just in case. *Let it not clot*; we hadn't a minute to change a clogged tube or decant my blood and add sodium citrate to keep it liquid. *Flow, flow, red waterfall, keep flowing into this woman. Don't let us have to cut this infant out of her.* Mother and child doing their best to *walk in the midst of the shadow of death*.

Could I see a slight flush rising in Honor White's chalky face?

Suddenly the woman blinked up at me.

You're all right, dear, I assured her.

(Not true yet; a hope in the form of a lie.)

I added, You should be feeling stronger soon.

She let out a husky scream.

The O'Rahilly baby in his crib gave a start and mewed.

Honor White tried to sit up.

Dr. Lynn ordered: Stay still.

Honor White began thrashing about.

I pressed my right hand over the needle in my left arm to keep it there and clamped my left hand over hers so she wouldn't yank out the tube. Mrs. White!

Was she going into convulsions, like poor Ita Noonan?

No, not that. Red-faced now, shuddering, she clutched her sides as if they might burst, then scratched at her face, her neck, panting, trying to say something. Pale hives rising.

Dr. Lynn muttered wrathfully, Transfusion reaction.

I was appalled. I'd only heard of this, never seen it.

Honor White was wheezing wildly as she clawed at herself, raising livid weals.

The doctor twisted the stopcock and tugged off Honor White's bandage.

Bridie struggled to hold the woman still. What's happening?

Something in Mrs. White's blood doesn't like mine, I admitted, even though I'm a universal donor.

Dr. Lynn muttered, There are always exceptions. We couldn't have known.

She whipped the tube out of the needle in Honor White's arm, and my blood jetted across the floor, unwanted now; noxious.

I pulled the needle and tube right out of my own arm and pressed hard on the puncture to stop the bleeding.

We could do nothing about the maddening itching—Honor White's body's way of trying to fight off my alien blood. She was gasping like a consumptive. I bent all my efforts on urging her to calm herself and breathe.

Dr. Lynn was scrubbing at the sink.

At a moment like this, why on earth did she need to wash her hands again?

Then I realised there was no hope but to get this baby into the air before the mother bled out.

I called, You'll find a sterile pair of forceps on the—

I see them.

Bridie and I gripped Mrs. White and held her as Dr. Lynn went in with the first branch of the forceps.

Honor White let out a long howl.

Then the other branch.

Dr. Lynn muttered, Yes. Staring into space as she tightened her grip and curled her index finger into the ring at the hinge.

I told Honor White, A huge push this time.

Though she didn't look as if she could even lift her head. Who was I to order this woman to go beyond her powers?

If you'd press on the uterine fundus, Nurse? asked the doctor.

I put my hand at the top of Honor White's bump, waited for the wave to take her, then bore down.

Urghhhhhhhh!

Steady, steady . . . and here comes the face.

Without rushing, Dr. Lynn guided the head out in her tongs.

New eyes blinking through a wash of scarlet, turned to the heavens. *Stargazer.*

Was the infant going to drown in its mother's blood? I flailed around to find a clean cloth and wiped the nose and mouth clear.

Dr. Lynn murmured, Wait for it. One more push.

I got behind Honor White and held her up to help her breathe. I swore, It'll soon be over.

(Thinking, *One way or another.*)

She stirred a little, and her eyes widened. She coughed with a sound of something ripping. On the next pang, she shoved back so hard, the bed rail bit into my ribs.

The whole baby slithered out of her.

Well done!

Dr. Lynn said, Congratulations, Mrs. White. You have a son.

I held out a blanket to take him.

Unprompted, he let out a cry.

At first I thought the doctor's forceps had cut his mouth. Then I recognised the kinked line—born harelipped.

But a healthy size for being a few weeks before full term, and a good hue.

Dr. Lynn was concentrating on stemming the bleeding. She massaged Honor White's collapsed belly from the top, persuading her uterus to squeeze out the afterbirth.

Now the cord's pulse slowed; this infant had had all he was going to get from it. I asked Bridie to bring me over the instrument tray. I tied the slippery blue rope in two places and scissored through.

Could you warm up a pint of saline, Nurse?

I bundled the White baby in a towel, set him in the crib, and told Bridie to watch him. Speak up if he seems to choke or changes colour.

I rushed to mix salt into hot water, then brought over the bottle. Dr. Lynn had already attached a fresh tube to Honor White's inner arm. I set the bottle up on a stand so the saline would pour into her.

She was less flushed, and she'd stopped scratching at her weals, but she was weak as a rag. What other damage had my unlucky blood done her?

Holy Mary Mother of God, pray for us sinners, she was whispering, *now and at the hour of our death, amen.*

There's the placenta now, excellent.

The meaty thing surged out, with a huge clot behind it.

Dr. Lynn lifted up the organ to check it was whole, then dropped it into the waiting basin.

I felt Honor White's pulse; still too high and too weak, an awful feathery dance.

Suture, please, Nurse?

I washed my shaking hands before I threaded the needle.

Dr. Lynn steadily sewed up the small incision she'd made in Honor White's perineum.

Bridie said, Your arm, Julia!

Inside my left elbow was trickling red where the needle had been. It's nothing.

But she went to get me a bandage.

It doesn't matter, Bridie. Leave it.

Let me just—

She tied it on me clumsily, too loose.

Over the next quarter of an hour, as we watched, Honor White's bleeding did taper off. Oh, the slow, painful relief of it. Little by little, her pulse steadied and dropped to under a hundred, and the speed of her breaths diminished too. She was able to nod, to speak. I didn't know if it was the saline, or divine mercy, or pure fluke.

I gave the White baby his bath with Bridie's help. How it drew the eye, this fellow's tiny gap—though only on one side, and the dip didn't reach the nostril. I'd heard the ancient Romans were so horrified by these babies, they used to drown them. This one was in the pink; no sign of flu, and my blood didn't seem to have done him any harm either, which suggested that his was a different type than his mother's. Funny to think the two of them had been one a quarter of an hour ago and now were severed forever.

Bridie whispered to me, Is he not quite finished, then?

His mouth, you mean?

Maybe because the doctor took him out before he was cooked?

Dr. Lynn said over her shoulder, No, it just happens, Bridie. Runs in families.

(Especially poor ones, though she wouldn't say that in front of Honor White. It was as if what the mothers lacked was blazoned on their children's faces.)

Honor White spoke up in a gravelly voice. What's wrong with him?

You have a healthy boy, Mrs. White, I told her, it's only that his lip is cleft.

I held out the wrapped pupa.

Her reddened eyes struggled to focus on his triangular mouth. Hand fumbling, she crossed herself.

Will I sit you up so you can hold him?

But her face closed like the lid of a desk.

Dr. Lynn murmured, She'd better stay flat to boost her circulation.

Right; sorry. (I should have remembered that.)

I'd have offered to lay him on his mother's chest, but maybe even his small weight would impede her wet breathing. So I held him right beside her instead, almost as near as if she were cradling him, his downy head not far from hers; I was ready to pull him away if she coughed.

She didn't move to kiss him. A tear ran out the side of her eye and down the gap between them.

Bearna ghiorria, murmured Dr. Lynn.

I knew a little Gaelic but not that phrase. What's that, Doctor?

She explained, It means a hare's gap. Bring him back in a month and I'll fix it for him, Mrs. White.

Which was kind but suggested she hadn't grasped Honor White's situation from the chart; both woman and child would be in the care and custody of the nuns.

Unless the doctor saw it as a matter of courtesy to speak to her as she would to any other new mother?

I hadn't had a chance to ask Honor White if she was meaning to nurse her baby, but anyway, he wouldn't be able to latch on with that split mouth. He'll need spoon-feeding, won't he, Doctor?

She weighed the question. Well, the palate's closed, at least, that's a mercy... he might manage a bottle if you put on a wide teat with a cross cut into it, Nurse, so long as you hold him well upright and keep the flow slow. I'll have Maternity send down their mixture.

Thanks.

Cleft lip could cause glue ear and speech defects, I remembered. But that was nothing to the way people would stare or avert their eyes or sneer at him as damaged goods. I thought of this scrap of humanity being sent back to the home with his mother in a week. It struck me that all the babies with unmarked faces would be chosen for adoption before him. Would he end up being nursed out for shillings with a stranger, as Bridie had been? Would that foster nurse know or bother to bring him in for surgery, or would he grow up an easy target for any bully?

Bridie announced, He has the same birthday as Nurse Power. Oh, and me! (Her eyes merrily meeting mine.) The first of November, a great date altogether.

Honor White said, very low: The Feast of All Saints.

I wondered whether it gratified her pious heart that he shared a feast day with the church triumphant in heaven.

Dr. Lynn straightened up and said, Well, everything seems to be in order. Good night, all.

She turned back at the door. I forgot to ask—how are you feeling yourself now, Nurse Power?

Fine. I hardly gave a cupful.

Still, you look done in. Sleep here to save the journey home and back.

Oh, but—

Did you know, Nurse, bacteriologists have determined that exhaustion lowers one's resistance to infection?

I smiled, giving in. Very well, Doctor.

We didn't have a telephone at home, but Tim wouldn't worry; he knew I sometimes needed to stay the night.

Honor White's eyelids were fluttering.

Before she dropped off, I cleaned her up and got her into the two binders, the abdominal one over her belly and the chest bandage because she wouldn't be nursing—but that one I wound much more loosely than Delia Garrett's so as not to restrict her breathing.

I spoke softly: I wonder would there be anyone you'd like us to send the good news?

A parent, a sister, a friend, even; I was hoping she could give me one name.

Honor White shook her head. Her lashes fell; she was sinking into sleep.

I was dizzy all of a sudden; I sat down by the desk. My arm hurt as if it had been caught on barbed wire, and a bruise was spreading.

If only the donation had done her some good, or no harm, even; *primum non nocere*. Instead, I'd watched my blood turn to poison and nearly kill her.

Bridie was holding out a cup of tea. You saved them both, you know.

Thanks, Bridie.

I gulped it down; it was sweet, at least. Really, it was Dr. Lynn who saved them with her forceps.

Not a bit. I was right there, and I say it was the pair of you.

I would have liked to hug her then.

Between the three of us, yes, I supposed we'd kept the

Whites alive, but I couldn't seem to take much comfort from that fact.

I said, The other day—yesterday, I corrected myself (was it only yesterday I'd met this young woman?)—you mentioned babies going *into the pipe*. What exactly did you mean?

Bridie shrugged. Mother-and-baby homes, Magdalene laundries, orphanages, she listed under her breath. Industrial schools, reformatories, prisons...aren't they all sections of the same pipe?

Rats in a flooded tunnel; the image turned my stomach.

I'm from the pipe, see, Julia, she said softly, and I don't suppose I'll ever get out.

Masked and draped, Sister Luke was standing in the door watching us drink our tea.

I jumped up, and my voice came out rusty: Evening, Sister.

And with that, another shift was over.

I brought her up to date on the day's two births, Mary O'Rahilly's and Honor White's. I advised her on how to feed the White baby: Sit him upright, and trickle it in or you'll choke him.

Where had Bridie disappeared to? It seemed out of character for her to shoot off without a word.

Then I caught myself—I'd known her only two days.

Sister Luke put one fingertip to the baby's scribble-shaped lip and sighed. Unlikely to thrive, of course, she murmured. I'll get Father Xavier in to baptise him.

I resented her defeatism. You won't have been trained in the care of newborns, I suppose, Sister?

Her lips tightened. I'm familiar with the basics.

Plenty of babies do very well being bottle-fed nowadays, and so, I expect, will Mrs. White's.

She conceded, Ah, I don't mean the disfigurement's going to choke him in itself.

Her voice dropped to a gossipy murmur. But our sisters who work with unfortunates tell me his kind generally have more than one hereditary weakness.

By *his kind,* she didn't mean the harelipped, I realised, but the illegitimate.

Often don't last long, poor things, as if they know they're not wanted...

I would have sorely liked to tell the night nurse she was wrong, except hadn't Dr. Lynn quoted a similar statistic about the mortality of children born out of wedlock?

I turned away. I took down my coat and said, I'll be staying in the nurses' dormitory tonight, Sister.

(I neglected to mention that the doctor had advised it because I might feel the aftereffects of having given blood; I didn't want her to question my capacities.)

Do have a midwife called down from Maternity if you've any cause for concern about Mrs. White, I added, or if Mrs. O'Rahilly needs help with her little girl.

Sister Luke nodded equably.

I hated the fact that I had to leave my patients in this woman's care.

Good night, Mrs. White. Mrs. O'Rahilly. Mrs. Garrett.

I paused for one more look at the White baby, whose mouth had the pursed curve of a sweet pea. Then I went on my way.

IV

BLACK

OUTSIDE THE WARD, I spotted Bridie's bright head. Was she waiting for me?

Thin coat folded over her arm, she was studying the latest poster.

THE GOVERNMENT HAS THE SITUATION
WELL IN HAND
AND THE EPIDEMIC IS ACTUALLY IN DECLINE.
THERE IS NO REAL RISK
EXCEPT TO THE RECKLESS
WHO TRY TO FIGHT THE FLU ON THEIR FEET.
IF YOU FEEL YOURSELF SUCCUMBING,
REPORT YOURSELF
AND LIE DOWN FOR A FORTNIGHT.
WOULD THEY BE DEAD
IF THEY'D STAYED IN BED?

Julia, she murmured without even turning her head. Is that true at all?

I asked, caustic, Which bit—are the dead to blame for dying?

The line I found most laughable was the one about lying down for a fortnight; who could afford or manage that without a houseful of servants?

She shook her head. Where they say it's *in decline.*

Propaganda, Bridie. Government lies.

She didn't seem surprised. It's like the song.

What song?

Bridie put her head back and gave the verse, full-throated, despite the fact that we were on a busy landing with people pushing past. *So stand to your glasses, steady,* she sang,

> *This world is a web of lies.*
> *Then here's to the dead already,*
> *And hurrah for the next one who dies.*

It made some heads turn.

I chuckled. Well, that's a jolly one.

The tune is, anyway.

You've a lovely voice, Bridie.

She puffed out her breath in scorn.

I don't flatter. Now, tell me, why did you scarper when Sister Luke came in?

Bridie looked back towards the door. So the old crow couldn't tell me to go straight to the motherhouse, *no dilly-dallying or shilly-shallying.*

I grinned at the imitation. Where are you going, then?

I'm not leaving if you're not. You need keeping an eye on, the doctor said.

I only lost half a teacup of blood.

Still.

I glanced down the stairs with yearning. I'd been looking forward to the walk to the tram to settle my nerves after the day. I suppose I must be tired, I said, but I don't feel as if I could sleep yet.

Bridie said, Me neither.

Well, the dormitory's upstairs if you mean to stay too.

She followed, asking, Will they let me in even though I'm only a helper?

I don't suppose anyone will make a fuss at a time like this.

Second floor, past Maternity. My ears made out the weeping of a mother in labour and the uncertain cry of another woman's newborn.

Bridie admitted on the third staircase, I am a tiny bit tired, actually.

I laughed, out of breath.

But not sleepy yet.

We got to the fourth floor, but the door I led her to had a notice tacked up: *Men's Fever (Overflow)*. A rumble of voices behind it.

Well, I said, that settles that.

Bridie's voice was disappointed: There's no dormitory anymore?

I suppose we'll have to head home after all.

I winced at my own word. Bridie didn't have a home, only a bed in a convent. Her life was ruled by the same order who'd run the so-called home she'd grown up in. A hidden, upside-down world where children had no birthdays and sisters were no longer sisters; just one part of *the pipe*.

Unless we go up on the roof for a bit of air?

I said it lightly.

Bridie looked taken aback.

I suppose I was feeling festive because it was my birthday. *Our* birthday. Also, it had been a good day. For all the slow misery of Mary O'Rahilly's obstructed labour, and the horror of Honor White's bad reaction to my blood, nobody had died. Not in our ward, at least; not in our small square of the sickened, war-weary world.

Bridie asked, Climb up the side of the roof, you mean?

I smiled at the notion. No climbing necessary. There's a flat part one can walk out on, between the pointy sections.

Well, that's a relief.

What I treasured about this young woman was that she never said no. She was game for anything, it seemed, including scrambling up the gabled roof of a four-storey building.

I grabbed a handful of blankets from a shelf as we were passing. I led Bridie through an unmarked door and up a narrow staircase. The last, smallest door seemed a dead end, but I'd been up here before when I needed a break, a breath, a cigarette, and a view of the city. I told her, It's never locked.

Out onto the tarred rooftop. It was a grand clear evening, for once, not a rag of cloud in the navy-blue sky. On a fine day in summer, there'd be little knots of staff basking during their dinner hour, but after nine o'clock on an autumn night, the two of us had the expanse to ourselves.

The old moon wrote its last faint C just above the parapet. A little streetlight leaked up from the hushed city below. I leaned my elbows on the bricks and peered down. I said, A walk would have been nice too. Maybe another day.

It hit me that once the hospital got back to its standards and routines, an unqualified skivvy would no longer be needed or, in fact, allowed. Odds were, Bridie would be thanked and discharged. Would I ever—no, how would I contrive to see her again?

I'm a grand walker, Bridie was saying, I can go on forever. Every Sunday at the home, we used to go five miles to the sea in a crocodile.

Ridiculously, I envisioned her in the belly of an actual crocodile. I tried to replace that picture with an image of a small

Bridie dancing on the shoreline, tossing stones at the waves, running into the water and screeching with delight.

You went bathing?

She shook her head. It was just for exercise. We had to turn around and walk right back. We weren't allowed to link arms or we'd get the strap, but we could chat without moving our mouths.

I didn't know what to say.

Face tipped up to the sky, Bridie swayed.

I took her elbow. Don't topple over the edge, now.

The stars are so bright, I'm dazzled!

I looked up and found the Great Bear. I told her, In Italy, they used to blame the influence of the constellations for making them sick—that's where *influenza* comes from.

Bridie took that notion in stride. As if, when it's your time, your star gives you a yank—

And she tugged as if reeling in a fish.

It's hardly scientific thinking, I admitted.

She said, Maybe not. But I have heard it's all set down up there.

What is?

The day each of us is going to die.

That's pure nonsense, Bridie.

She lifted and then dropped her bony shoulders. I don't have to be scientific; I'm not the nurse.

You've the makings of one, though. If you wanted.

Bridie stared, then laughed that off.

I did realise that this job was too grim for most people, all the stinking and leaking and dying. Mine was a peculiar vocation.

You know, Bridie, I mark down every patient I lose.

Where? In a book?

I think you saw me doing it.

I pulled out my watch now, without looking at the time, and dropped it in her palm, facedown.

Bridie weighed it in her hand. Would this be solid silver?

I suppose so. It was my mother's.

(I added that so she wouldn't think I'd earned enough to buy myself such a thing.)

She murmured, It's still warm from you.

The chain between the two of us was a taut umbilicus.

I put my finger to one of the bockedy scratched circles on the watch back. Every full moon means a patient of mine who's died.

But not through your fault.

I hope not. It's hard to be absolutely sure. In this job, one has to learn to live with that.

She asked, And the little curved pieces?

They're crescent moons instead of full ones.

The babies?

She never missed a trick, this one. I nodded.

Bridie peered more closely now. Some are only little scratches.

Those ones were stillborn. Or miscarried, if far enough on that I could tell whether it was a girl or a boy.

So you scar your precious watch for all of them because you feel bad?

I shook my head. I just...

Bridie suggested, Want to remember them?

Oh, I remember them anyway. Often I wish I didn't.

Do they haunt you, like?

I struggled to find the words. I have a sense that they want to be recorded somewhere. Need to be. Demand to be, even.

Bridie stroked the silver curve. It's a sort of map of the dead, then. A sky full of moons.

I took the watch back and tucked it into my pocket. I told her, I'm often just as haunted by the ones who live. Mrs. White's boy, for instance.

Bridie nodded.

I keep thinking, instead of him going into *the pipe,* if some nice young couple—like the O'Rahillys, say—if they didn't mind his lip, and adopted him…

Bridie grimaced. Mary O'Rahilly's a sweetheart, but he's a thug.

I was knocked off balance by that matter-of-fact sentence. Her husband?

Well, he wallops her, doesn't he?

She read my appalled face and saw that this was news to me. Oh. Couldn't you tell?

She wasn't triumphing at all; she was just thrown by my naïveté.

It added up. Young Mary O'Rahilly's timidity, the many things that seemed to make her husband cross…and the old blue marks on both wrists. She'd claimed to *bruise easy,* and I, gullible as a probie on her first day, I'd left it at that.

Bridie, I breathed, you know things you shouldn't. Especially not at *about twenty-two.*

Her half smile was rueful.

I admitted, No one's ever lifted a hand to me in my life.

That's good, she said.

I'm beginning to know enough to know that I know nothing.

Bridie didn't contradict me.

I moved along the flat middle of the roof. I found a pitched section and put down one of the blankets against the slope. I squatted to sit, tucking my skirts around me to keep the cold out, and leaned back on the clammy slates.

Bridie fitted herself beside me.

Button up your coat to keep warm, I advised her. And here, lean forward—

I swept a second blanket over our heads and down behind us like a cloak. No, a magician's cloth. I shook a third out to cover our knees.

Tell me about it, I said into the silence. Your—the home. If you don't mind?

The pause was so long, I thought Bridie probably did mind.

Then she said, What do you want to know?

Anything you remember.

I remember it all.

Her face worked as she thought about it.

She said at last, Old pee and rubber, that's what I smell when I think of it. So many of us had accidents in the night, see, that at a certain point they said we could just sleep on the waterproof undersheets and spare the laundry.

It was in my nostrils now, that acrid reek.

There was this one teacher who'd come into class, going like this—Bridie wrinkled her nose in imitation. Every day she'd call out, Who can I smell? Who can I smell? But the thing was, Julia, we all smelled.

That's terrible.

She shook her head. What was terrible was how every one of us would throw a hand in the air, eager to call out another girl's name, name her as the smelly one.

Oh, Bridie.

A long minute stretched while I let all this sink in.

She said, Then there's the beatings. I can feel them in my bones.

I cleared my throat. Beatings for what?

She shrugged. You might be made an example of for sleeping

242

in the wrong position, or sneezing at mass. Writing with your left hand, losing a stud off your boot. Having hair that was curly, or red.

I reached out to the faint fuzz of amber escaping from her pins. Why on earth—

They said it was a mark of badness and hung me up by my bun from a coat hook.

I pulled back my hand and put it over my mouth. Couldn't you have told someone about the mistreatment? A teacher at school, say?

Her smile was dark. Oh, Julia. Any lessons we had were in the home—it was the school too, see?

I saw.

But in fairness, they weren't all divils there, she told me. A cook we had in my last years, she took a liking to me. She'd lay the apple skins on the very top of the scraps so I could nick them when I carried the bucket to the pigs. And one time a whole half a boiled egg.

My mouth was flooded with sour.

Bridie went on. I was no hand at knitting Aran jumpers or embroidering vestments, so I was put on novenas. We nibbled on candles those days, or paper, or glue, anything to put in our stomachs.

Novenas? I repeated. As in nine days of prayer?

Bridie nodded. People paid the convent to have them said for special intentions.

That flabbergasted me, the notion of children praying on an industrial scale, children so hungry they'd eat glue.

She added, I loved it the odd time they hired me out to farms, though. I could snatch a few berries or a turnip here and there. Cattle feed, even.

I tried to picture that, the small redhead worming her way

between two cows to scrabble in their trough. When did you start work?

As soon as we were dressed in the morning.

No, but what age, roughly?

Bridie didn't answer, so I rephrased it: Don't you remember a time before they made you knit or weed or say prayers?

She shook her head a little impatiently. The home needed running. We had to clean and cook and mind the little ones as well as do the money jobs to earn our keep, see?

Such lies! I exploded. The government pays per head.

Bridie blinked.

From what I've read, the monks or nuns just run these places for the state. They get a lump sum for each child in their custody every year to pay for food and bedding and whatever else is needed.

Is that right? Bridie spoke with an eerie calm. We were never told.

I realised it was the same shameful trick used in the institution a few minutes' walk away through these dark streets, the place where women such as Honor White were obliged to work off the costs of their own captivity for years on end.

Enough, said Bridie.

But—

Julia, please, let's not waste any more of this fine night raking over bad times.

I tried. I gazed up at the sky and let my eyes flicker from one constellation to another to another, jumping between stepping-stones. I thought of the heavenly bodies throwing down their narrow ropes of light to hook us.

I'd never believed the future was inscribed for each of us the day we were born. If anything was written in the stars, it was we who joined those dots, and our lives were the writing.

But Baby Garrett, born dead yesterday, and all the others whose stories were over before they began, and those who opened their eyes and found they were living in a long nightmare, like Bridie and Baby White—who decreed that, I wondered, or at least allowed it?

My stomach growled so loudly, Bridie giggled, and I did too.

I remembered what had been sitting in my bag all day. I asked, Peckish?

Why, what've you got there?

Chocolate truffles from Belgium and an Italian orange.

Bridie marvelled, No!

Birthday presents from my brother, Tim.

The fruit was easier to peel than I'd expected. Its perfume spritzed off under my thumbnail. Behind rags of white, the flesh was so dark in the starlight, it looked nearly purple.

Bridie peered at it. Ah, wouldn't you know, after all that, it's a rotten one.

It is not! Smell it.

She looked revolted but leaned in for a sniff. Her face lit up.

I said, Blood oranges are called that because of the colour inside. Ever so sweet, and hardly any seeds.

The segments parted in my fingers. I ripped the thin membrane. The sacs ranged from yellow through orange to maroon, almost black.

Bridie bit a segment warily. Oh—the juice almost leaked from her mouth, and she had to suck it back—that's only glorious.

Isn't it?

Happy birthday, Julia.

I licked trickles of juice off my hands in a way that would have caused Matron to sack me on the spot. Yours too, now, remember? The first of November.

The first of November, she repeated solemnly. I won't forget. Happy birthday, Bridie.

No sound now but the small wet noises of the orange being devoured between us.

You're awfully easy to talk to, I found myself saying. Since Tim came back from the front, he doesn't.

Bridie didn't ask, *Doesn't what?* Instead, she asked, Doesn't talk to you?

To anyone. Not a word anymore. As if his throat's been cut—except the damage is all in his mind.

I wasn't sure why I felt compelled to blab all this, to set one small pebble of pain on the scale against Bridie's boulders.

It's not something I usually tell people, I added.

Bridie asked, Why not?

Well. A sort of superstitious fear, I suppose, that once I say it in so many words, it'll be true.

Bridie put her head to one side. Isn't it true already?

Yes, but…more official. Permanent. I'll be *Julia with the mute brother.*

She nodded. Does that mortify you?

That's not it.

Grieves you, Bridie suggested.

I nodded, swallowing.

Well, she murmured. Lucky you, I say.

Lucky for having a mute brother?

Having a brother, she corrected me. Any kind.

She was right, I told myself. This was how Tim was. This was the brother I had now.

After a pause, she said: Or having anyone.

Oh, Bridie!

She did one of her little monkey-like shrugs.

I cleared my throat raggedly. Tim still has his sense of humour.

Well, then.

Also a magpie he's very fond of.

There's posh, she said teasingly.

He's a great gardener and a good scratch cook.

The magpie?

My laughter echoed across the jagged roofline.

I divided the truffles. We scarfed up one each, then had a game to see who could take longest to melt her second one on the heat of her tongue.

Bridie said thickly, This is some condemned man's last meal, all right.

I thought of the patient whose mind was turned by the flu, the one who'd jumped to his death from a window. But I didn't say a word. Let Bridie enjoy her truffle.

I was cold but I didn't care. I turned my face up to the starry sky and blew out a long steamy plume.

Did you know, other planets have lots of moons instead of just one?

Bridie said, Come off it.

It's a fact. I got it out of a library book. Neptune has three, and Jupiter eight—or, no, scientists just found the ninth by taking a picture with a very long exposure.

Bridie tilted her head to one side, as if I were pulling her leg.

It occurred to me that Jupiter's ninth moon might not in fact be the last; the astronomers might keep discovering more of them as the centuries slowly wheeled by. Maybe if they got stronger telescopes they'd glimpse a tenth, an eleventh, a twelfth. It made my head spin, the shining plenitude up there. And down here. The dancing generations, the busy living—even if we were outnumbered by the quiet dead.

A man was caterwauling on the street below. I said, We should drop something on that fellow.

Bridie laughed. Ah, stop. I like an old song.

Would you dignify this one by the name?

It's "Are We Downhearted?"

It's drunken gibberish.

She sang, *Are we downhearted?*

She waited for me to give the response. Then answered her-self with the punch line: *No!* On she went: *Then let your voices ring, and all together sing. Are we downhearted?*

On the third verse, I finally supplied the *No!*

The time rolled by. At some point in our long and rambling conversation, Bridie and I agreed it must be well after midnight.

All Souls' Day now, I remembered. We're supposed to visit a graveyard.

Does a hospital count, since there's always people dying in it?

Let's say it does. Oh, I should say a prayer for Mammy.

Bridie asked, Was it in hospital she took her fever after your brother was born?

I shook my head. At home. It happens every day, the world over—women have babies and they die. No, I corrected my-self, they die of having babies. It's hardly news, so I don't know why it still fills me with such rage.

Bridie said, I suppose it's your fight.

I looked sideways at her.

What you said to Mr. Groyne about women being like soldiers, laying down their lives? Well, your job's not to bear the babies, it's to save them. And the mothers.

I nodded. My throat hurt. I said, All of them I can, anyway.

Bridie crossed herself. Bless Mrs. Power, mother of Julia and Tim.

I bent my head and tried to join in the prayer.

Bless all the departed, she added.

Silence like silk around us.

Bridie remarked, These have been the two best days I've ever had.

I stared at her.

The time of my life. Such an adventure! A couple more people are alive because of us—because you and me were here and did our bit. Can you credit it?

But—the very best days, really, Bridie?

Well, and I've met you.

(Her five syllables, like blows to my chest.)

You said I was a tonic, Julia. Indispensable. Didn't you put balm on my hands when you didn't even know me? Gave me your comb. And a birthday as well. When I broke the thermometer, you said it was your own fault! You've taught me so much in two days. Made me your helper, your runner. Made me matter.

I was speechless.

I thought again of what a good nurse Bridie might make. Has the order never proposed to have you trained in anything?

She made a face. They placed me in service when I first came up to Dublin, but the lady sent me back—said I had a lip on me.

Yes, I could see there was a spark about Bridie that the meaner kind of employer would resent.

I sometimes go out to char by the day, she said. Hotels, schools, offices.

And the wages you get—

Bridie's face made me realise that she never saw a penny. She said, We still owe the nuns for our rearing and education.

My voice was furious. If the order takes your pay, that's bonded servitude. Are you boarders not free to leave?

I don't know all the ins and outs of it, Bridie admitted. Let's talk about something more fun now.

She was shivering, I saw. I huddled farther down and pulled her under the blankets.

The stars inched across the sky. I told Bridie the plot of every Mary Pickford film I'd seen. Then of other films, anything I thought she might enjoy.

She enjoyed them all.

At one point we were talking about children. I volunteered, I won't be having any myself.

No?

I don't know that I ever wanted to marry, exactly. But in any case I've missed the moment.

Bridie didn't say, *Thirty's not old,* as any other woman would have. She just looked at me.

I said, I was never exactly beautiful, and now—

But you *are* beautiful.

Bridie's eyes, the gleam of them. And you haven't missed *this* moment, she told me.

Well, I suppose not.

She took hold of my face and kissed me.

Not a no, not a word, not a movement to stop her, nothing. I just let it—

Her—

I let the kiss happen. Never before, never this way. Like a pearly moon in my mouth, huge, overwhelming, the brightness.

This was against every rule I'd been reared by.

I kissed her back. The old world was changed utterly, dying on its feet, and a new one was struggling to be born. There might only be this one night left, which was why I kissed Bridie Sweeney, held her and kissed her with all I had and all I was.

Lying on the cold slant of the slates, trying to catch our breath.

My eyes brimmed.

Bridie noticed at once. Ah, don't cry.

It's not—

What is it, then?

I said rashly, I bet your mother remembers your real birthday. There must have been a moment when you were put in her arms and she thought, *Oh my.*

A grim chuckle from Bridie. *Oh, my burden,* more like.

Oh, my treasure, I said. (Taking her hands.) The sweet weight of you on the day you were born—imagine.

Bridie put her mouth to mine again.

We got colder and colder as the night wore on. We kissed and we talked, on and off. Neither of us mentioned the kissing so as not to burst the bubble by touching it. So as not to think about what it meant for the two of us to kiss.

We got onto the war, and I found myself telling her about Tim's best friend, Liam Caffrey, how the two fellows had signed up together, bold as brass, grinning away in the photograph that still hung a little tilted, the only picture on my brother's wall. I told her, Liam didn't make it home.

What happened to him?

He was shot in the throat last year at the Battle of Jerusalem. (I moved Bridie's finger to the dip at the base of my own throat. The same spot where Tim wore his little touchwood, which had saved his skin, perhaps, though not the rest of him.)

She wanted to know, Was he there, your Tim?

As near as you are to me now. Splattered with bits of his friend.

Oh, janey mac, poor lad. Poor lads.

It struck me now that war might just have heated and forged that friendship into something harder to name, impossible to describe. Was I a fool not to have thought of that before? It wasn't something I could imagine ever asking Tim, any more than I'd know how to tell him about this night on the rooftop with Bridie.

No matter how cold we got, she and I didn't stir from that spot. Every so often our mouths were speaking so close, they stopped for a while and kissed. I was so happy I thought I'd burst, and in the moments between the kissing I was almost more so.

When had that spark between us first caught, glowed, begun to singe? I hadn't noticed; I'd been too busy. With births coming pell-mell after deaths, when would I have had time to wonder at something as unimportant as my own new feelings, much less worry about them?

We were both yawning. I said, This was mad, coming up here. You need your sleep.

And you don't?

I've been trained to stay up, hardened—

I'm harder, Bridie said with a grin, and younger and tougher.

Point taken.

Sure we can sleep when we're dead, she told me.

I was groggy but exalted, felt as if I'd never sleep again.

But we must have lapsed into silence and dropped off without realising it, because I woke when Bridie moved beside me against the pitched roof. I straightened my stiff neck. The Great Bear had crawled across the sky; hours must have passed.

Cramp in my leg! Bridie gasped as she straightened it.

I admitted with a shiver, I can't feel either of mine. I thumped one foot on the slates; it felt as if it were someone else's.

I'm awful thirsty, said Bridie.

I wished I had another orange for her. Do you want to go down to the canteen for a cup of tea?

I don't want to go anywhere.

Her eyes were so fond, they made me dizzy. It was as if this rooftop were an airship floating above the soiled world, and nothing could happen as long as we stayed up here gripping each other's icy fingers so hard we didn't know whose were whose.

After a bit, I insisted we stand up for a minute to get the blood flowing. We levered each other to our feet, shook ourselves doggishly. Even danced a little, stiffly, laughing, our breath making puffs of white on the dark air.

I'd like to go to that place where you lived, Bridie, and knock it down. Tear it apart, brick from brick.

It was stone, actually.

Stone from stone, then.

She said, What bothers me most to remember is the little ones wailing.

I waited.

Your charge would cry and cry, see, and there was nothing you could do.

Your charge?

Whatever toddler they put in a crib beside your bed to look after once you got big.

What do you mean by big—fourteen, fifteen?

Bridie's lip pulled up on one side, almost a smile. More like eight or nine. And here's the thing—if your charge got into mischief, you'd both be punished. And if she took sick, that was on you too.

I struggled to take this in. You're saying you'd be blamed for her illness?

Bridie nodded. And the little ones were sick all the time. Loads of them went in the hole at the back of the buildings.

I'd lost the thread. You're saying they caught something from playing underground?

No, Julia! That's where they got put...after.

Oh. A grave.

Bridie said, Just one big hole, with nothing written.

I thought of the Angels' Plot in the cemetery where Delia Garrett's unwoken girl would be buried. Small children did die, poor ones more often than others, and unwanted ones even more often than that. But...

The injustice of that, I said, to hold an eight-year-old child accountable for a toddler's death!

Well, said Bridie flatly. I have to tell you, the odd time I was so hungry, I couldn't help robbing my charge.

Robbing her of what?

She hesitated, then said, I'd eat her bread. Drink half the milk from her bottle and fill it up at the tap.

Oh, Bridie.

We all did it. But that's no comfort.

My eyes were prickling. This young woman had survived by whatever means necessary, and I found I couldn't wish that it had been otherwise.

I've never told anyone these old stories, said Bridie.

(Old stories, she called them, as if they were legends of the Trojan War.)

She added, I probably shouldn't be telling you either.

Why not?

Well, you know what I'm like now, Julia.

What you're like?

Bridie said it very softly: Dirty.

You are not!

Eyes shut, she whispered: Things happened.

To you?

Things were done to lots of us. Most of us, I bet.

My pulse was thumping. Done by whom?

She shook her head as if that wasn't the point. A workman, a priest maybe. A minder or teacher, she'd pick one girl to warm her bed and give her a second blanket after.

I was sick to my stomach.

She added, Or a holiday father.

What on earth's a holiday father?

A local family would request a child for the weekend, *to give her a little holiday,* like. You might get sweets or pennies.

I wanted to block my ears.

She went on, One of the fathers gave me a whole shilling. But I couldn't think what to do with that much money or where to hide it, so I ended up burying it in the ashpit.

Bridie, I said. (Trying not to weep.)

It's probably there still.

None of this dirt is yours, I told her. You're as clean as rain.

She kissed me, but on the forehead this time.

Voices on the roof behind us; strangers coming out of the same small door we had.

Bridie and I lurched apart.

I said in a loud and false voice, Well, I suppose we'd better get some breakfast.

(I promised myself that there'd be more time for kisses and for telling all the stories.)

By the time Bridie and I collected our blankets and picked our way past the orderlies, they were lighting their cigarettes and agreeing with each other that it would be over any day now. Uprisings in various German cities, the tossing down of bayonets, secret negotiations, the kaiser on the very brink of abdication...

I hoped the dark hid my flush.

Fancy a smoke, girls?

No, thanks, I told him politely. I held the door for Bridie but she stumbled into the jamb. Careful!

She laughed. Clumsy me.

I said, That's what we get for staying up all night out in the cold.

But I found I was wide awake, entirely alert.

On the main staircase, as we went by the big windows, I looked down at the electric beams of a motor launch creeping by. No, a motor hearse. Another funeral, then; the day's cavalcade was starting up before sunrise. As if some dread angel were flying from house to house, and there was no mark one could put on one's lintel to persuade him to pass over.

Two haggard older doctors passed us as they plodded upstairs.

One of them said, I was pulled over for having only one light on my car, and I found myself rather hoping they'd send me to jail so I could have a rest.

The other's laugh had a hysterical edge to it. I must admit, I'm sucking Forced March like barley sugar.

When they'd passed, Bridie asked me, What's Forced March?

Pills supplied to soldiers, or anyone who needs to stay awake and sharp. Powdered kola nuts and cocaine.

Her eyebrows went up. Do you take them, Julia?

No. I tried once, but I got a racing heartbeat and the shakes.

She covered a long yawn.

Are you shattered, Bridie?

Not a bit.

In the lavatory, we splashed our faces with water, and she bent down and lapped at the stream from the tap, puppyish.

At the mirror, using my comb to neaten myself, I met my eyes. I was old enough to know my own mind, surely, and to be aware of what I was doing. But I seemed to have stumbled into love like a pothole in the night.

On the landing, yesterday's poster hooked my attention:

WOULD THEY BE DEAD IF THEY STAYED IN BED?

I had an impulse to rip it down, but that probably constituted conduct unbecoming to a nurse as well as treason.

Yes, they'd be bloody dead, I ranted silently. Dead in their beds or at their kitchen tables eating their onion a day. Dead on the tram or falling down in the street, whenever the bone man happened to catch up with them. Blame the germs, the unburied corpses, the dust of war, the random circulation of wind and weather, the Lord God Almighty. Blame the stars. Just don't blame the dead, because none of them wished this on themselves.

In the basement canteen, Bridie and I lined up for porridge.

She didn't want any sausage; she seemed fuelled by hilarity this morning.

I asked her in a low voice, What's the worst that could happen if you just never went back to the motherhouse?

Sure where would I go, Julia?

I had an idea. I wanted to ask her to come home with me tonight and meet Tim. But would that sound rash, even unhinged? I couldn't decide how to phrase it; the words died on my lips. I told her, I'll think of something.

Yoo-hoo, you're in early.

Gladys! I blinked at my pal from Eye and Ear. All I could add was Yes.

She asked, Keeping your chin up?

Rather.

Gladys frowned a little as if she sensed something off about me this morning. She sipped her coffee. Her eyes didn't even go past me to the young woman with the cracked shoes; she wouldn't have had any reason to guess that Bridie Sweeney was anything to me.

The queue loosened ahead of us.

I took two steps forward and gave Gladys a wave. Well, ta-ta.

When she'd left, I wondered how I should have introduced Bridie.

And what in the world would Gladys have thought if she'd seen us kissing on the roof? More than that, what would she have done?

I'd stepped so far away from my old life, I wasn't sure I could ever go back.

When Bridie and I entered Maternity/Fever together, Sister Luke looked up from the desk. She didn't like our being friendly, that much was obvious. She asked, Well rested, I hope, the pair of you?

I assured her that we were. If she didn't know about the nurses' dormitory having been shut, I wasn't going to mention it.

The small room stank of eucalyptus. Honor White was out of view behind a steam tent of sheets, but I could hear her coughing. Her baby was in his crib, bundled legs stirring.

Sister Luke reported that he'd taken his first two bottles all right.

I had to grant the nun this much—her prejudices didn't get in the way of her looking after patients.

Bridie poured herself a glassful from the jug of boiled water and drained it with a gasp. Then she set to work tidying up the ward like an old hand.

Delia Garrett told me, I'm leaving today, Nurse Power!

Really?

Dr. Lynn was in, and she says I'll do better convalescing at home.

It was unorthodox but I couldn't object, given the state of the hospital. The Garretts were comfortably off enough to hire a private nurse, whereas for most of our patients, this was their only chance to be looked after.

Sister Luke told me, Father Xavier was gone last night, and he's out at a funeral at the moment, but I'll see can I find another priest to christen that one. (Nodding at the White baby.)

Once the nun had left, I met Bridie's eyes. Her smile was dazzling.

She asked, What now?

In her steam tent, Honor White was crimson. I decided it was time to get her out.

I wiped her face with a cool cloth. Is that any better, Mrs. White?

She only muttered another of her prayers.

I checked her chest binder. Barely damp; her milk hadn't come in yet. I loosened the fabric further so it wouldn't constrain her noisy breathing. Bridie, could you ever make Mrs. White a hot lemonade while I check on Mrs. O'Rahilly?

The young mother was nursing her little girl, whose head was rounding out nicely already. Mary O'Rahilly's face was serene, and the tray beside her looked as if she'd eaten well. But my eyes went compulsively to the shadowed insides of her wrists—the blue marks.

As if she'd read my mind, she mentioned him. Mr. O'Rahilly's coming for Eunice tomorrow, she said, for her to be christened. They'll let him in as far as the visitors' lobby, and she'll be brought down.

Very good.

I was watching her face. Was she longing to go home to her husband, dreading it, both?

Stay out of it, Julia. Marriage was a private business and a mysterious one.

I turned to Delia Garrett. I see you're packed up already. I'll change your binder before I dress you.

When I unwound her bandage, it came away soaked with milk.

She kept her face averted.

Such a waste, those plumped-up breasts; I wondered how long it would take them to register and accept that there was no one to feed.

I wrapped Delia Garrett up again with a fresh bandage. Then I looked in her bag and pulled out a loose dress.

Not that old thing!

I found a skirt and blouse instead, and Bridie and I got her dressed, very gently.

I looked back at Honor White, who'd already dropped into a doze, her lemonade untouched on the cabinet. Sleep was the best thing for her, I supposed; we had no medicine any more effective.

In his crib, her boy made a catlike sound as his legs stretched. No need to carve a crescent on my watch for this one. Despite being premature, he was doing grand. Already his asymmetrical mouth hardly startled my eyes anymore; just two pieces of lip that didn't quite join up, a brief hiatus.

It occurred to me that this tiny stranger had some of my blood in his veins. Would he always be kin to me under the skin?

Shall I show you how to feed him, Bridie?

Do.

I found the crosscut teat and bottle where Sister Luke had left them in soda after boiling them. I shook up the jar of infant mixture (pasteurised cow's milk, cream, sugar, and barley water, according to the label), then diluted it with warm water, not cold, so as not to chill his stomach. I fitted the teat onto the soldered spout.

I had Bridie take the White boy in the crook of her left arm. He tried to curl up like a grub, but I made sure his neck was straight. I let the liquid down gradually into the twist of his mouth, slowing the flow by putting my finger on the teat's second hole as if I were playing the tin whistle.

Bridie murmured, Look at that. Can't suck it exactly, but he's glugging it down, no bother to him.

Little by little, the White boy took his whole meal while the two of us watched. He swallowed as if he knew he had only one task in the world and his future depended on it.

I heard baritone singing in the passage. *Two little boys had two little toys . . .*

Groyne, of course.

I took the drowsing baby. Could you go and shush the man, Bridie?

She hurried out.

But rode back in the next minute in the wheelchair Groyne was pushing. Bridie was holding imaginary reins, pretending to giddy-up while the two of them carried on the song.

Did you think I would leave you dying,
When there's room on my horse for two?
Climb up here, Joe, we'll soon be flying,
I can go just as fast with two.

I said without heat, This is a sick ward, you pair of foolish gamallooks.

The orderly neighed softly and tipped the chair back on its little rear wheels. Carriage for Mrs. Garrett.

Bridie climbed out, laughing sheepishly.

When I turned to apologise to Delia Garrett, she was weakly smiling. She said, I sing that one to my little girls.

Won't they be delighted to have you home?

She nodded, a sudden tear spangling off her chin.

I put down the White baby and got Delia Garrett into the wheelchair, then hung her bag on the handle. Her hands lay in her lap, her blouse loose on her belly. She looked pretty in a half-destroyed way.

Thank you, Nurse Julia, said Delia Garrett. Thank you, Bridie.

Goodbye, we chimed.

Best of luck, Mrs. O'Rahilly.

The younger woman couldn't say *You too* to this bereaved mother, so she only smiled wanly and nodded at her.

Groyne pushed Delia Garrett off down the passage.

Bridie and I turned to each other.

Oh, the secrecy and heat of that glance.

Then, without a word, we made up the empty bed on the right, to be ready for whoever would arrive next.

When the sun came up a little later, a band of light cut in the ward's window. Bridie looked see-through to me today, as if made of bones and light, wearing her flesh like a dress.

Bridie sneezed so suddenly that Eunice jerked and fell away from her mother.

Sorry, said Bridie, it's the sunlight.

I told her, It sometimes makes me sneeze too.

Mary O'Rahilly reattached the baby's mouth to her nipple, expert already.

Honor White was sleeping, and there was no other patient to hear, so I found I couldn't pass up this opportunity to talk to Mary O'Rahilly.

I leaned over her bed and said under my breath (since I

wasn't supposed to be saying this at all), May I ask you something, dear? Something rather personal.

Her eyes went wide.

Does Mr. O'Rahilly ever . . . lose his temper?

A carefree wife might have answered, *Doesn't everyone?*

But Mary O'Rahilly shrank back a little, which told me
Bridie had guessed right.

Coming round to the other side of the bed, Bridie asked: He
does, doesn't he?

The woman was barely audible. Only when he's taken spirits.

I told her, That's an awful shame.

Bridie pressed on. How often?

Mary O'Rahilly's eyes slid back and forth between us. It's
hard for him, being out of work.

Oh, I know, I said. It must be.

She assured us, He's very good to me most of the time.

I'd ventured into these deep waters with no plan for getting
out the other side. Now that Mary O'Rahilly had confessed the
truth, what in the world was I going to advise her to do? She'd
be taking her baby home in six days or less, and neighbours
made a point of never coming between man and wife.

I made my voice firm. Tell him you won't stand for any more
of that, especially not now there's a baby in the house.

Mary O'Rahilly managed an uncertain nod.

Bridie asked, Would your father take you in if it came to it?

She hesitated, then nodded again.

Tell your husband that, then.

I pressed her: Will you?

Bridie added sternly: For Eunice. So he'll never do the
same to her.

Mary O'Rahilly's eyes were wet. She whispered, I will.

The baby pulled her head away and whimpered.

That ended the conversation.

Hold her upright now, I told Mary O'Rahilly, lean her face in your hand and rub her back to help her burps out.

I looked over at Honor White. Still out like a light, her head flopped sideways on the pillow.

No. Not sleeping.

My throat locked. I leaned over to examine her face. Eyes open, not breathing.

Bridie asked, What's the matter?

I slid my fingers under the wrist that lay on the sheet. Still warm, but no pulse at all. I tried the side of Honor White's pale throat too, just to be sure.

Eternal rest grant unto her, I whispered, *and let perpetual light shine upon her.*

Ah no! Bridie rushed over.

I stroked Honor White's lids shut. I crossed her white hands on her breast.

I swayed; suddenly I couldn't hold myself up. Bridie hauled my head down onto her shoulder and I held on tight enough to hurt. I could hear Mary O'Rahilly weeping over her baby girl.

I made myself pull back, straightened up. Bridie, could you ever go for a doctor?

When she was gone, I stared at the White boy. His little snuffles and tentative flailings. Had my donated blood and all our efforts only rushed his mother into the arms of the bone man?

Dr. Lynn came in looking worn. Nurse Power, what a sad thing.

She checked the dead woman no less thoroughly for it being hopeless. Then she filled in the certificate.

I had to ask, in an uneven voice: Was it the transfusion reaction, would you say?

The doctor shook her head. The pneumonia's strain on her heart, more likely, exacerbated by labour, haemorrhage, and chronic anaemia. Or possibly a blood clot leading to a pulmonary embolism.

She drew the sheet up and over the statue's face, then turned her glinting glasses on me. We're doing our level best, Nurse Power.

I nodded.

And one of these days, even this flu will have run its course.

Really? Mary O'Rahilly asked. How can you be sure?

The human race settles on terms with every plague in the end, the doctor told her. Or a stalemate, at the least. We somehow muddle along, sharing the earth with each new form of life.

Bridie frowned. This grippe's a form of *life*?

Dr. Lynn nodded as she covered a yawn with her hand. In a scientific sense, yes. A creature with no malign intention, only a craving to reproduce itself, much like our own.

That thought bewildered me.

Besides, pessimism's a bad doctor, she added. So let's keep our hopes up, ladies. Now, Mrs. O'Rahilly, I'll have a look at you and your bonny newborn.

After the doctor examined Mary O'Rahilly, she peered into the White baby's mouth. Has he kept a feed down?

I told her, Three.

Good lad. *Filius nullius* now, I suppose, she added soberly — nobody's son, a child of the parish. I suppose he'll be sent over to the institution where she was staying?

Into the pipe, I thought. I nodded.

The doctor said under her breath, Once this is over, Miss Ffrench-Mullen and I are hatching great plans to found our own hospital specifically for the infants of the poor.

How splendid!

Won't it be, won't it just. Rooftop wards, good nurses of any denomination, all the women doctors we can hire, nanny goats for fresh milk...

I caught Bridie's eye and almost laughed; it was the nanny goats.

Dr. Lynn added, Also a holiday home in the country to restore the mothers.

Mary O'Rahilly said, That sounds lovely.

I'll send up orderlies for Mrs. White, the doctor told me on her way out.

No next of kin on the woman's chart, I remembered. That meant—I flinched—a pauper's burial.

I took the nail out of the wall and readied my watch for the scratch.

Bridie whispered: Can I do it?

If you like.

I passed over the watch and nail.

She turned away from Mary O'Rahilly discreetly. She found a space and scored the silver with a deep, neat circle for Honor White.

I wondered how many more mothers I'd have to mark on my watch over the decades to come. The lines would overlap, lying together, tangles of hair. My words came out huskily: Such a number.

Bridie said, But think of all the others. The women going about their lives. The children growing.

I stared at the White baby. Arms little thicker than my thumbs flung wide on the crib mattress as if to embrace the world.

Groyne marched in, carrying a stretcher as he might a shield. Nurse Power, I hear you've lost another one.

That made me sound like a careless child dropping pennies.

Behind him, O'Shea clasped his hands to hide their tremor.

Groyne looked at the cot on the left. Ah, so the scarlet woman's gone west.

I ignored that slur on Honor White and wondered who'd told the orderlies she wasn't married.

In the shades now, he said to O'Shea with a melancholic relish. Riding the pale horse…

I asked, Is it all a pure joke to you, Groyne? Are we just meat?

Everyone stared at me.

After the event in question, you mean, Nurse? He slashed his throat with one finger, smiling. In my view, we are. Napoo, finito, kaput.

He tapped his sternum and added, Your humble friend included.

I couldn't think of a riposte.

Groyne made me a stiff little bow and laid the stretcher on the floor.

O'Shea helped him set Honor White's draped body down on it, and they carried her out.

Her baby, in the crib, showed no sign of knowing what he was losing.

I busied myself stripping her cot.

Bridie asked softly, Why are you so hard on Groyne?

I bristled. Don't you find him grotesque? The constant ditties, the morbid vulgarity of the man. Went off to war but never got within whiffing distance of a battle, and now he swans around here, the greasy bachelor, trying out his music-hall numbers on women in pain.

Mary O'Rahilly looked disconcerted.

I knew I shouldn't be speaking this way in front of a patient.

Bridie said, He's not a bachelor, actually. What's the word? Not just a widower, but someone who used to be a father.

My heart was hammering. When was this?

Years and years ago, before the war. Groyne lost his whole family to the typhus.

I cleared my throat and managed to say, Sorry, I wasn't aware. I suppose the word is still *father,* even if...how many children?

He didn't tell me.

How did you learn all this, Bridie?

I asked had he a family.

I was so ashamed. I'd assumed Groyne had made it to this point in his life unscathed because he'd come home from the war with a steady grip, an unmelted face, his conversational powers unimpaired. I'd never managed to look past the jokes and songs to the broken man. Hale and hearty and in torment; trapped here without those he loved, serving out his time. Groyne could have drunk away his military pension, but no, he was here every day by seven a.m. to carry the quick and the dead.

Mary O'Rahilly said, I don't mean to bother you, Nurse Power...

After some hemming and hawing she admitted that her nipples were very painful, so I took down a jar of lanolin to rub into them.

I checked Honor White's baby but his nappy was still dry. So weak and small he looked to me all of a sudden; was Sister Luke right not to rate his chances?

I said to Bridie, We need to baptise young Mr. White.

Now? she asked in a startled voice. Us?

Well, there's no priest at the hospital today, and any Catholic's allowed to do it if it's urgent.

Mary O'Rahilly asked with an uneasy thrill, Have you christened babies before, Nurse?

Not yet, but I've seen it done on a few.

(*Dying ones,* I didn't say.)

I can remember the words, I assured her.

Bridie objected: But we don't know what she wanted to call him.

True, and that troubled me. Honor White had been so veiled and bleak, and I'd thought there'd be time . . .

Bridie said grimly, Still, I suppose it's better we pick a name than the staff wherever he ends up.

I asked her, Will you be godmother?

A half laugh.

No, but will you, Bridie? It's a solemn thing.

As if she were at a circus, Mary O'Rahilly cried, Go on!

So Bridie scooped up the White boy and stood like a soldier.

I wondered if we should play it safe with one of the more common saints. I said aloud, Patrick? Paul?

John? That was from Mary O'Rahilly. Michael?

Dull, dull, Bridie complained.

I stared into his small face. Maybe a nod to the final tweak the potter had given the clay? Harelipped; what was that Gaelic phrase Dr. Lynn had used for it, *bearna* something? I said, Let's call him Barnabas.

Bridie considered the baby clasped in her left arm. I like that.

Mary O'Rahilly said, Rather distinguished.

Bridie turned her head sharply and let out a huge sneeze, her sleeve flying up to cover it. Sorry!

Then she sneezed again, even louder.

Mary O'Rahilly asked, Are you all right?

I've just picked up a bit of a cold. Must have sat in a draught last night. (Bridie winked at me.)

I remembered the roof. Was I blushing?

I began in a ceremonial tone, Bridie Sweeney, what name do you give this child?

She said solemnly, Barnabas White.

What do you ask of God's church for Barnabas?

Ah . . . baptism?

I nodded. Are you as his sponsor ready to—

(The traditional phrase was *Help the parents*.)

—help Barnabas?

I am.

In the absence of holy water, ordinary boiled would do. I fetched a basin and poured water into a glass. I asked, Hold him over the basin, would you, Bridie?

I steadied my hands and my voice. This next bit, the Latin, was the most important. *Ego te baptizo, Barnabas, in nomine Patris*—

As I trickled it over his forehead, I thought he might furrow his brow, but no.

Et Filii—

I poured again.

Et Spiritus Sancti.

A third time, trickling the clear liquid, calling down the Holy Spirit on the boy.

Bridie broke the silence: Is it done?

I nodded and took Barnabas out of her hands.

She drained the rest of the glass in one gulp.

I blinked at her.

Sorry, I've that mad thirst on me still.

My pulse skidded with fright.

A pink sheen across her freckled cheeks; two spots of colour high on her cheekbones. She'd never looked prettier.

I put Barnabas down in his crib and set the back of my hand to Bridie's forehead. A little feverish. Are you feeling poorly?

Bridie admitted, A bit dizzy, that's all.

She refilled the glass from the jug and knocked that back in one long swallow, her throat contorting as it worked.

I said, Easy, easy.

A whoop of laughter. I can't seem to get enough water.

It was then that I heard it, the faintest creak as she spoke, an infinitesimal music from deep in her lungs, wind in a far-off tree.

I guarded my expression. Any trouble catching your breath at all?

She yawned widely. Only because I'm tired. And my throat always gets a bit scratchy when I've a cold.

But her nose wasn't running as it would in the case of the common cold.

My mind ticked like an overwound clock, checking off each sign I'd observed without registering it till now:

Sneezing.

Sore throat.

Thirst.

Dizziness.

Restlessness.

Sleeplessness.

Clumsiness.

A *touch of mania.*

I found I didn't want to name it. But that was superstition. I said briskly, Well, it can't be this flu, because nobody gets it twice.

Her mouth twitched.

Bridie!

She didn't answer.

All at once I was a raging fury. You said you'd had it before, you'd had it ages ago.

(The first morning, she'd told me that. Two mornings ago— was that all? It felt like a lifetime since she'd sauntered into my ward unmasked, unprotected.)

271

Bridie's eyes slid away. That could have been the ordinary old flu I had then, I suppose. Or maybe it's only the ordinary old kind I'm getting now?

I had to bite my lip to stop myself from saying, *The only flu anyone's catching these days is the dangerous kind.*

Christ Almighty. Two days for incubation, which meant she'd likely picked it up right here, in this little hothouse of contagion.

I tried to keep my voice unshrill. Are you aching at all?

One of her shrugs.

I put a hand on her elbow. Where, Bridie?

Oh, a bit here and there.

She touched her forehead, her neck, the back of her skull.

I wanted to pound her; I wanted to embrace her. Anywhere else?

Her hand moved to her shoulder blades, the small of her back, the long bones of her thighs. She twisted away and sneezed convulsively against her sleeve.

A little sheepish, she said, Well, seems as if I've got it, all right. Or it's got me.

It struck me that the dots of colour were more red than pink, almost gaudy; face paint in a Christmas pantomime. (Had Bridie ever been taken to a pantomime?) *Red to brown to blue to black.*

Mary O'Rahilly was telling her, This grippe's not so bad, I've had worse before.

The young mother meant well, but I could have shaken her.

In a matronly tone, I made myself say, Indeed, you'll be fine, Bridie.

She was starting to shiver, I noticed.

Rest, that's the thing. Let's get you into bed right away.

She said, Where?

For a moment I was stumped, and then I nodded at the empty cot on the right, the one that had been Delia Garrett's, with sheets and blankets that Bridie had smoothed with me only this morning.

But...I'm not having a baby.

The fact was I couldn't bear to send her off downstairs to Admitting, where she might have to hang around for hours. Delay could be dangerous if this was a bad case, which odds were it wasn't, but just to be on the safe side...making do, desperate times, the higher duty of care. (Who was I arguing with?)

I told her, It doesn't matter. Here, put this on—

I found her a starched nightdress on the shelf. Can you manage?

A loud sneeze drowned out Bridie's answer. Sorry!

Punished for sneezing at mass, I remembered.

She turned her back modestly and started unbuttoning.

I found her a clean handkerchief, slid a thermometer under her tongue, and began a chart as if she were any new patient. *Bridie Sweeney. Age twenty-two (approx.).* So many details I didn't know. It galled me to give her address as the motherhouse of Sister Luke's order. *Admitting physician*—blank. I tried to remember when I'd put the thermometer in her mouth—could one minute have passed yet? Time was moving so peculiarly. I bent and touched Bridie's jaw. Open up?

Her dry lips parted, releasing the thermometer; her lip clung to the glass as I lifted it out, and a bit of skin tore, releasing a bubble of blood.

I dabbed the glass and read it: 102.6. High, but actually not particularly high for this flu, all things considered, I told myself.

I hurried out the door. I pushed past nurses and doctors and shuffling patients in the passage. I leaned into Women's Fever, and because I couldn't for the life of me remember the ward sister's name, I called, Nurse? Nurse?

The small nun didn't like that form of address. What is it, Nurse Power?

My runner's not well, I said in a high, falsely casual voice. Could you spare someone to fetch a doctor right away?

I didn't say for what patient; I couldn't admit that I'd put a volunteer helper into a bed when she hadn't even been admitted.

The nun sighed and said, Very well.

I bit back the word *Now*.

When I got back to my ward, Bridie was under the covers already, her clothes folded on the chair.

(I realised she'd grown up knowing she'd be beaten if she dawdled.)

I was in no state to be in charge of this ward, given that I was so frightened I could hardly breathe, but it wasn't as if there was anyone else. *Needs must.* I propped Bridie up on two pillows. I fetched four sulphur-reeking blankets from the press. I made up a hot whiskey, very strong. Bridie's respirations were just a little fast, and her pulse was only slightly high. I wrote down all the figures, trying to think scientifically. No cough, at least.

Bridie shifted between the sheets. She asked, But what if a real patient needs the bed?

Shush, now, you're as real as any. High time you had a rest after all the racing around for me you've been doing. Enjoy a little kip.

My tone was incongruously playful.

I added, You must be sleepy after sitting up all night on the roof.

Bridie's chapped smile was radiant.

I twisted around suddenly. Mrs. O'Rahilly, I wonder, would

you mind if I moved you to the far bed to make a little more room here?

Mary O'Rahilly blinked. Certainly.

(Whenever I leaned over Bridie, I thought I was doing a good job of keeping the panic from showing on my face—the panic but not the love. I couldn't bear anyone to see the way I was looking at her.)

So I helped Mary O'Rahilly out of her sheets and into the cot by the wall. I did spare a thought for the two babies. I pushed Eunice's crib between her mother's cot and the emptied middle one, to move her away from Bridie's sneezes. Then I shoved Barnabas's crib alongside it, but too hard, so both babies were slightly shaken, and Eunice sent up a whimper.

I was busy trying to remember, if I'd ever been told, whether a faster onset of the flu necessarily meant a worse case. Might Bridie blaze through the thing and be back on her feet and laughing in a few days?

To keep off the chill, I draped a cashmere shawl around her head and neck.

Her teeth were chattering. Lovely!

I laid the blankets over her and tucked them around her narrow, shaking frame.

She joked, I might get *too* hot now.

It's good to sweat it out, I told her. More water?

I hurried to pour a glass.

Bridie sneezed five times in a row into her handkerchief. Sorry—

I cut her off. You don't have to be sorry for anything.

I flung her handkerchief in the laundry basket and gave her another. Was I imagining it or was the colour spreading towards her porcelain ears? And rather more like mahogany now? *Red to brown to*—

Drink your whiskey, Bridie.

She gulped her drink. Spluttered.

I scolded fondly, Little sips!

She gasped. I thought it would taste nicer than it does.

I could hear the effort in her voice, the precariousness of breath. I said, You know, I don't think you're getting *quite* enough air, so your heart's beating faster to try and make up for that. Let me just pop this behind you...

I grabbed a wedge-shaped bedrest and pushed it between her and the wall, then put a pillow in front of that. Lie back now.

Against the pillowcase, her hair stood out like the setting sun. She let out a ragged breath.

I took hold of her fingers. I whispered, Really, whatever possessed you to lie about having had this already?

Creakily: I could tell you needed another pair of hands.

She strained for the next breath.

I wanted to help, she said. Help *you*.

But you'd met me only half a minute before.

Bridie grinned. If I'd admitted I hadn't had it yet—

(Panting now.)

—you might have sent me away. There was work to do, work for two.

I found I couldn't speak.

Bridie wheezed, Don't fuss, now.

(As if she were the nurse.)

No need to fret. I'll get through this.

If I was hearing her right. She breathed the words so lightly, I had to stoop right down with my ear to her mouth.

Her tone was odd. Elated, that was it. I'd once attended a talk by an alpinist who reported having experienced a euphoria in the upper peaks, where the air was thin. While on the mountain, he hadn't recognised it as a symptom of anything, or perhaps he'd been too caught up in the adventure to care.

I took her temperature again. It had jumped to 104 now.

That's not Bridie Sweeney?

The voice behind me was Dr. Lynn's.

I kept my eyes on the chart as I summarised the case at top speed.

The doctor interrupted before I finished. But she should be in Women's Fever—

Please, Doctor. Don't move her.

She tutted, already putting the stethoscope down the back of Bridie's nightdress. Deep breath for me, dear?

I could hear the awful rasping from where I stood. I said, She has no cough—isn't that good?

Dr. Lynn didn't answer. She was turning Bridie's hands over; they were puffy, I saw now, and not just from the chilblains. She murmured, Edema—fluid leaking into the tissues.

How had I not spotted that?

I made myself ask, What about her—

I couldn't get out the syllables of *cyanosis.*

—her cheeks?

Dr. Lynn nodded gravely. Well, if you stay nice and quiet, she told Bridie, with a bit of luck...I've seen it go back to pink.

How often had the doctor seen that, though, compared with the number of cases in which the stain had deepened? *Red to brown to blue to—*

Stop it, I told myself. All Bridie needed was *a bit of luck,* and who deserved it more?

Dr. Lynn took hold of Bridie's chin. Open up for me a minute?

Bridie gaped, showing the dark tongue of a hanged woman.

The doctor didn't comment. She turned to me and said,

You're doing all you can, Nurse Power. Keep up the whiskey. Now I'm afraid I'm needed in Women's Surgical.

But—

I promise I'll be back, she told me on her way out.

For something to do, I took Bridie's temperature's again; it was 106. Could that be right? Pearls of sweat standing out on her face, appearing faster than I could wipe them away.

Stay nice and quiet like the doctor said, I murmured. Don't try to talk, and you'll get better all the faster.

I dabbed iced cloths on her magenta cheeks, her forehead, the nape of her neck. It occurred to me that Bridie wasn't coughing because she couldn't; she was being choked by her own rising fluids. Drowning from the inside.

Hours rolled by like one long, impossible moment. Every now and then, moving like an automaton, I made myself perform one of my other duties. I gave Mary O'Rahilly a bedpan when she ventured to ask; I checked her binder, changed her pad. Barnabas woke and cried a little. I changed his nappy and made up another bottle for him. But all the while, all I knew was Bridie.

Her cheeks were nut brown all the way to her ears; you couldn't call it any shade of red, and her breath was a rapid, wet grinding. She couldn't hold her whiskey cup anymore, so I knelt on the bed beside her and held it to her cracked lips. She took sips between her raking breaths. She sneezed five times in a row, and suddenly the handkerchief was smeared with red.

I stared at the linen. One broken capillary, one of thousands, millions in her resilient young body. Blood meant nothing. Birthing women often thrashed about in puddles of the stuff and were perfectly well the next day.

I think I need the—

What, Bridie?

No words came out.

I guessed. A bedpan, is it?

A tear slid out of her left eye.

I checked, and she'd wet the bed. Don't worry your head, it happens all the time. I'll have you dry in two ticks.

I tilted Bridie's light, limp frame at just the right moment to roll the dry sheet on at the left side and the wet one off at the right. I undid the tapes of her nightdress—glimpsing her pale flanks and what looked like an old scar—and got a clean one on her.

I asked her, Can you see me all right? Am I blurry?

She didn't answer.

Her temperature was down to 105. My voice soared with relief: Your fever's breaking.

Bridie gaped like a fish. I wasn't sure she'd grasped what I'd said.

I checked her pulse; it was still fast and the force felt low to me. I had to stop her going into shock, so I ran to make up a pint of saline. I filled our largest metal syringe, willing my hands steady.

Even in her confusion, Bridie quailed at the sight of the needle.

I told her, It's only salt water, like the sea.

(Had doctors made visits to her so-called home? Had Bridie ever had an injection in her life?)

She whispered, You're putting the sea into me?

I ordered myself not to hurt her, got the needle into the vein on the first try.

I watched; I waited.

Still one hundred per cent alive, I repeated in my head, even if her lips were turning a beautiful shade of lavender, almost violet, and her swollen eyelids so smoky, shadowy, like Mary Pickford's on the silver screen.

The saline didn't seem to be working; her blood pressure was still dropping.

When ought purple be considered blue? *Red to brown to blue to black.* What exactly had Dr. Lynn said about the blue cases, their chances of pulling through?

Bridie gasped something.

I thought it might have been *Sing.* You want me to sing?

Maybe she was delirious. Maybe it wasn't even me she was addressing. Anyway, she couldn't answer, because all her effort was bent on that next breath.

I would run to Women's Surgical and drag Dr. Lynn back with me.

Bridie, I'll only be gone a minute.

Did she even hear?

I fled the room. Turned left, went down the passage very fast.

Back the other way, there was some commotion. It didn't matter.

But then it got louder and I looked around and saw Dr. Lynn coming down the stairs in an apron with a trace of red on the bib, each arm in the custody of a helmeted constable. How clumsily the trio descended; the men were holding her too firmly and she was briefly lifted off her feet.

Dr. Lynn!

The doctor stared through the knot of gawkers that stood between us. She had the most baffling expression—mingled frustration, regret, sorrow, even (I thought) laughter at the absurdity of the situation. I realised she couldn't help me, and she couldn't help Bridie, because her time was up.

The men in blue steered the doctor around a corner, out of sight.

When I stumbled back into the ward, Bridie was the colour of a dirty penny. Her eyes were wide with what looked like terror.

I gripped her damp hand. You'll be grand, I swore to her.

One of the babies started crying and I thought Mary O'Rahilly might be too, but I didn't turn my head from Bridie. Her wheezes were laboured and shallow, almost too fast to count. Her face was dusty blue.

I waited.

I watched.

The bone man was in the room. I could hear him rattling, snickering.

But Bridie's powers of endurance were extraordinary, weren't they? She was *younger and tougher* than me, she'd gloated. Deprivation and humiliation had been this girl's meat and drink; she'd swallowed them down and turned them to strength, mirth, beauty. Surely she could survive this day as she had all the other ones?

It was only a path through the woods, I told myself. Tangled and faint and looping but a path just the same, and didn't every path have an end? Like the forested hills around Dublin where we'd walk one day, Bridie and I, joking about how scared I'd been when she got the flu. She'd come home and meet Tim and his magpie. She'd lie beside me in my bed. There'd be all the time in the world. We'd take a ship to Australia someday and walk in the perfume-clouded Blue Mountains. I pictured us strolling through eucalyptus groves, entertained by the exuberant flutter of strange birds.

A little red froth leaked out the side of her mouth.

I wiped it away.

In my mind's eye, the track through the woods was getting dimmer as the branches closed overhead. More of a tunnel now.

I thought of running in search of another doctor to inject Bridie with something, anything. But all stimulants would do was buy her *a few more minutes of pain*—wasn't that what Dr. Lynn had told me?

The tunnel straightened. The two of us knew right well where it was going.

Bridie whooped and coughed up dark blood all down her neck.

I held her in my arms as crimson bubbled from her nose. I couldn't find a pulse in her skinny wrist. Her skin was clammy now, losing all the heat it had hoarded.

I did nothing, only crouched there counting her fluttering sips of air—fifty-three in a minute. How fast could a person breathe? As light as the wings of a moth; as loud as a tree being sawn down. I kept count, totting up Bridie's breaths until the small, noiseless one that I realised, a few seconds later, must have been her last.

My eyes were dry, burning. I turned them towards the floor. It was Bridie who'd mopped it earlier; I tried to find her silvery track.

Nurse Power, please. Get hold of yourself.

Groyne; when had the orderly come in?

His tone was oddly kind. Stand up now, would you?

I dragged myself to my feet; I was daubed with blood from bib to hem. I let go of Bridie's hand and set it down on her ribs.

Groyne's face caved in. Ah, not the Sweeney girl.

Mary O'Rahilly was sobbing behind me.

The orderly was gone without another word.

I began with Bridie's fingers. I wiped them clean, then lavished balm on the irritated red skin on the backs. Traced the raised circle left by ringworm—the faint marking of an ancient fort on a hill. I moved the cloth down her arms, the smooth one and the rippling, burnt one.

A pot of soup, she'd told me on the first day.

How naïve of me to have assumed that it was an accident. Much more likely that at some point in Bridie's penitential upbringing, an adult had thrown scalding soup at her.

In came Dr. MacAuliffe.

I barely said a word.

He listened for a nonexistent pulse. He lifted Bridie's right eyelid and shone his torch in to confirm that the pupil didn't contract.

It was the faulty paperwork that threw him. You're telling me she was never actually admitted to this hospital?

I said, She worked here for three days. Tirelessly. For nothing.

It must have been my tone that shut MacAuliffe up. Under *Cause of death*, he scribbled, *Influenza*.

Then he was gone and I carried on.

There were few stretches of Bridie's body left unmarked; preparing it for burial was like finding chapter after chapter of a horrifying book. When I peeled off her second stocking, I noticed a toe at an odd angle—an old break left unset. On her ribs, snaking around from her back, an ugly red line; it had healed in the end, as most things did. I bent down and kissed the scar.

From her cot, Mary O'Rahilly spoke up shakily. Nurse Power, can I please go home? This place—

It was a healthy instinct, the desire to grab her baby and escape. I said, without turning my head, Just a few more days, Mrs. O'Rahilly.

I found a starched nightdress to put on Bridie. Laid her limbs straight, put her hands together, interlocked her fingers.

Groyne and O'Shea came in with the stretcher and set it along the empty middle bed.

I couldn't look as they lifted Bridie onto it. I couldn't not look.

I got a clean sheet and covered her up.

Groyne put his hand on my shoulder, making me twitch. We'll take care of her now, Nurse Power.

Silence filled up the ward again once they were gone.

At some point Barnabas started crying. The noise abated. I looked and saw that Mary O'Rahilly was rocking him in her arms, shushing him.

When Sister Luke came in, I stared, because I didn't know what she was doing here so early. But the square of window was quite dark, and my watch, inexplicably, said nine o'clock.

Mary O'Rahilly was still holding Barnabas against her chest.

The nun sighed. Well, I heard about poor Sweeney. Such a shock! Truly, *we know not the day nor the hour.*

My rage was stuck in my throat.

The night nurse hung up her cloak; adjusted her veil and mask; bound on an apron. I see the little botch is hanging on?

She took Barnabas from Mary O'Rahilly and put him in the crib as if tidying up.

I managed to get up, then; I took one step and then another.

I stared down at the bloom of Barnabas's jumbled upper lip. It came to me that it was a sign, a seal set on this boy. I said, There's nothing wrong with him.

Above the mask, Sister Luke's brow arched sceptically.

A wild idea was flowering. I thought to myself, *If Tim—*

No, it wouldn't be fair to my brother. I'd no right.

But I pressed on regardless.

I told the nun, I'm going home tonight.

Her nod was cursory; she thought I meant just to sleep.

I spelled it out: I'm taking my annual leave.

Ah, no, I'm afraid we're all very much needed here for the duration, Nurse Power.

I untied my apron and tossed it in the basket. I said, If it's a sacking matter, then let them replace me.

Your job's not to bear the babies, Bridie had told me, *it's to save them.*

Well, maybe save just one. For Bridie. I had this peculiar conviction that she'd want me to keep Barnabas White out of the pipe.

Before I had time to lose my nerve, I got an old Gladstone bag from the back of the press and filled it with basic supplies: nappies and pins, baby clothes, two of the special bottles with wide teats, the big jar of infant food. That maddeningly popular song went round in my head: *Pack up your troubles in your old kit bag.*

Sister Luke was studying me. Finally she asked, What do you think you're doing?

I'm bringing the baby with me.

I put an outdoor dress over Barnabas's other layers.

The nun clucked her tongue. There's no need for that— arrangements will have been made to take him over to the mother-and-baby home.

I swaddled Barnabas in two small blankets and pulled down a woolen hat almost to his eyes.

I went to put on my own coat and hat, and when I turned back the nun was standing in the way. Nurse Power, this infant isn't yours for the taking.

Well, he doesn't seem to be anybody else's, does he?

Do you mean to say you're putting yourself forward as a foster mother for him?

I winced. I said, I won't be asking for pay.

What would you be after, then?

I reminded myself that Sister Luke meant well; she thought her duty was to protect this human scrap from all hazards, including me.

Just to mind him, I said. Raise him as my own.

She plucked at her mask as if itched. You're sounding overtired and distraught—quite understandable after the day you've had.

If she said Bridie's name, I was going to fall apart.

We're all tired, Sister. I'm going home to sleep now, and Barnabas White is coming with me.

Sister Luke sighed. We celibates tend to suffer the odd flare-up of maternal instinct. But a baby's not a plaything. What about your work here?

I said, I have a brother who'll help.

(How dared I make that claim on Tim's behalf?)

I'll come back to work after my week's leave, I promised rashly. Now let me by.

The night nurse drew herself up. You'll need to speak to Father Xavier, as he's the acting chaplain. Any Catholic born in this hospital comes under his aegis.

I found myself wondering who'd put us all in the hands of these old men in the first place. Isn't he out at a funeral?

He's back now—up on Maternity.

Through my teeth I said, Very well.

Reluctantly, I set Barnabas on his back in the crib, looking muffled up enough for the Arctic. I grabbed his chart and headed out the door to find the priest.

The Maternity ward upstairs was long and cavernous. How were they managing for an obstetrician now that Dr. Lynn had been hauled off to Dublin Castle? I passed a score of women grunting, gasping, turning, sipping tea or whiskey, kneeling up, nursing their fragile cargo, weeping. *Woe unto them that are with child.* Also joy. Woe and joy so grown together, it was hard to tell them apart.

I found Father Xavier praying with a patient. He straightened up when he saw me and came over, wiping his dripping nose with a handkerchief.

I wanted to be clear, so it came out curt: I'm taking a baby home.

His grey tufted eyebrows went up.

I went through the cold facts of Barnabas White's case.

The priest fretted, You're young to be shouldering such a burden.

I'm thirty years old, Father.

What if you go on to marry, Nurse Power, and you're blessed with some or many of your own?

I couldn't simply say, *I want this one.* I tried to put it in terms the priest might respect. I told him, His mother died on my watch earlier today. I have a conviction that this task is laid on me.

Hmm. Then the old priest's tone turned more practical. I know you nurses are all of good character, regular massgoers. My concern's more on the other side.

I was suddenly too tired to follow.

He spelled it out: The mother was unfortunate, to say the least. What if it turns out, upon further inquiry, that the father was a brute, or degenerate—bad stock, don't you know?

The little fellow can't wait while we investigate his pedigree!

Father Xavier nodded. But do bear in mind, he's certainly not of your class.

I don't believe an infant has a class.

Well, now, that's all very forward-thinking. But the fact remains, you wouldn't know what you'd be getting.

I remembered the dark wells of the baby's eyes. I said, Nor does he.

This time the priest didn't say anything.

Good night now, Father.

I moved towards the door as if he'd given his agreement. I heard Father Xavier's steps behind me. Wait.

I spun around.

What are you going to call him?

He's already been baptised Barnabas.

No, I mean...maybe it'll be best if you let the neighbours think he's a cousin from the country?

I considered that for the first time, the stain of being what some called *an adopted*.

A fresh start, see?

The priest meant well.

So I told him, I'll think about that.

I took a step back and Father Xavier's hand went up as if to stop me. But no, he was sketching a blessing on the air.

My legs shook a little going down the stairs.

For a moment I thought I'd turned in the wrong door. No, it was Maternity/Fever, but a stranger was in Sister Luke's place, giving Mary O'Rahilly a spoonful of something.

Where's Sister Luke?

The nurse I didn't know said, Running a message.

There was little Eunice in her crib, but the other one was empty. My pulse thumped.

Mary O'Rahilly hissed: Sister Luke took him, Nurse.

I whirled on my heel.

So the nun meant to hand him over to his keepers herself, just to spite me?

I dashed down the stairs. (Was there a hospital rule I hadn't broken yet?)

I stepped aside to let two men carry a coffin in the doors—lightly, an empty one. Then I pushed out into the chill and galloped down the street.

The night was dark, quite moonless. I turned one corner.

Two.

A sudden misgiving. Had I misremembered the way to the

mother-and-baby home listed on Honor White's chart? Or confused it with another? I froze, scanning the dim line of buildings. Was that it, standing tall and stony at the corner?

I spotted the white bulk of Sister Luke gliding towards the gate with the Gladstone bag over one arm and a small swaddled shape tucked into the other.

I didn't call out; I saved all my breath for chasing them.

As my steps slammed up the footpath behind her, the nun turned.

No mask now; Sister Luke's lips were thin and her one eye bulged. Nurse Power, what in the name of God do you think you're—

What are *you* doing?

She nodded up at the grey facade. Clearly this is the place for the child till things are sorted out. Best for him—for you—for all concerned.

I stepped close so I was only inches away from her. I have Father Xavier's say-so. Give me the baby.

The nun's grip on the sleeping Barnabas tightened. To be perfectly frank, Nurse Power, you don't seem in a fit state. That poor girl today, I know it must have been upsetting—

Bridie Sweeney!

I roared the name so loudly that people hurrying by turned their heads.

I added, more quietly: One of twenty slaves kept at your convent.

The nun's mouth opened and shut.

Underfed, I said. Neglected. Brutalised all her life. What was Bridie to you but a dirty orphan—free labour, and you took the wages she earned too. Tell me, when you sent her to serve in my ward, did you even think to check whether she'd had this flu?

Barnabas's eyes popped open; he blinked around at the tarnished city.

Sister Luke said, You're raving. Quite unhinged. What has Bridie Sweeney to do with this boy?

I didn't know how to answer. All I knew was that their two souls were tethered in some way. One barely born, one gone too early; they'd shared this earth for a matter of hours. It was some kind of bargain, that was all I was sure of; I owed this much to Bridie.

I told her, I have permission from the priest. Give him over now.

A moment. Then Sister Luke set Barnabas's blanketed form in my arms and the bag by my feet.

He mewed. I tucked him inside my cape to shield him from the November air.

The nun asked coldly, What are you going to tell people?

I didn't have to answer her. But I said, That he's my cousin from the country.

A snort. They'll think that means he's yours.

I registered her snide implication.

Maybe even that your brother's the father, she added in a worldly tone.

Shame—but then my wrath pushed it away. To defame such a fellow as Tim, who couldn't answer back.

I didn't waste any more words on her. I seized the bag and strode off down the street. I watched my shoes land on each paving stone, being careful not to stumble and drop what I carried.

What was I doing, bringing a frail baby home to inflict on my frailer brother, who didn't take well to noise or disruption? Hadn't Tim been through more than enough already—what right had I to drag him into this story?

But he was such a tender fellow, I argued in my head. A natural at nurturing; he didn't even need speech to look after me so well. If any man could rise to this strange occasion, it was Tim.

Small, practical worries crept in too. Once I got off the tram I'd have to walk the rest of the way home; I couldn't get on a cycle with the baby.

And what would I say, how would I begin, once I let myself into the hall? *Tim, you wouldn't believe what—*

I met this girl—

Tim, wait till I tell you—

This is Barnabas White.

I was in no condition to persuade my brother with argument or eloquence. Was this anything like Tim's state when he'd emerged from the trenches, baptised in the blood of the man he loved? If I ever told anyone what had happened to me—the fever dream of the past three days—it would be Tim.

Maybe these hushed thoroughfares looked so foreign because I was showing them to Barnabas. A stranger come among us, unheralded; an emissary from a far star, reserving judgement. Breathe in the fresh air now, Barnabas, I whispered to the downy top of his head. It's a while more till we're home, but not too long. We'll go to sleep then, very soon. That's all we have to do for tonight. And then when we wake up tomorrow—we'll see what we'll see.

So I carried him along through streets that looked like the end of the world.

AUTHOR'S NOTE

The influenza pandemic of 1918 killed more people than the First World War—an estimated 3 to 6 per cent of the human race.

The Pull of the Stars is a fiction pinned together with facts. Almost all details of Bridie Sweeney's life are drawn from some of the rather less harrowing testimonies in the 2009 Ryan Report on Irish residential institutions: https://industrialmemories .ucd.ie/ryan-report/. She and Julia Power and the rest of my characters are invented, with the sole exception of Dr. Kathleen Lynn (1874–1955).

In the autumn of 1918, Lynn was vice president of Sinn Féin's executive and its director of public health. When she was arrested, the mayor of Dublin intervened to have her released so she could keep combatting the flu at the free clinic she'd set up at 37 Charlemont Street (leased by her beloved Madeleine Ffrench-Mullen). The following year, on the same premises, Lynn founded her children's hospital, St. Ultan's, with Ffrench-Mullen as its administrator. In the general election that followed the armistice of November 11, 1918, Lynn campaigned for their friend Countess Constance Markievicz, who became the first woman elected to Westminster, and

Lynn herself won a seat in the new Irish Parliament in 1923. She and Ffrench-Mullen lived together until Ffrench-Mullen's death in 1944. Lynn worked on into her eighties at St. Ultan's, campaigning for nutrition, housing, and sanitation for her fellow citizens. To those interested in her and in the diaries she kept over four decades, I recommend Margaret Ó hÓgartaigh's *Kathleen Lynn: Irishwoman, Patriot, Doctor* (2006) and the 2011 documentary *Kathleen Lynn: The Rebel Doctor*.

Influenza viruses were not identified until 1933, when they were discovered with the help of the newly invented electron microscope, and the first of the flu vaccines that protect so many people today was developed in 1938.

Symphysiotomy (dividing the ligaments holding the pubic bones together) and pubiotomy (sawing through one of the pubic bones) operations were performed in Irish hospitals most frequently between the 1940s and 1960s but as early as 1906 and as late as 1984. Since the 2000s, this has been the subject of bitter controversy and legal conflict.

The film Bridie and Julia discuss, the silent short *Hearts Adrift* (1914), made Mary Pickford a huge star, but all prints seem to have been lost.

In October 2018, inspired by the centenary of the great flu, I began writing *The Pull of the Stars*. Just after I delivered my last draft to my publishers, in March 2020, COVID-19 changed everything. I'm grateful to my agents and to everyone at Little, Brown; HarperCollins Canada; and Picador for pulling together to bring out my novel in this new world in a mere four months.

Above all, thank you to all the health-care workers who risk so much and into whose hands we give ourselves. Midwife Maggie Walker was kind enough to take time during quarantine to correct some of my misunderstandings, and as on previous occasions, I owe so much to the corrections of the doubly extraordinary physician/copyeditor Tracy Roe (working through a pandemic this time). On a personal note, I'm grateful to the midwives at Womancare and Dr. Kaysie Usher of London Health Sciences Centre for the babies you've caught and the mothers (me among them) you've saved.